Praise for *Love Is an Algorithm*

'Warm, funny, emotional, propulsive and real—a beautiful love story.' JESSICA STANLEY, author of *Consider Yourself Kissed*

'Smart, funny, immensely readable, and deeply insightful about how we make art, fall in love, and connect with each other in the age of AI. With its sharp humour and delightful dialogue, *Love Is an Algorithm* was exactly the book I needed—I tore through it.' ELSE FITZGERALD, author of *Everything Feels Like the End of the World*

'Robson has crafted a compelling love story examining intimacy, vulnerability, and communication in the modern age.' MARGARITA MONTIMORE, author of *Oona Out of Order*

'A cutting satire of tech startups, New York City, and dating, this novel is necessary reading for anyone trying to figure out who they are and what they want in the era of social media. In this funny, fast-paced, and intimate tale, there might be AI but there's nothing artificial about emotion.' KYLE CHAYKA, author of *Filterworld*

'Joyful, generous and smart—an absolute delight moment-to-moment, full of fun and charm, but also sharp and perceptive about creative work, our dependence on technology, and some of the ways relationships can go awry.' HOLLY GRAMAZIO, author of *The Husbands*

Laura Brooke Robson grew up in Oregon, studied English and Creative Writing at Stanford and has spent some time Australia. She is currently based in New York. She is the author of two young-adult novels, and her adult debut, *A Curse for the Homesick*, was published to stellar reviews in 2025.

LOVE IS AN ALGORITHM

LAURA BROOKE ROBSON

TEXT PUBLISHING MELBOURNE AUSTRALIA

The Text Publishing Company acknowledges the Traditional Owners of the country on which we work, the Wurundjeri people of the Kulin Nation, and pays respect to their Elders past and present.

textpublishing.com.au

The Text Publishing Company
Wurundjeri Country, Level 6, Royal Bank Chambers, 287 Collins Street, Melbourne Victoria 3000 Australia

Copyright © Laura Brooke Robson, 2026

The moral right of Laura Brooke Robson to be identified as the author of this work has been asserted.

All rights reserved. Without limiting the rights under copyright above, no part of this publication shall be reproduced, stored in or introduced into a retrieval system, or transmitted in any form or by any means (electronic, mechanical, photocopying, recording or otherwise), without the prior permission of both the copyright owner and the publisher of this book.

Published in the USA by Park Row Books, Harper Collins, 2026
Published in Australia, New Zealand and the UK by The Text Publishing Company, 2026

Cover design by Imogen Stubbs
Cover images: background by Pixel Buddha/Creative Market, heart by Samolevsky/Creative Market

This is a work of fiction. Names, characters, places, and incidents are either the product of the author's imagination or are used fictitiously. Any resemblance to actual persons, living or dead, businesses, companies, events or locales is entirely coincidental.

Printed and bound in Great Britain by Clays Ltd, Elcograf S.p.A.

ISBN: 9781923058804 (paperback)
ISBN: 9781923059658 (ebook)

A catalogue record for this book is available from the National Library of Australia.

EU Authorised Representative: Easy Access System Europe—Mustamäe tee 50, 10621 Tallinn, Estonia, gpsr.requests@easproject.com

For Greg

Sounds like a good idea :)

LOVE IS AN ALGORITHM

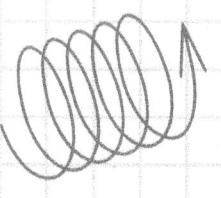

First

FIRST

1

Eve meets Danny in a park at sunset for an outdoor concert, and though it's their first date, it doesn't feel like a first date because they've been friends for ten years, so they spend the whole opening act making jokes about their fellow concertgoers—"Oh my god, has Gen Alpha brought back deerstalker hats?"—while the sides of their arms brush suggestively, and by the time the headliner comes on, they have fallen into an easy comfort, which she likes—she likes that the music means something to him the same way it does to her, and she likes the way his lips silently shape the lyrics, and she likes the way the New York summer heat clings his shirt across his shoulders and his chest, but then (!) what she finds she likes even more is taking off that shirt—in his bedroom, with the hum of the city fluttering through the windows as he kisses her collarbone, stomach, hip—and by the next morning, she is certain of her feelings, ecstatic with them, but she's worried she's been too much too fast until he kisses her softly at the subway station and asks, at the risk of showing, like, all his cards, if she is free for dinner, and she knows she is in love with him, or at least as in love with a person as you can be on a first date, which sounds ridiculous, but then again, maybe the people who think it's ridiculous just don't have love stories as good as this one.

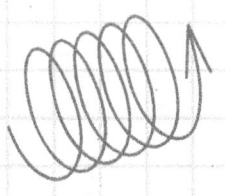

ski rat

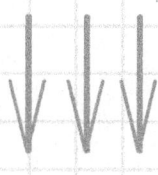

1

When Eve was twenty-two, she moved to Colorado. It was Fletcher's idea.

Fletcher is a full-time consultant and a part-time ultramarathoner, and when he and Eve started sleeping together in their senior year of college, all their friends were like, "Fucking finally!"

Now Eve is twenty-six. Location: laminate bar/table, plastic IKEA stool. View out the window: pitch black. Breakfast: semi-frozen toaster waffle; peanut butter. Company: Fletcher on the stool next to her.

It makes for an awkward eating arrangement because they have to turn if they want to speak. Fortunately, Fletcher does not like to speak before his races. Is this fortunate? She can't stop hearing her friends saying, *Fucking finally.*

"D'you think there's a technical term for the pockets in a waffle?" Eve asks.

Fletcher shifts; the stool creaks.

"I mean, pockets, maybe. Divots? Belly buttons?"

"You could look it up," Fletcher says.

Eve types. "Hi, Mr. AI. Waffle pocket name, please. Mmm, okay. Mr. AI suggests *wells*. Do we like *wells*?"

Fletcher places a hand on Eve's shoulder, which requires him to set down his waffle and shift his stool. His hand is gentle. His voice is calm. "Babe," he says, "I don't mean to shut you down, but if we could just do silence. That would be awesome."

Eve finishes her waffle and puts the dishes in the sink. She gets in the driver's seat of their Subaru Forester, nicknamed Gus, so Fletcher can ride shotgun and retie his shoelaces. This is the seventh weekend this year they have allocated to an ultramarathon. Fletcher consistently places in the teens. It is currently 4:49 a.m., and they will likely get back around midnight. For the duration of the three-hour car ride, there will be no music, and neither of them will say a word.

2

There are two versions of this story. Version One: Fletcher and Eve have a great relationship. Version Two: Fletcher and Eve should break up. Eve has the sense that both of these stories are provisionally true; it's just a matter of time before she finds out which one will win out. Version One: They get married. Version Two: They end it.

Both stories have plenty of supporting evidence:

Version One: Fletcher and Eve have a great relationship
- They never fight
- They divide chores equitably
- They like each other's families
- They have sex at least twice a week
- They have similar beliefs and plans (liberal, agnostic, want two kids)

Version Two: Fletcher and Eve should break up
- Fletcher is boring
- Eve is annoying
- Fletcher is petulant
- Eve is condescending
- In five years of dating, they have never really been sure of each other

Lately, Eve's been wondering what people mean when they talk about love. Because a lot of people say, "When you know, you know!" But a lot of people also say, "Relationships are work." She keeps going to weddings where the couples claim they knew right from the start: *That's the love of my life.* At the same weddings, drunk aunts say the infidelity stings less if you expect it. It seems impossible to Eve that we could all go through life with so little understanding of how happy other people's relationships actually are.

3

Eve idles the car in a dirt lot as Fletcher gets out. He pauses. Taps the window. Eve rolls it down and he says, "Can you please bring the NSAIDs to the third checkpoint?" Fletcher doesn't use brand names for things, as if they live in a world of copyright violence where Pfizer men will rappel down from the trees if he dares utter an "Advil."

"I would love to," Eve says. "I would love to bring the nonsteroidal anti-inflammatory drugs to the third checkpoint."

"Cool cool," he says, and then he lopes to the start line with his little neon vest all stuffed with Maurten gels.

Version One: Eve is so charmed by her athletic, earnest boyfriend. Version Two: No one has ever looked sexy in a hydration vest.

On the drive to the third checkpoint, where she was asked to wait with two cheese quesadillas and a two-liter bottle of flat Coke ("cola"), Eve rolls down the windows and scream-sings high notes at the edge of her vocal range. She catches a glimpse of herself in the rearview mirror and must admit she looks like a Woman on the Edge. When Eve was growing up—Manhattan, Upper West Side—and then in college, she had a carefully constructed look. Neon nail polish, gold jewelry, long wool coats in the winters, and crocheted everything in the summers. Now her roots are growing out and she always has a sports bra tan. All her makeup has expired. She is wearing silver earrings because Fletcher once mentioned, offhandedly, that he liked silver better than gold. It's not so much that Eve doesn't like this version of herself—it's that she doesn't remember agreeing to it. It feels like a version of herself that happened rather than one she made on purpose.

She parks at the aid station and leaves Fletcher's quesadillas and Coke on a folding table with the volunteers, all of whom appear to be injured runners. Fletcher won't arrive for two hours at the earliest, so Eve takes a wander down the crisscrossing tracks until she finds a stream. The air is cloudy with a thin, fine dust, and clumps of unmelted snow hide in the roots of the pine trees. There is so little oxygen up here. Everyone is always going on about the mountain air, but Eve has always found the air at sea level extremely palatable.

She puts in an AirPod, brushes the dead pine needles from a flat rock, and sits with her legs stretched in front of her.

"Autocrat," she says. "Auto . . . craaaaaat."

The AirPod is looping a guitar riff from a song she wrote last year that everyone agreed was unsalvageable. It was a love song. A bad sad song is still interesting, but a bad love song is unforgivable. There is a version of this story where Eve writes a song about the smell of pine trees; about kissing Fletcher at the finish line; about love. Eve knows because she wrote it last year and everyone hated it.

"Nonsteroidal," she says. "Strava royal. Strava. Roooooooyal." The guitar loops again. The inside of her brain shudders with a perfect yesness, like she has just sealed the lid on a to-go cup. *Click*. Strava royal, nonsteroidal, always get your way. Ski rat, autocrat, daddy's Piaget.

She records it once and then rests her phone face down on her thigh and stares at the stream. It's not wise to make fun of one's boyfriend in song. A nice girlfriend wouldn't call her boyfriend an autocrat; then again, a nice boyfriend probably wouldn't treat his girlfriend like a subject. Is she being unfair? Are her standards too high or too low? What is love, actually? Maybe none of us know; maybe we all just keep dating people until we find a definition we're willing to live with.

Eve hears a crack. A stick breaking. She glances up, expecting a runner. No one is there.

She returns to her phone, and then she catches a shift in her peripheral vision. A flash of bronze in the underbrush. This time, when she looks up, she sees two black-rimmed eyes staring at her from the other side of the stream.

So it's a mountain lion, actually.

"Holyfuckingshit," she says. She scrambles to her feet and holds her arms above her head in an attempt to look taller. "No. No, no."

The mountain lion's head vanishes as it crouches beneath the bushes, but Eve can see the tail slink closer. The tail vanishes. Just underbrush. Silence.

"Hey," Eve says. She tries to clap, but it doesn't make any sound because her stupid phone is in her hand and she's afraid that if she puts it in her pocket she will look temporarily small. "Hey!" She wants to run. She's almost positive you're not supposed to run.

And then, to her left, on her side of the stream, Eve hears a meow.

Slowly, she turns. There, in the underbrush, are four small eyes.

Okay, yep, she's going to run. Mama cougar separated from her cubs seems unlikely to be scared away by Extended Mountain Pose. Eve starts walking backward, trying to scale her way up the steep dirt track. The mother still has not reappeared on the other side of the water.

And then she does.

She leaps across the stream.

And Eve thinks:

- *Fuck, this is actually happening*
- *She is aiming for my head*
- *I am actually going to get killed by a mountain lion*
- *I thought you were, like, thousands of times more likely to be killed by a vending machine than a wild animal*
- *It's true what they say about time slowing down*
- *Fucking wildlife*
- *Fucking Colorado*
- *Fucking Fletcher*

The mountain lion's claws rake Eve's shoulders. What happens next is either a reflex or an accident. Eve's arm swings down to shove the mountain lion away, but her phone is still death-gripped in her hand, and that's what connects with the side of the mountain lion's nose. Eve has dropped her phone on her face many times; the pain is universal.

The mountain lion rears back, and Eve scrambles up the hill. They watch each other as Eve takes another step.

"I'm going to go," Eve says. She tries to lift her arms to look big again, except one of her arms won't move. Her shoulder is bleeding melodramatically. Another step. The mother doesn't move.

"Leaving. Never coming back. Okay?"

One of the cubs mewls again, and Eve flinches. The mother's tail flicks.

"My mom simply would never have done this for me," Eve says as she crests the ridge. "Goodbye. Thanks so much! This has been so fun."

Eve keeps walking backward, counting her steps. At thirty, she turns and begins striding deliberately—*not running, we're not scared, we're not running*—to the aid station. When she gets there, two women with crutches leap to their unsteady feet.

"Hi," Eve says. "I think I need a tetanus shot . . . ? Or rabies, or something. I don't know. Anyway, I'm going to throw up, I think—just a warning." And then she does. Fortunately, the aid station is prepared for this eventuality. Ultrarunners throw up all the time.

4

The race organizers catch Fletcher at the second checkpoint and mention to him, "Oh, hey, your girlfriend had a little run-in with the local wildlife." When he shows up at the recovery tent where Eve is lying on a cot, she realizes she didn't expect him to come. She didn't want him to. Because if he had kept running, it would've made for a great grievance. *I got attacked by a mountain lion and my boyfriend kept running.* That's the kind of thing you could break up with someone over. That's the kind of thing that would settle it.

He sits lightly on the edge of her bed.

"You okay?" he says.

What a banal question. She has just been *attacked* by a *giant cat* and he goes with "you okay?"

"Would you still love me if I developed cougar-like superpowers?" she asks.

He lifts the collar of her shirt; a race shirt she was given despite not racing (imagine). He hmms quietly.

"You know," Eve says, "jumping, big claws, a way with younger men."

"What have they done to treat this?"

"They cleaned it and put on antiseptic. But they said I should call my doctor once we get back to service."

"That seems fine."

"Not if my doctor is a younger man."

Fletcher looks at Eve for a long moment, and Eve looks back. She thinks of those first months they were together, the *fucking finally* months, when they trailed each other around campus to study dates and lawn parties. He always seemed so amused by her; so willing to wait patiently while she stood in the spotlight. Her boyfriend before Fletcher had been jealous and prickly, so in comparison, being with Fletcher had felt like breathing clean air. It did not occur to her until much later that some people are in relationships where they are more than just tolerated.

"Okay," Fletcher says finally. "Well, why don't we drive you home, then."

For a moment, Eve thinks he's suggesting a road trip. They are going to New York! But that's not what he means by home. He means, of course, the Boulder house with the laminate countertops. The place she has chosen to live.

They get in the car and Eve puts on a Stella Seaport album that was big when they were in college. Stella Seaport got huge overnight but has never lived up to her potential. Someone on Reddit recently suggested that maybe the same thing had happened to Eve Olsen; too big too fast.

Eve's first album, *PRELAPSARIAN*, came out just after she graduated college, the same month she moved to Colorado. Her sophomore album is still forthcoming.

"Would you be upset if I sang about you?" Eve asks.

"What do you mean?"

"If I wrote songs about you. Because, like, if I wrote about having sex or fighting or being in love, everyone would assume I was talking about you."

"I mean, I wouldn't love it."

"Okay," Eve says. She picks at the gauze at the edge of her bandage. "Why not?"

"What do you mean, why not? Who would want that?"

"I don't think I'd mind."

"Of course you would," he says tiredly.

"I think I'd like to be a muse. To know someone cared that much, you know? To know I'm living in someone's brain."

"Mmm."

"You don't agree?"

"I don't know, Eve."

"Are you afraid I'd make you look bad?" Eve asks. "If I sang about you? Or is it just a general vulnerability thing?"

"I haven't really thought about it."

"I just wish you would interrogate your feelings."

"This is starting to feel very therapy."

"How would you know?" Eve says. "You've never been to therapy."

"Not everyone needs it."

That's when the semitruck in front of them blows out a tire, skids into the median, veers sideways, and launches upside down through the air. In the moment before impact, Eve thinks:

- *Seriously, what the fuck*
- *Gus the Subaru is so not going to make it out of this*
- *I think the universe is trying to tell me something*
- *There's a nonzero chance I die in the next five seconds*
- *If I don't, I am moving back to New York*

Impact. Eve's neck snaps back and the airbag erupts. Everything smells of burning rubber. She hears a ringing, and as the sound moves through her she feels an epiphany about that word, *ringing*, because the sound seems to spin in circles, pitching higher, waning, coming back again. She's enringed by it. Then her heartbeat returns. She hears it, fluidlike, inside her skull. There are two versions of this story, and in one, Eve is dead, and in the other, Eve is alive, and that's what this album is going to be about. It will start with a ringing, and it will end with a breakup. It's suddenly so clear. Fucking finally.

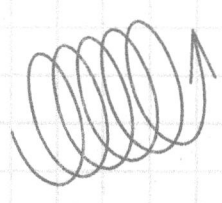

The Bug in the System

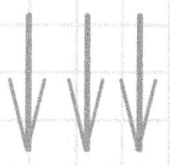

1

Danny is buying a twelve-dollar coffee when his dad calls. He didn't realize the coffee would be twelve dollars when he ordered it, but the ice cost extra, as did the oat milk, as did the caramel foam (yes), and then Danny left a two-dollar tip because he worked in a café in high school and now will spend the rest of his life trying to make empathetic eye contact with every barista he ever meets.

His dad, Cal, is a man who believes in instant coffee from a Costco tub. It's all very embarrassing.

"Hey," Danny says, stepping to the side by the straws and stir sticks. "Everything okay?"

"Why do you always ask that? You worry too much."

"Sure," Danny says. "But is everything? Okay?"

"Oh, just fine. But my life is boring. How're things with you?"

"Dad, you called me."

"Can't I say hi to my favorite son?"

The barista announces that there is a large iced oat latte with salted caramel foam for Danny.

"Wowzers," Cal says. "Fancy."

Danny takes the drink and ducks out onto the street. Commuters are bustling their way home, but it's still bright out; after the cavern of winter, the spring days just go and go.

"Yeah," Danny says. "Well, I was falling asleep at my desk, and I have a dinner tonight."

"Like a date?"

Danny hesitates. "Yeah. Like a date."

"With?"

"The app matched us."

"Gonna take her somewhere fancy?"

"A taco truck, I think."

"Well, you just remember, it's polite to pay. You can be a feminist and still pay."

"Okay," Danny says. "Good tip. Hey, I should probably let you go."

"Oh! I'm sorry! I didn't mean to interrupt your day."

"It's fine, Dad, I just need to get on the subway now."

"Yes, sorry, I know you're so busy!"

Danny takes a deep breath. "I love you. Talk to you later."

In the crowded car, Danny finds himself standing beside a mother-son duo who are both wearing those Balenciaga shoes that look like wet suit booties. They cost $900; Danny knows this off the top of his head, though he has never had the faintest inclination to purchase them (because they look like wet suit booties). On the seats, there are two elderly gentlemen looking at their phones. One is a new iPhone, $1300; the other is a foldable Samsung, $1500. Leaning against the door with nary a care in the world is a man dipping his Pringles in Trader Joe's hummus. This is an unhinged snack. Danny stares at the man for a long moment, wondering about the logistics; Trader Joe's surely does not sell Pringles, so the man must have made two stops. Also, there is no way a Pringle has the structural integrity to hold hummus. Danny does not usually move away from people on the subway, but this man seems unsafe. Pringles: $3. Trader Joe's hummus: $4. The ad running along the top of the subway car encourages passengers to take control of their finances and start investing in crypto now. Danny's phone buzzes and it is an email from Chase saying his automated credit card payment has gone through. He gets a text from his gym saying his monthly membership has been automatically renewed. He gets a notification from the Sweetgreen app saying he has been rewarded with a discount for spending so fucking much on salad this month here in the financial capital of the world.

2

> **Maple**
> **Compatibility:** *81*
> **Convergence:** *Friendships, lifestyle, words of affirmation*
> **Divergence:** *Texting style, conflict resolution, family plans*

At the food truck near Danny's apartment, he and Maple both order soyrizo tacos, and Danny pays.

Maple says, "That's really considerate, but you didn't have to."

"Yeah." Danny laughs to seem amenable. "Wait, what?"

"It's cool if you eat meat," Maple says. "You don't have to abstain just because of me."

"Oh. No, I'm a vegetarian."

Now Maple laughs. "Wait," she says. "Oh, actually? Sorry."

"Do I seem like I wouldn't be?"

"For sure," Maple says.

Danny files this away for future inspection. He did not know he exuded carnivorousness. Just something to worry about!

So far, Danny and Maple have only messaged briefly in the app. Danny sent a tepid question asking if she missed Oregon—her profile said she was from Portland—and she responded:

> **Maple:** Hi Danny! Want to just meet Thursday at 7-ish? I don't think you can tell if someone is a fit until you meet in person, and I'm too busy for small talk (haha). I am friends with Gigi and she says you are a good person. Let me know!

Danny said he also hated small talk. That was a lie. Why would he want to go on a date with a stranger? That sounds terrible. What if she believes the world is a simulation? What if her comfort show is *The Big Bang Theory*? What if she asks Danny about his relationship with his mom? What if their food never comes out and Danny makes a joke that the taco truck is going to give him abandonment issues and she says abandonment can be really serious, actually, so forgive her for not laughing, and then Danny has to say no, don't worry, my mom left when I was twelve and I haven't heard from her since? What then, Maple? Maybe they should have figured this out over text.

They take their buzzers to a free picnic table, and Maple positions her extremely large tote bag on the seat next to her.

"So you work with Gigi's fiancé?" Maple asks.

"Do you know Julian?"

Maple shakes her head. "But I'm curious about Pathos. I signed up because it's related to my research."

"Your research?"

"I'm finishing my PhD."

Danny asks what she's studying, but she's distracted by something in her bag. She frowns and adjusts something. He assumes it's her phone. He waits for an answer, but then a taxi and a Citi Bike collide in the bus lane. Both men start hurling profanities.

"Oh my god," Maple says. "I hate this city. You get it."

"Ha," Danny says. "Wait, what?"

"I just mean, it's no Portland. God, don't you miss the trees? The mountains?"

The mountains? Where the bears are? "Totally," Danny says.

Maple peers inside her bag again. Danny touches his phone in his pocket but doesn't pull it out. He finds himself experiencing the date from outside of himself, as if he is narrating it in the future to whomever he is actually meant to be with.

"So, do you believe in soulmates?" Maple asks. She delivers this line clinically; there is no implication she believes Danny is hers.

Danny scratches his neck. "I mean. I'd like to."

"Interesting."

"Is that surprising?"

"Deeply," she says.

A carnivorous, cynical man. Danny plans to throw away this shirt.

"Because of your app," Maple says. "I've read about it. If you can measure your compatibility with anyone, surely you'd see plenty of people are equally compatible."

"Well, it's not really permanent compatibility so much as compatibility in a given moment."

"And love at first sight? What's your stance?"

"I think it's a stretch," Danny says. "Why? What do you think?"

"I believe more in love at first smell."

"I don't know that I'm particularly attracted to smells," Danny says.

"You are. Everyone is. You just might not notice. Shh."

He blinks.

"Not you." She gestures to her bag. "I had to bring my prairie voles home from the lab for the long weekend."

This is exactly the sort of thing one can preestablish during small talk.

"Yeah, no, sure," Danny says. "I have a family of chipmunks in my backpack."

"Do you want to meet them?"

This seems to be a rhetorical question. Maple sets the capacious tote on the table. Danny looks inside and sees a gray plastic crate with two rodents. While this is probably a health code violation, the prairie voles are essentially semispherical mice with nubbly tails. There's just no way around it. They are, like, so cute.

"Some people are weird about rodents," Maple concedes.

"I'm more weird about bugs myself."

"Mammalian bias," Maple says. "Why are you weird about bugs?"

"Scuttly."

"Prairie voles pair bond for life," she says. "The soulmate thing—that's what I'm doing for my PhD."

"They're soulmates? The prairie voles?"

"Depends how you define soulmate, but yeah, basically. They give each other all the happy brain chemicals. They're not going to cheat on each other. No laws or religious doctrine required."

"Does this mean you believe in soulmates?" Danny asks.

"Not in the, like, 'our souls are split in two and we wander aimlessly looking for our other half' way. It's not predestined. It's retroactive. I believe in inventing a soulmate."

"Huh," Danny says.

Maple sips her beer then sets it down again. "Look, my therapist says it's really important that I start respecting my attachment style, and I think you're probably too closed off and avoidant for me."

"Really," Danny says. Kyra, his last ex, thought he was anxious and needy. He tries not to take this as a win.

"So I think we won't be seeing each other moving forward. Best of luck with life, though!"

He is relieved and disappointed when she walks away with her tacos. Relieved that he will not have to send a "thanks but no thanks" text in three days. Disappointed that he has been rejected. There is something especially scathing about being rejected by someone you did not want to ask out again in the first place.

3

Quinn
Compatibility: *90*
Convergence: *Hobbies, favorite media, attachment styles*
Divergence: *Sleep schedule, sex drive, sense of humor*

Danny meets Quinn in Central Park for "stargazing." Frankly, he thinks this is a weird date. What stars? This is Manhattan. It gets weirder when he arrives at the park and finds her standing at the edge of the water with a paddleboat.

"We'll be able to see the stars better from the water," she says. This seems unlikely, and, furthermore, Danny is pretty sure no paddleboat rentals are still open at 8:00 p.m. Maybe this is his own fault for suggesting an 8:00 p.m. date, but in his defense, he had a work dinner and sort of assumed this would just be a drink.

What Danny realizes immediately is that he is super not attracted to Quinn. There's not a good reason for it. She's conventionally attractive in all the normal ways, but she's wearing a newsboy cap and Danny just doesn't want to sleep with anyone who might suddenly shout, "Extra, extra!" He feels guilty for not finding her hot and hopes she also finds him physically neutral. He is of average height and average build. His eyes are neither light nor dark. His skin is white but tan. His hair is cut in the usual way. Once, after losing each other at a concert, Julian asked him, "Can you start wearing one of those striped *Where's Waldo* shirts?"

Danny and Quinn get in the paddleboat and push anemically offshore.

"So," Danny says, "who got you on Pathos?"

"I went to college with Chloe," Quinn says.

Chloe is Danny's CMO. Very nice! Completely normal! Danny tells himself that a friend of Chloe's is probably fine.

"So," Quinn says. "What's your Myers-Briggs type?"

Danny laughs. Quinn stares at him. Whoops! Not a joke!

"Oh," he says, "I'm not actually sure."

"Really? But you make an app that pairs people up with their most compatible matches."

"Yeah, but we use, like . . . different metrics."

"What metrics?"

"Oh," he says, "you know, kilometers, liters. That sort of thing."

Quinn stares at him.

"Because those are metric units," Danny says.

"No," Quinn says. "I got it."

On the bright side, the app seems to have correctly predicted that Quinn and Danny do not share a sense of humor. On the less bright side, it's unclear to Danny where their ninety out of one hundred compatibility is coming from. A few weeks back, Danny got in an argument with Julian—Danny's cofounder—about how to weigh the various compatibility categories. Danny thinks the current algorithm overvalues similar taste—whether you like the same TV shows and music—and undervalues basic communication goals. He suspects this is because Julian and his fiancée, Gigi, share a love for critically acclaimed satires about the American elite but have never figured out how to vulnerably communicate with each other.

"So, what do you do in your spare time?" Danny asks.

"I love to journal."

"Oh, supercool. So you, like . . . write down what happened that day?"

"Mostly my feelings about what happened."

"That's great. Seems like a healthy habit. Do you do it every day?"

"For an hour or two."

"Oh," Danny says. "No. That's inconceivable."

He means this to be a joke. A little playful teasing! Quinn (and

Danny probably could have anticipated this) does not seem to find this funny.

"The app said we had similar hobbies," Quinn says. "What are your hobbies? Since self-reflection is clearly not one of them. That was a joke, to clarify."

"Right," he says. "Ha! Um. I like to run?"

"I used to like running. But then I tore my ACL and now I can't anymore."

"Oh, but that'll heal, right?"

"Maybe," she says. "But I don't like running anymore."

At the end of the date, she jokes that this was fun and they should do it again. He laughs. It turns out that was not a joke.

4

Nellie
Compatibility: 94
Convergence: *Work ethic, politics, moral compass*
Divergence: *Travel plans, disposition, willingness to compromise*

Danny almost cancels at the last minute but appreciates that he already knows the date will last only forty-five minutes. Nellie sent him a calendar invite.

They do the perfunctory hug at the door of Our Lady of Perpetual Breakfast. It's a diner in Chelsea where Danny has spent more money than he has spent at possibly all other New York establishments combined. It's in an old Catholic school—the building was converted thirty years prior—and there are still stained glass windows and retro drinking fountains. The old chalkboards are scattered around the diner, some displaying daily specials, others displaying customer graffiti. One near the back says GIGI AND JULIAN AND DANNY LOVE OLOPB!!! Gigi wrote it last night. Danny really can't express just how often he finds himself here.

Nellie props her sunglasses on top of her head and looks around. "Huh," she says. "How'd you find this place?"

"My friend Gigi used to work here. When she first moved to the city. She lives a block away now."

"Cool, cool," Nellie says. "Been meaning to try it. Anyway, so I'm going to have to keep my phone on."

"Yeah, no worries. You work in finance, right?"

She quickly types an email, which he takes as his answer. He rocks onto his heels and waits. When she looks up again, he begins his shuffle toward the nearby empty booth, and she follows. Danny waves at Ed, who has worked at the diner for its entire existence, and Ed lifts a coffeepot.

"What's your name?" Nellie asks.

"What?" Surely she knows his name—it was on the calendar invite. "Danny?"

"Like, full name."

"No, it's actually just Danny. It's not short for Daniel, or long for Dan, or anything."

Nellie makes a scooping gesture of the air. "I mean last name."

"Oh. Aagaard." He spells it for her. All those *a*'s.

"You were first for everything," Nellie says. "Students with alphabetically earlier names get better grades. What are you, Norwegian?"

"Sort of," Danny says.

"Sort of?" Nellie looks like she's interested in parsing this but ultimately gets distracted by her phone. When she speaks again, she says, "So, Pathos?"

"Yeah."

"I asked to join the beta because we're thinking of investing."

"Oh, shit, really?"

"But dating apps are a broken business model," she says. "The incentives are wrong. The second you get someone into a good relationship, you've lost a customer. It's a fundamental bug in the system."

"Right, but the thinking is, then their friends hear about how they got such a good match from us, then their friends hear . . ."

Nellie's phone buzzes. She taps out another email, hits Send, and blinks up at him like she forgot he was there.

"It's like trying to be a subscription fridge service," she says. "You don't need a new fridge every month. You just need a good one that won't break. All dating apps run into this problem."

"We're hoping to compete on the quality of the matches."

"And have they been?" she asks. "High-quality matches?"

"It's so hard to quantify a connection that way," Danny says.

"Yeah. But that's your job."

5

When Danny gets back to Julian's apartment, aka the de facto Pathos headquarters, he goes to Julian's office and lies on the floor. It has never made sense to Danny that Julian is able to afford a two-bedroom in Chelsea with real wood floors and an elevator from this century, and he suspects that Julian's parents have something to do with it. That, or Gigi makes more as an influencer than Danny realized. Danny would love to have rich parents and a rich girlfriend with whom he could split rent. Danny lives in a one-bed in FiDi, which he thought sounded corporate and impressive when he first moved in, but now he realizes it's just windy and barren of grocery stores. Before all that, years ago now, they were roommates on the Lower East Side. Julian was working in finance. Danny was doing grunt-work coding for a series of failed fintech start-ups. And then, three years ago, Julian had this idea for a dating app that gave users way more data—"Hinge but make it Spotify Wrapped," Julian had said—so they spent a year working nights and weekends before they had enough seed money to go full-time. While Danny's fellow grunt-work coders have begun collecting a portfolio of stock options and annual bonuses, Danny still finds himself making the same amount of money he made right out of college. It's enough to buy an iced oat milk latte with caramel foam, but not so much that you won't feel guilty when you do it.

"You good, man?" Julian says.

"Hnnnnngh," Danny says.

"Didn't you have a coffee date this morning?"

Danny presses his fingertips against his eyelids. When they named their start-up two years ago, they went with Pathos, as in *inspiring emotion*. They would draw feelings out of people! Danny can't help but reflect now that *pathos* has the same root as *pathetic*, which feels, alas, incredibly apt.

"I think our app is broken," Danny says.

"That is so not the attitude," Julian says.

"Our metrics are wrong. There's no way I was in the eighties, much less the nineties, with any of these women."

"Have you considered that you're not giving anyone enough of a chance? Maybe you're being too picky."

"How does one know if one is being too picky, though? Maybe we should all be picky."

"'*One*,'" Julian mimics. "You sound like my sister."

Danny props himself up on an elbow. Julian has swiveled around in his chair so he's facing away from the desk, and he has his ankle up on one knee. "How is Eve?" Danny asks.

"She's moving back, actually. Did I tell you that?"

"Really?"

"Yeah, she and Fletcher got in a huge car crash. They broke up in the hospital."

"Is she okay?"

"Physically, yes. But we talked on the phone yesterday and she was all evangelical about dispensing relationship wisdom. She said she would 'no longer abide a relationship that was not spectacular.' Hey, maybe I'll get her on the beta when she comes back. It'd be funny if you two matched."

Danny is stuck on that phrase: *a relationship that was not spectacular*. "Do you think most people would describe their relationships as spectacular?"

"I mean," Julian says, "Gigi and I are spectacular."

"But you've obviously had some doubts. At some point."

Julian squints. "Not really."

"Not even when you fight?"

"We like to think of it as us against the problem."

"You never once worried she was going to break up with you?"

"Gigi and I trust each other completely."

"Do you think that's normal?"

"I think it's special," Julian says. "I think a lot of people have settled for a lot worse. I wish everyone could have what Gigi and I have."

It would be annoying if he wasn't so earnest.

6

That night, on the walk home, Danny's dad calls. Danny almost doesn't pick up; feels too guilty; answers.

"Hey, buddy," his dad says. "How are all those dates going?"

When Danny was a teenager, his dad was forever interrogating him about who he liked. Anyone in any of his classes? Was he going to homecoming? Would he ask someone to be his date? Danny is aware that it's a blessing to have a dad who cares about his life. But what Danny remembers most about these interrogations is the edge of panic in his dad's voice—the fear that Danny would fall in love and make a new family and never come back. Now, when he looks around the city—at the thirty-million-dollar homes and the two-dollar pizza slices—he is suffocated by the fear of losing this place: of ruining the company and emptying his bank account and limping back to Montana. People love to ask Danny if he misses Montana. Danny cannot imagine missing feeling so alone.

"Nothing to report," Danny says. "Hey, did you hear Julian's sister is moving back? She got in some massive car accident. Also something about a cougar? I don't know, Julian exaggerates."

"She's okay, though?"

"Yeah, it sounds like she's fine."

"You going to ask her out?"

"Who, Eve?" Danny squints. "I think she just had a big breakup. Also, I don't know how compatible we are. Like, I love Julian, but I wouldn't date him."

"Well. Sure. I mean, as long as it's not on my account."

"I have no idea what you're talking about."

"Just because of, you know, your mom, Eve's family, you know. Baggage! Don't we all have it."

"That literally didn't even cross my mind," Danny says.

"I just thought, maybe, since you used to be so self-conscious going over to their house. Because they have so much money. And you used to worry about that all the time."

Danny stands on the edge of the curb and waits for the light to change; for the stream of cars to dam. The woman on the sidewalk next to him is wearing an engagement ring the size of a small planet. Danny says, "I don't really think that way anymore."

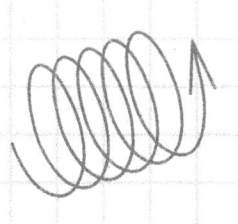

The Wound

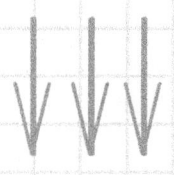

1

Two years out of college, Eve got a remote job at a B2B tech start-up that specializes in helping other B2B tech start-ups identify data vulnerabilities. She understood very few of these words at the time but has always been great with bullshit.

The company, Rampart, allows her to work remotely. She mostly writes their content, but occasionally, they have her design social media graphics because young + female = good with fonts? Eve doesn't love it. But when *PRELAPSARIAN* came out, she only made enough money to keep her dream alive, not her body. Rampart became her side hustle. She can churn out SEO-friendly articles like a machine. No one hides a witty Easter egg in a social media post like Eve. It's easy to evoke emotion in potential customers because humans hate feeling vulnerable; they don't like to hear that their data is exposed like an upside-down turtle. The word *vulnerability*, Eve has learned, comes from the Latin *vulnerabilis*: "wounding."

Eve is in the Denver airport waiting for her flight to JFK when her Rampart email spontaneously logs her out. That's fine; she was mostly writing lyrics in her Notes app, anyway. She tries to log back in but can't get through. Maybe something's wrong with the Wi-Fi in here. Back to lyrics.

VULNERABILITY: When *PRELAPSARIAN* came out, the big review site called it "humid" (which they meant as a compliment) and "guarded" (which they meant as an insult). "Moments of insight are eclipsed by stilted overproduction—descriptions of heartbreak and first love feel like they were written by six men in a boardroom." There was no boardroom. Eve is all six men.

In the past four days—and that's how long it has been since the car accident, four days to end things with Fletcher and pack up all her belongings while they took turns sleeping on the couch—she has written nine songs. She needs at least one more. She knows how the album starts but she needs a final track. Something with hope, but not in a bleh way. No one wants to be called saccharine.

This is the first time she's written songs like this, fluidly and confidently, since she was a teenager. Maybe they have only taken four days to write, but they've also taken four years to write—four years of Boulder, four years of feeling trapped, four years of Fletcher asking her not to write songs about him. Her computer is littered with snippets of half-finished projects, and she feels less like she's creating something and more like she's snapping pieces into predetermined places.

VULNERABILITY: If Eve does not turn her relationship with Fletcher into art, then she wasted half of her twenties.

Eve gets a text from Diego, her work friend.

Diego: Rampart email being weird for you?

Eve tries to log in again. No luck.

Eve: server down maybe?
Diego: Dunno, I'm getting weird vibes
Diego: I heard there was some big meeting this morning
Eve: ooooo keep me in the loop pls

Eve shuts her laptop and gets in line to board. She wonders if it's true that she's too guarded. *PRELAPSARIAN* contains no direct references to sex even though that's what the entire album is about: coming of age, wanting and being wanted, wondering whether your desires are weird. But the album isn't meant to be feelings-y; it's meant to be clever. So it's full of allusions to Milton and Melville and Miller, canonical references she amassed over an English lit/history double major. She sang about temptation in the Garden of Eden, but she couldn't bring herself to write about her own body touching and being touched. She could not bear the thought that her family would listen to it.

VULNERABILITY: Once, Josh—Eve's first serious boyfriend, early college—rolled to face her in the extra-long twin bed and said, "It's weird how you spend all this time writing songs about feelings but I never actually know how you feel about anything." Fletcher never asked Eve how she felt. He did not care to know. For a long time, this felt like the perfect solution.

Just as Eve is hoisting her carry-on into the overhead bin, her phone begins to buzz. She slides into her seat and answers in a whisper.

"Hey!" Shannon says. Shannon is Eve's best friend; they met on the first day of rush freshman year, promptly quit the process, and spent the rest of college being smugly anti–Greek life. It's unclear to Eve who she would've become had Shannon's last name (Offenbach) not been alphabetically adjacent to hers.

"I'm just getting on the plane," Eve says.

"What did Rampart say? I'm asking as your friend, obviously. Consider my reporter hat discarded."

"What," Eve says, "are you talking about?"

"About the data breach."

"What data breach?"

"Oh," Shannon says. "Oh no."

The woman seated next to Eve gives her a look (fair enough) and Eve tilts her head toward the window.

"Can you give me the thirty-second recap?" Eve says.

"Someone hacked the shit out of Rampart, and seeing as their whole business model was to, like, not get hacked, rumor has it that the company will essentially not exist this time tomorrow."

"Wow," Eve says. "That was only ten seconds. Fifteen, tops."

"Are you okay?"

"Oh, I'm totally panicking."

"Deep breaths. This will be fine."

VULNERABILITY: Just before Eve finished college, she got a record deal. It was nothing huge, but, you know, still a record deal. Her dad looked at the projected numbers and told her he would get her a job at his bank. She said A) that was nepotism, and B) she wasn't interested. He told her she was irresponsible and childish. She told him twenty-two was the perfect age to follow your irresponsible and childish dreams. He said, "If you do this, you need to know you will not see a single cent of my money. We're not your patrons. You're an adult now. And you can't stay in this house." So Eve moved to Boulder.

"In the spirit of full disclosure," Eve says, "my bank account is a teensy bit very depleted at present."

"And you definitely can't stay with your parents while you find a new job?"

"Definitely not."

"I would say you could stay with me," Shannon says, "but my landlord is so weird about guests. We could sneak you in and out under cover of night?"

"I'll talk to Julian when I land. I was going to stay with him until I found a place anyway. Maybe I'll just . . . stay a few extra days."

Eve very much hopes "days" does not mean "weeks." Or "months."

"Is that going to be okay?" Shannon asks.

"Positive thoughts," Eve says.

"What if," Shannon says, "and this is just an idea, no pressure, but what if you wrote a super fucking awesome album and then released a song and it went totally viral and then everyone realized how neat you are and you made a shit ton of money?"

VULNERABILITY: Eve will not make it as a musician. There's this idea in creative professions that if you just keep knocking on the door long enough, it will eventually open. But Eve is beginning to wonder if it's less like knocking on a door and more like panning for gold in a river. Not all rivers have gold.

They're somewhere over Ohio when the plane hits turbulence. Eve is not usually a nervous flier but she is entirely convinced she's about to die. A mountain lion and a car crash in quick succession will do that to a person. And her fear—as the seat belt light comes on, as the captain says in a too-tight voice that flight attendants should take their jump seats—is that she will die with this album still halfway trapped inside her. What if she dies and it never becomes real?

She opens the Notes app in her phone and writes a song about hope.

The title of the song is "retrocognition." She's pretty sure *retrocognition* is a synonym for *hindsight* but decides she will need to verify this upon landing. It's apt because this album feels retro—new wave, synth-pop, indietronica. She types the word at the top of her Notes app and it feels gut-right: "retrocognition." Lowercase intentional.

The song comes like it's been there all along.

It's directed at Fletcher. What a feeling—to remember the dead dreams you once had for the future. It's like watching an episode of *The Jetsons* in the 2020s. Oh, to remember what we thought we could be.

In the song, she tells Fletcher she hopes he finds someone who makes him happier, which is true. It's all right. They put up a good fight. She hopes he really loved her but that he loves the next girl more. At least they'll always have hindsight.

When the plane does not, in fact, crash, the fasten seat belt sign turns off and Eve makes her way to the bathroom. She whisper-sings "retrocognition" into her phone in one take so she doesn't forget how it's supposed to sound.

As soon as they land at JFK, Eve sends everything she has, all ten songs and the lyrics and the bits of sound she's been splicing together, to her manager with the subject line: *Do we think this sounds okay?*

Her manager emails back while Eve is at baggage claim.

Halfway through but yes. Have a new producer in mind. When can you be in New York?

It's all so exciting and distracting that Eve can almost ignore the other email she has received, this one from the CEO of Rampart. It uses a lot of corporate jargon to express deep regret.

Diego: Well, nice working with you
Diego: Let me know if you have any job leads
Eve: rip
Eve: o'er the ramparts we watched crash and burn
Diego: Hey, wasn't your brother's company a client?

Eve says, "Uh-oh."

VULNERABILITY: Eve has heard murmurs from Shannon that things are not going so well at Julian's app. Investors are concerned. You know what would be a really inconvenient thing to happen to a precariously situated dating app? An app with an enormous amount of sensitive, personal, and highly traceable user information? A data breach. That would be, as they say, a big fucking vulnerability.

It's unclear to Eve how, exactly, she's going to get her assorted suitcases from the Jamaica AirTrain to the E—or the LIRR?—and she's considering if she will regret spending a hundred dollars on an Uber when the automatic doors open and through them emerges Shannon with a cardboard sign. It says WELCOME HOME NEVER LEAVE ME AGAIN!!! Shannon spots Eve, brandishes the sign overhead, does a little dance, shoves the sign in the recycling, and jogs to help Eve with her bags.

"I love you so much," Eve says.

"I know! Hug, please."

They catch up on the train to Julian's even though they're always in semiconstant contact and there's not that much to catch up on. Shannon gives Eve her phone to read an article she's drafting on facial recognition software. Eve gives Shannon her phone to listen to the disjointed files she has tentatively labeled *ski rat*.

"Eve, this is, like—" Shannon says.

"Surely they must be regulating who has access to facial recognition," Eve says.

"You've gone indietronica. I love it."

"Anyone can just download this software?"

"We're going to talk about your thing for a minute," Shannon says, "but thank you."

Eve concedes: "I think I had all these songs in the back of my mind, but I didn't want to write any of them because I thought it would hurt Fletcher. Or myself."

"Let me see the lyrics," Shannon says.

Eve shares the folder. She knows Shannon will return the songs with notes: "Hard to parse this" and "Cliché" and "Singsongy rhyme." Shannon has never once sent a grammatically accurate text, but that's mostly irony. No one gives better edits.

At the apartment, Julian lets them in. He hugs Eve then holds her at a distance, blinking down with pale lashes like little filaments of glass.

Julian is twenty-eight. Very tall, very thin, very pale. He is beautiful like a Victorian ghost. He wears casual clothes but steams and irons all of them. He has been reading *The Power Broker* for the past four years. On his nineteenth birthday, he got a tattoo on his rib of the Augustus Saint-Gaudens golden statue of Diana in the American Wing of the Met—that was where their grandmother took them for lunch growing up—and he cried because he regretted it so completely. In the bottom drawer of his nightstand, he keeps a deflated stuffed polar bear named Professor Snowflake Van der Doodle. When they were kids, he would sort all their Halloween candy so Eve could have all the best pieces. He is Eve's favorite person.

Shannon has to get back to work, so she hugs them goodbye and leaves.

"I should get back to work, too," Julian says. "We're in a bit of a shit show. On account of a data leak. Perhaps you're familiar."

"Really," Eve says, "so sorry about that."

"Grab whatever you want from the kitchen. Gigi's at a work lunch. You just missed Danny. No pressure, but remind me how long you're staying?"

"So, Shannon's lease ends in a month . . ."

"Ah."

"But I can, like, totally couch surf for a while."

"You're not going to couch surf," Julian says. "Just be really nice to Gigi."

"Done. I promise. So nice. I love Gigi."

Gigi is grumpy and gorgeous and terrifying, but Eve has always felt like she and Gigi *could* love each other if given enough time, so this is not so much a lie as it is willful optimism.

"Right," Julian says, "just please don't take her coffee? Or her shampoo. Oh my god, do not eat her pita chips. Gigi loves pita chips."

"I'll be invisible," Eve says. "A little mouse."

"A little mouse who doesn't eat pita chips."

Eve salutes. After a pause, she adds, "Thanks for not suggesting I ask Mom and Dad."

"They'd say no."

"Yeah. Ever think that's kind of weird?"

"All the time, Eevee. Now please let me work."

2

The month goes by like this: Eve thinks about music. Her manager gets in touch with a new producer, someone who's been doing promising work with the label that put out *PRELAPSARIAN* and ostensibly wants to put out Eve's sophomore album. The producer is no-nonsense—a sixtysomething man who wants to get in, make the music, and get out again, with no diversions for friendship along the way. Eve keeps her head down in the studio and follows instructions. At the label's request, she begins teasing songs on her long-dormant social media. Some fans are excited. Many seem to have vanished in the wind. Eve didn't have that many to begin with, and it's been a long four years of nothing.

Whenever she's not working on the album, Eve applies to another soulless tech copywriting job. AI has rendered them scarce. She applies to other jobs, jobs for which she is wholly unqualified, and imagines what her life would look like if she really did have a passion for data analytics. She tries to be out of the apartment as much as possible, so she writes in the library and has lunch with her parents, who do not offer use of her childhood bedroom. Julian and Gigi introduce Eve to Our Lady of Perpetual Breakfast, and Eve decides she has never loved a dining establishment so thoroughly. A Catholic school! Turned diner! You can eat right there in the confessional booth. It is perpetually cacophonous: the clanging AC, the clatter of silverware echoing off the ceilings, the weird whistling of wind coming from who knows where. Eve has never consumed so much drip coffee.

In the evenings, she eats ice cream in the park with Shannon and they talk about AI-driven linguistic adaptations and which of their college classmates are most likely to break up. It feels like—ah. Eve had friends in Colorado, but she didn't have Shannon. Shannon Offenbach is singular: She grew up near Santa Cruz in an "intentional living community" (commune) founded by born-again hippie Silicon Valley ex-pats. It was endlessly dramatic and contentious, which means Shannon is better than anyone Eve knows at resolving fights. Sophomore year of college, they were required to write their "personal superpowers" on the paper name signs on their doors, and Shannon wrote: "I will mediate your problem for one (1) beer." Her father is a professor and foremost expert on Euclidean geometry in the flora of Big Sur. Her mother is a former tech lawyer who now represents the "intentional living community" (commune). The first time Eve met Shannon's parents, she was overwhelmed by how loud and chaotic they were. And then she fell in love with them. She wished they were hers even as she felt guilty for wishing it. It's obvious, in retrospect, that some parents really love each other, but the realization never occurred to Eve until she saw Shannon's parents holding hands on the walk to dinner.

There is much that feels magic to Eve about her friendship with Shannon, but the thing she treasures most is that Shannon makes her a better person. Shannon prods at Eve's assumptions about the way the world works and gets her to interrogate what she takes for granted. Eve grew up around a mostly silent dinner table, but with Shannon, she feels as if they could talk forever and never run out of things to say.

Eve gets home after one of these ice cream evenings with Shannon to find Julian in the kitchen making dinner and Gigi doing yoga in the living room.

"Danny?" Gigi says, then looks up from her downward dog. "Oh, hey. He just left. I thought you were him."

"I can't believe we still haven't overlapped," Eve says. She goes to the kitchen.

"Danny?" Julian says. He turns. "Oh."

"Just me."

"You just missed him again. He has a date."

Eve hoists herself on the counter. "Like an app date? By which I mean, obviously, a date wherein you eat only appetizers."

"That was so stupid. That's such a Danny joke."

"I did not remember that Danny had such a refined sense of humor. It's someone he met on your app, though, right?"

Julian nods. "You should get on Pathos. It's been long enough post-Fletcher, yeah?"

"I mean, it hasn't been that long, but I also feel like we were spiritually broken up for the last two or so years."

"So get on Pathos."

"Are you trying to make me a guinea pig?"

"Well, *I* can't use it. I'm engaged to a literal goddess and I really don't want to cross her."

From the other room, Gigi says, "Figurative."

"Come on," Julian says. "It's better than all the other dating apps. We'll tell you all the ways you're actually compatible with people."

"I don't want an app to tell me how to feel. I want to tell myself how I feel."

"Because you've done such a good job of that in the past?"

Primly, Eve says, "We should all endeavor to be lifelong learners."

VULNERABILITY: Eve is embarrassed how many people have told her, "Well, obviously you and Fletcher were never going to work." Obvious to whom? And for how long? And what does this indicate about Eve's ability to choose her next partner?

3

It's decided that they're going to release "rings" first, which will be the first song on the album. It's about the stories we tell ourselves about our lives; about waiting for either a breakup or a proposal to tell you if your love story was a good one. As a courtesy, Eve sends it to Fletcher before she posts the first snippet on Instagram.

> **Eve:** It's not meant to be about you, but it's about how I felt when I was with you, so of course some details leak over. Let me know if you want to talk about it more. I hope you're well
> **Fletcher:** I just listened. I actually do feel like this is quite personal.
> **Eve:** I appreciate that, but it's music, and it's my subjective experience, and this is my career.
> **Fletcher:** For someone who loathes being vulnerable as much as you, I'm surprised you're willing to force someone else to be so vulnerable in a public forum
> **Eve:** Are you asking me to not release the song?

Fletcher doesn't respond again. Eve releases the song.
And her fans. Love it.
People are using it in Instagram Reels that have nothing to do with the vibe of the song—it really takes off in the fashion sphere—and then more people are streaming it, and then they're announcing the full album will be out in two months' time. Out of nowhere, fan accounts spring up calling themselves Evils, Evenings, Eevees—which has always been Julian's nickname and no one else's. Eve feels

like she is on a roller coaster click, click, clicking up—that the trajectory of her career is suddenly, without warning, pointing directly at the sky.

VULNERABILITY: What the hell is she going to write about for her next album?

4

Eve and Shannon go out to celebrate and drink too much champagne, and when they say goodbye on the C train, they're both happy-teary and can't quite remember how they ended up this way. Julian and Gigi are out of town visiting wedding venues, so Eve plans to luxuriate in the empty apartment all weekend. She will make herself her traditional post-drinking snack: a peanut butter spoon. As she walks up the stairs to their apartment, she thinks: *I am finally in the version of the story I always wanted.*

   She unlocks the door and shoves it open with her shoulder, but where she expects darkness, there is actually light, and where she expects an empty apartment, there is actually a man at the sink holding a glass of water and staring at her with probably more than the appropriate amount of shock, but it is shocking, like a physical shock when they look at each other, and obviously it's not first sight because they've known each other for ten years but it feels like something fundamental has just taken shape in the space between his eyes and hers, but then again, maybe Eve is just getting carried away because who believes in all that, just nonsense, really, except for right now when it feels like the truest thing in the world when Danny finally finally finally says, "Eve?"

Questions and Answers

1

RIGHT NOW

A QUESTION: DANNY

Danny finds himself staring at Eve. Eve! Eve Olsen! He's not sure why he's so surprised to see what she looks like. He has known her, after all, since he was a freshman in college, for ten years. When he first saw her, he thought she looked like Julian—the same fair hair and brows, the same ski slope noses, the same posture, an exclusive of the wealthy, simultaneously upright and effortless. But now Danny does not think Eve looks like Julian at all, because Eve is—well, because Eve is gorgeous, messy, and sunswept. Julian is none of those things! Eve has this look on her face like Danny has caught her in the middle of a thought. A moment of inspiration. *Oh*, he thinks, *oh shit*.

"Danny!" Eve says. She throws her arms around him and he did not know she was this tall, but she is, they are nearly the same height, and her arms are around his neck. She smells like eucalyptus.

"The one and only Eve Olsen," he says. Jesus Christ. *The one and only?* It's giving circus.

Eve laughs with something like delight and takes a step back. She claps twice, looking at him. "How are you? How have you been?"

"I'm good. Great. But how are you? I heard you were in an accident?"

She waves him away. "Cosmic intervention! How's app life? Introduced any true loves lately?"

"Unfortunately, our app seems to be about as good as the other apps at finding successful matches, which is to say: not very good. I should know. I am guinea pig number one."

"Oh, yeah, hey—sorry to hear about Kyra."

"Oh, it's totally fine. That was, like, two years ago."

"That long, huh? Wow."

"I mean, like a year and a half. Sorry to hear about Fletcher."

"Really," she says, "don't be."

He hesitates. It's obvious he's going to ask her out. What's the worst she could say? No? Actually, the worst she could say is yes, and then they'd have the greatest first date ever seen, and then they would have a slow and pastel summer full of park picnics and falling in love, and then in a year's time they would move in together, and then Danny would take her back to Montana to meet his dad, and they'd make each other laugh and Danny's dad would say, "Hey, kid—you chose well," and Danny would look at her and know that she had made him braver and smarter and kinder, had helped him grow into the person he'd always wanted to be, and she would look back at him the same way—and then, three years on, he would get down on one knee and tell her she was the love of his life and would she please make him the happiest man on earth and she would say, "I'm so, so sorry, but no."

But fuck it.

"What are you doing Saturday?" Danny asks.

2

TWO YEARS AGO

AN ANSWER: DANNY

The snow comes early that year. Four days before Christmas, down it wafts in glittery flurries, icing the fire escapes and dusting the trees. Danny waits for Kyra just outside her subway stop, up in the cold and the slush with the Christmas music leaking out the nearby coffee shop every time the door pushes open. He exhales, and his breath fogs.

"Hey, cutie," Kyra says.

He looks down—he is not particularly tall but Kyra is tiny—and smiles at her. There she is, like magic. She is wearing earmuffs, and there is a snowflake quickly melting on the tip of her nose. Danny leans to kiss her, and she tilts her chin up.

"Where are we going?" she asks.

"Sheep Meadow?" Danny says. "Look at the snow?"

"You're so Montana."

"Everyone likes snow in Central Park."

"Still. So Montana. When we're there, are you going to start doing cowboy things?"

"Hey," Danny says, "I'll have you know I come from a line of crunchy woodsy Montanans. Entirely distinct from cowboy Montanans."

"Are we going to cook a moose on the range?"

"Moose hunting is restricted by permit. But if you're lucky, we might cook tofu in the air fryer."

Kyra slips her mittened hand into Danny's gloved one, and they start crunching through the frost. It's that perfect, brief glow you only get in the first hours after a New York snow—when all that is white has not yet become gray and slushy. They cross a street populated by slow-moving carriages, horses clip-clopping on the pavement, and pedicabs playing carols. The open spaces between sidewalks are full of children on sleds and dogs in plaid jackets.

Kyra hums contentedly. They have, at this point, been together for three years. Three years exactly. They met at a Christmas party when she spilled an entire bottle of peppermint schnapps on Danny's shirt. She tried to help him clean it. They ended up kissing in the building's basement laundry, where someone had hung mistletoe. At this point, they have told and retold this story so much it has the polished choreography of a stand-up routine. In this age of app dating, how precious is this? A real-life clumsy meet-cute. They always conclude with her saying, "He smelled like a drunken elf for a week." And him saying, "Totally worth it."

For the first time, they have elected to spend the holidays together. They will go to Bozeman for Christmas, and then to Kyra's parents' in Philadelphia for New Year's. When they made these plans in September, Danny felt consumed by the trepidatious butterflies he thought were the exclusive purview of a relationship's beginning. He felt, again, like he was on a roller coaster. But now, the question is not "will they won't they?" but "forever or just for now?" *Forever*, he thinks. That's what it means, doesn't it, that Kyra wants to spend Christmas in Montana? In October, he and Julian went ring shopping. Julian brought along his new girlfriend, Gigi, to weigh in.

And now there is a diamond in a red velvet box in Danny's pocket.

Kyra is saying something, and Danny's having a hard time paying attention. His stomach keeps swooping. He laughs, and it sounds canned—a studio audience laugh.

They stop at a tree, bare bark all dusted with snow, and Kyra puts her hands in her pockets and grins up at the branches. This, this! This is what Danny loves about her. She is so infinitely astounded by the world. He has dated people before, and this is not the first time he's been in love, but he feels a certainty in this moment that those loves were a cheap facsimile of the real thing.

An elderly couple walking their elderly dogs plod slowly past. They smile at Danny and Kyra, and Kyra smiles back, and Danny shifts his weight from foot to foot. Finally, they move along, and there's a sudden moment of privacy, and Danny takes a breath.

"Kyra," he says.

"Danny."

"Meeting you, three years ago, was the best thing that ever happened to me. You make me a better person. I love you, but I also admire you, and I appreciate you, and I'm just so grateful you're in my life."

Kyra has gone very still. Her head is tilted slightly to the side. The elderly couple with the dogs is circling back around. Why are they coming back? Danny puts his hands, which are numb, in his pockets and feels the shape of the box.

"I want to be with you forever," he says. "That's all I want. I had no idea a person could feel as much love as I feel for you. I think it's the kind of thing that only happens if you're lucky. Once in a lifetime."

"Danny," she says quietly.

He begins to lower his knee.

"Danny, please stop."

He straightens.

"I don't—" Kyra looks over her shoulder, like someone might be coming to her rescue. The elderly couple is now watching one of their dogs take a shit in the snow. "This isn't what I want."

"Oh," Danny says. Slowly, slowly, he takes his hands out of his pockets. "Like . . . now? Or . . . ?"

"We're way too young."

"Are we? Okay. I just—sorry." Sorry? What kind of person apologizes for having their heart broken? Danny, that's who.

"I have so much that I still want to do," Kyra says. "I have to live in Paris!"

Kyra has never before mentioned Paris. "Okay," Danny says. "Okay, sure, let's move to Paris."

"No," she says, with more conviction now. "No, and I want to get an MBA, I want to run a marathon! Oh my god, I've never even done anal!"

The elderly couple looks up, then at each other, then back at Danny and Kyra.

"Do you want to do anal?"

"I don't know!" Kyra says. "I can't get married to someone who's too afraid to ever try anything new."

"You don't want to marry me because I have never suggested we do anal."

"Could you stop saying that word?"

"Okay," Danny says. "Sure. I would love to stop saying *anal* in the park."

Now Kyra is laughing, which means that Danny is also laughing. His eyes are watering, but he's also laughing. It's just so cold out.

She touches her mittens to her cheeks. She's crying, too. Danny's instinct is to reach out for her, but he knows that he should not. That he will never comfort her again.

"I'm so, so sorry," she says. "But no. I can't be with you forever. I do love you. But I just think you're—we're. We're missing something."

"Nice save," Danny says.

"I just mean for me, there's—look. Danny. You will be perfect for someone. I know that. I'm sure of that. But I think for me, if we're together, I'll just always wonder if there's more out there."

"How long have you been wondering that?"

"I guess the whole time," she says.

"What were we missing? What's the more you need?"

"Danny."

"It'll help if I know, right?"

"You're just so—close. All the time. I feel like I don't have any room to breathe. I'm always worried I'll do something wrong and hurt your feelings. I just need someone who pays less attention."

They have had a version of this conversation before. The subtext is that Danny is anxious, but he doesn't know how not to be. He went to therapy for two years, back when everyone was going to therapy for two years, but he felt like it only made him more anxious—anxious to share every tiny revelation to prove that he was becoming more than he had once been.

"But maybe I didn't really realize how strongly I felt it until you said what you said. About this love being the kind of thing you only find once in a lifetime. I think, for me, this just doesn't feel like—the happily-ever-after. The magic thing. And I bet it doesn't really feel like that for you, either."

"How do you know?" Danny says.

"I guess I don't," Kyra says. "I guess you never really know what another person is feeling."

"I guess not," Danny says.

"I'm so sorry."

"Don't be."

Carefully, cautiously, Kyra rises to her toes and kisses Danny's cheek. Then she turns to go. She walks quickly away from him through the park. He watches her go. His skin is numb where she kissed it.

There are logistics to be untangled here. Plane tickets, a lease. Custody of Ticket to Ride and the fiddlehead fern named Sebastian. Friends one will keep, or the other. Changing of emergency contacts. The slow unpicking of two lives very nearly braided together forever.

Danny senses there is a lesson to be learned here. Something about wariness, something about treading carefully, something about not getting your hopes too high. He does not yet know how this will feel in one, two, thirty days' time, but right now he is in the eye of the hurricane, and there, he has the clarity to make a single wish: Let it be a lesson he does not learn.

3

ELEVEN YEARS AGO

A QUESTION: EVE

August. Upper West Side. The air hangs heavy with a primeval, humid fog.

Eve (fifteen, rising high school sophomore, dance team participant, in possession of two overdue library loans and no boyfriend) stands outside the church her family has attended since she was born. The deep green leaves of the sidewalk honey locust trees droop with moisture. From this angle, Eve can see two of the seven grotesques on the church's Gothic facade: lust and wrath. Inside, she can hear the subdued murmurings of a service about to begin. She looks at her phone, which says 10:43. The bell will toll at 10:45, and then she will be late, which she often is. This makes her father, Phillip, angry. Julian tells Eve to please not provoke him, but Eve can't help it. She provokes because she feels she is, at all times, near some terrible breaking point. Once, last Christmas, when conversation devolved into politics and Eve told Phillip his views were reductive and fascist, he lifted a hand to chest height. Nothing happened. Eve looked at him, and his hand, and then he walked away. She later tried to tell her mother about it, and Julian, and they both thought she had imagined it. Eve thinks it would be easier if Phillip did something truly fucked-up once so she could finally stop waiting for proof, and so she would have an excuse for the low-grade dread she feels every time she stands near him.

At 10:44, Eve ducks inside and walks to her family's pew. She slides into the empty space on the edge beside Julian, who shakes his head. Their parents are on his other side. Phillip looks at her, narrows his eyes, and then turns back to the choir at the front as they begin their processional hymn. They are all dressed in black; it is impossible to tell where one body ends and another begins. Immediately, it's too hot, and Eve feels sweat tracking down the back of her neck. Her thighs stick to the wood.

This pew has been the Olsen pew for a hundred years. The original patriarch lived here on the Upper West Side with his modest scaffolding empire and his upright little family. They were not a stylish family because they were too busy going to church and abiding by prohibition. The business fell to the heirs, who managed well enough, and then it fell to their heirs, Eve's grandfather's generation, and that was when it all went to hell. Eve's grandfather was a profligate spender, a debauchee, a man about town. His siblings exited the family business and made their own money elsewhere, but Eve's grandfather slowly and steadily drove the scaffolding business into the ground—which is not where you're meant to put scaffolding. He was married five times, always to a younger and more doe-eyed actress, singer, dancer. Phillip watched his father become the laughingstock of the family. While Phillip's cousins went to the Hamptons, to the Cape, to the Caribbean for the summer, he stayed in his same apartment full of lost grandeur and sweat. Eve never met her grandfather; he died when Phillip was in college. But she feels as though she knows her grandfather through the imprint he has left on Phillip. She thinks of this line of men, the good and the bad, as the source of her father's seriousness, his fragility, his intensity. The reason he works so hard. The reason he is so easily offended, as if any social gaffe could derail them at any moment. He sees himself as a self-made man, which is not true: Though his father had nothing left to leave him, Phillip still had a network of uncles at law firms and banks to give him the lucky break of his choosing. But he has none of the ease of old money. While Eve's cousins sneak into hotel bars and do yearlong stints in Paris and upstate rehab clinics, Eve and Julian go to school and go to church. They will not ruin what their father has clawed back. In a generation's time, when the other Olsens have squandered what they have, Eve and Julian will be the two great-great-grandchildren left standing. This has never been up for debate.

The service opens with a hymn. For the joy of human love, brother, sister, parent, child. Et cetera. They pray. Then the reverend begins his sermon, which he calls "The Price of Knowledge."

"My friends," he says—and then he tells the story of Adam and Eve. This is of particular interest to Eve, for obvious reasons. While it makes sense to Eve that her parents would have given her the name of a biblical woman, it does not make sense that they chose one so badly behaved. It speaks to a fuck-the-man edginess Eve has never known her parents to possess. As far as she's concerned, her parents both came out of the womb dressed for Wimbledon.

The reverend goes on: When Satan appears, he approaches not Adam but Eve. Some interpretations claim this is because women are weaker. But who among us would turn to our wives, daughters, colleagues, friends, and think them weak?

Eve glances at her father, whose hands are clasped. His thumb rubs the links of his watch.

No—Satan came to Eve because Eve was willing to ask questions. What is the price of consciousness?

Those among us with children, the reverend says, may know how it feels to watch a young person—so confident, so undaunted—lose that innocence. But when we lose our childlike innocence, what do we gain? Ah. That's the question.

Every day, we are faced with decisions. Not just of right and wrong, moral and amoral, but decisions to lean in or turn away. Do we ignore suffering? Or do we seek to understand it? Do we prioritize comfortable ignorance? Or do we venture into the wilderness—that uncomfortable place where we question the status quo?

There is beauty in childlike innocence, as there is beauty in all stages of life. But it does not do to yearn for the garden. There is much—very much—to be grateful for in our knowledge of good and evil. And now that we have the knowledge, we must use it. As Eve before us, we must be curious. We must be curious how best to be—and how best to love each other. Do not move through the world like a child, assuming love will last no matter the circumstances. You must remain kind. You must tend to your love as you would tend to your home. It is where you live.

Let us pray.

When the service ends, Eve waits for her parents to go to the fellowship hall for coffee before she wends her way to the front of the church. She reaches the reverend, who smiles at her.

"Eve Olsen," he says. "How fitting. What can I do for you?"

"How can you say the Bible treats Adam and Eve equally? Isn't the pain of childbirth women's punishment for Eve being disobedient?"

"Ah," he says. "You've found something I've been grappling with, too."

"How am I supposed to buy into something that seems to pretty fundamentally claim women are worse?"

"Well, I'd disagree with your premise, and we could go into that. But maybe the real question is—do you want to buy into it?"

"You don't care if I don't?"

He smiles. "Coffee calls. Walk with me."

"You really don't care if I don't think the Bible is accurate?"

"I care in that I'm curious. I like to hear how young people make meaningful decisions. But I don't plan to convince you one way or another."

"Why would God put the tree there if they weren't supposed to eat it?"

"That's a good question. Maybe they were."

"That's pretty sneaky and vindictive. You know, like entrapment."

"Well, when you put it that way."

"Do you think there's such a thing as too much knowledge?"

He hums softly, a single note. "No, as long as the knowledge is accompanied by equal wisdom. But knowledge without wisdom is dangerous."

"Like if I had the science to engineer a superweapon and didn't have the wisdom to not deploy it all over everyone."

"Exactly," he says. "When we seek knowledge, we also must accept responsibility. Not just for how to use the knowledge, but for how the knowledge might change us."

"Like if you figured out your dad was cheating on your mom."

The reverend's eyebrows lift. "Yes," he says. "Something like that could be difficult knowledge to bear."

Someone bumps Eve as they near the coffee urns, and she has to duck out of the way. It's one of her mom's friends, or, more accurately, a woman her mom doesn't like but who is active in the same circles. The reverend is waylaid by an elderly couple who always sit at the very front, so Eve gives up her interrogation and goes outside, where she sits on the stone steps in the shade. It has gotten even hotter. The sky hangs gray and low. Rain. Any minute now.

When her parents appear, Phillip walks past her without looking down. She assumes he didn't see her. A minute later, her mom, Cecilia, appears, hurrying after Phillip. She does look down at Eve—and she says, "Can't you just be *nice*?"

Eve blinks. *Nice*, she thinks. Is she nice? It's such a severe criticism from a parent—much worse than being called bratty or ungrateful.

Julian comes next. He helps Eve to her feet and says, "Oh, boy, this is a bad one."

"What did I do?"

"You said something to Reverend Palmer."

"I was just asking questions. It was literally a sermon about asking questions. He's not mad at me."

"Look, I don't know. Let's just go home, okay?"

"What the fuck, though," Eve says.

Julian lifts his arms above his head. They walk the long way—east to the park, then along the uneven stones. It's so humid, Eve feels like she's underwater. Even the pigeons are panting.

"He's mad at me because I made some point about a dad cheating on a mom," Eve says.

"You think Dad's cheating on Mom?"

"I was literally just using a random example," Eve says. Then: "I don't know. I wouldn't put it past him."

"Come on. They're not that bad."

"Would *you* want their marriage?"

"Tempting," Julian says. This is sarcasm. "I still don't think either of them would have an affair."

"Then why's he so mad?"

"Because he's Dad."

It would not be until Eve met Shannon's family that she understood the difference between *Dad* and *a dad*. As in—this is not what all dads are like.

"Don't worry," Julian says. "He'll forgive you the next time you get an A on a test."

"And get mad again the next time I offend him."

"Thankfully," Julian says, "there are plenty of tests."

When Eve and Julian get home, Julian goes straight to his room. Eve hesitates at the entrance to the kitchen, where she can hear the clattering of dishes. She considers going upstairs, but she wants to get this over with. She goes into the kitchen.

Cecilia is filling two mugs with hot water from the kettle. Phillip is reading the paper at the table. Neither of them looks at her.

"Hey," Eve says. "Everything okay?"

"Fine," Cecilia says. Phillip says nothing.

"I was just worried that maybe I said something wrong?"

"Let's move on," Cecilia says. Phillip says nothing.

"So . . . we're all okay?"

"I think it would be for the best if we all got along," Cecilia says. And Phillip says: nothing.

"Dad?"

He flips the page. He does not look at her.

"Phillip."

He flips the page again.

At dinner that night, Phillip does not speak to her a single time. She asks Cecilia and Julian if they see how ridiculous this is. Julian lifts his hands placatingly, almost in prayer. Cecilia says, "Can you please just stop?" And it's clear that Eve is the one who is meant to stop.

Eve's father doesn't speak to her for two weeks.

That was the last time Eve went to church. After that Sunday, she stops showing up. Phillip can't tell her she must attend because that would require words, and Cecilia can't force her because that might make the attack of silence obvious to the public. So Eve never goes back.

The shame of it, though, is that she doesn't blame the church, or the reverend, or the contents of his sermon. She likes his measured way of speaking, his gentle intellectualism. Like the faith of so many children, Eve's is collateral damage, ceded to piss off her parents.

When Phillip finally acknowledges her, it's in the morning. He asks if she'll be home after school; someone needs to let the window guy in.

"No," Eve says, "I have dance."

"Oh," Phillip says. "Well. Julian, then." And then he leaves for work.

That's it.

Eve eats the rest of her cereal and stares at the clock ticking above the pantry. If she's angry at her dad, she is equally angry at her mom, who chose to marry him. She wonders if she will ever marry someone. Perhaps no. She thinks of the reverend's warning to remain curious and kind. Whatever her parents' marriage is, it's neither curious nor kind. Maybe it will be fucked forever. Maybe this is just what men do to women they say they love. Maybe, if Eve falls in love with some guy, she will let him walk all over her. Maybe she hasn't learned any other way. Maybe the happiest version of Eve's life, she thinks, is the one where she never lets herself love anybody at all.

4

RIGHT NOW

AN ANSWER: EVE

"Saturday?" Eve says.

"Yeah," Danny says. "I have two tickets to this outdoor show. I don't suppose you know the band Snowy Owl?"

"I *love* Snowy Owl."

"Oh, well, I mean, if you wanted to come. Could be fun."

Danny seems to be blinking at about twice the frequency of normal. Eve is charmed by his nervousness, but also, she is charmed by his familiarity. This is not a stranger but Danny, her Danny. And she is surprised how unbruised she feels post-Fletcher. Like maybe no one can really hurt her. So you know? What's the harm? Eve is not the type to have her heart broken.

"I would love to," she says. "Like a date?"

He is beautiful when he smiles. Like the sun. "Yeah," he says. "Like a date."

It feels as if this is the very beginning of a story, the story, the start of everything. They open the book, flip to the first page, here we go: Chapter 1.

Roller Coaster

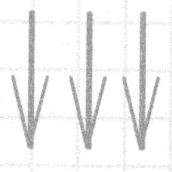

1

It's been a month. But. They still haven't yet had the what-are-we talk. The DTR. The boyfriend/girlfriend label assignation. Which is fine, superfine, awesome. Danny wonders if they don't need to have it at all because they just understand each other innately. They're always on the same page! How could there possibly be the time in the day for Eve to go out with anyone else? It is really so supercool that they can just trust each other from the start.

2

HIGH

Eve asks Danny if he wants to get dinner spontaneously on a Wednesday night. Danny is working from a booth at Our Lady of Perpetual Breakfast, just ordered fries, had planned to work until ten or eleven. Furthermore, he feels it seems a little desperate to accept an invitation on two hours' notice. He says yes anyway.

She has to grab a piece of stray mail from her parents' house, so she asks if he wants to meet her there. Sure! He spends the ride on the C to the Upper West Side fretting about the fact that he is wearing five-inch-inseam floral-patterned shorts about which Chloe, his CMO, said, "Hey, hey, pool party people."

Danny rings the buzzer of the Olsens' 87th Street brownstone and takes a step back down the stairs. The first time he came here, he was eighteen. His exact words to Julian were "Sick house, man." So true.

Phillip, Julian and Eve's dad, opens the door wearing slacks. He looks at Danny's shorts and says, "Daniel! Well. Always a pleasure."

Danny trails him through the entranceway. It has always seemed impossible to Danny that the Olsens' house could be so bright while sitting wedged between buildings on either side. Everything is white and mirrored.

They find Cecilia, Julian and Eve's mom, leaning against the island with her laptop open to an art website. All the art seems to be metacommentary—photos of paintings of sculptures—though what commentary this provides is unclear.

"Sweetheart, hello," Cecilia says. She kisses Danny's cheek. "Are you and Eve going swimming?"

"No, these shorts are just like that."

Cecilia laughs. Does she know Eve and Danny are dating? *Are they dating?* Like, they're going on dates, but are they *dating* dating? Julian has always said that Eve doesn't get along with their parents, but still, this is the sort of thing one tells their parents, yes? Danny has told Cal about Eve.

Footsteps on the stairs.

Eve springs forth in a red sundress with sunglasses on her head. "Sorry, okay, ready, bye Mom, bye Dad, let's go."

On the way out the door, before they have quite cleared the threshold, Eve takes Danny's hand. It's the first time they've ever held hands. She wouldn't do this in front of her parents if she didn't like him, or so he assumes.

They go to a ramen place and the couple next to them spends the whole time breaking up. Eve keeps frantically texting Danny under the table.

Eve: omg do we think he cheated on her
Eve: holy shit with her bridesmaid??
Danny: I think it was with his groomsman
Eve: a queer love story!!!
Danny: But still cheating
Eve: pls be an ally danny

When they exit the restaurant, they walk with her arm around his waist and his around her shoulder. She says, "Please don't cheat on me with a member of my wedding party."

"Are we getting married?"

"I don't know, probably."

"Huge! Congrats to us."

"Ha ha," Eve says.

He kisses her temple, and she leans against his shoulder.

"Uh-oh," she says.

"What's up?"

"I'm very fond of you."

"Is that an uh-oh?"

She wraps herself around him; buries her nose against his collar. "Huge," she says.

When you know, you know—that's the wisdom Danny has always heard, and this feels a lot like knowing.

3

LOW

Eve and Shannon and some of their college friends go away for a weekend. It's some sort of coed bachelor/ette party; Danny is fuzzy on the details. On the first night of Eve's absence, Danny is lying in bed working, which he knows is bad for his sleep but so is everything. He keeps checking his phone to see if she's texted him. Obviously she's superbusy and he shouldn't be weird about it. But what if Fletcher is there and she has fallen rapturously back in love with him? What if she's currently realizing she is so much happier single? What if the degree to which Danny is overthinking all of this is a sign that he should end things because he cannot possibly keep feeling this unhinged? What if!

Right before Eve left, Danny spent the night at Eve and Shannon's apartment, and there was a cockroach in a glue trap. Eve dispatched it with no-nonsense efficiency; putting the trap in the trash, taking the trash to the curb, replacing the trash bag, and washing her hands. Danny stood against a wall the whole time trying not to look like someone who could feel a hundred little legs scuttling over his skin.

"You're so funny," Eve said. "You've lived in New York for six years."

"Let us not acclimate to the will of the cockroach," Danny said.

"Doesn't Montana have bugs?"

"I don't want to talk about it. Also, I'm very brave about rats, so. Can't win them all."

He keeps thinking about this and wondering if he is a fake New Yorker, or if Eve thinks he is.

So those are the things running through his mind as he tries to write this code. Would you believe—it looks very bad. Inevitably, someone else on the team will give him shit about it when they can't understand what he was trying to do. He leaves a comment to really show them who's boss:

```
// DA
// This works but is garbage :)
```

He sends Eve two memes on Instagram, and then he finds a third that's funnier than the first, but he feels he has already used his allotted messages for the night. He should not let her know that he has nothing better to do on a Friday than write code and think about her. He saves the third meme to send after an appropriate interval.

He rereads their most recent text exchange:

Eve: getting on the plane oooo
Danny: Have fun! May all your dreams come true, etc
Eve: give new york a good-night forehead kiss for me
Danny: I wouldn't want to lead her on

Eve didn't respond to the last message. Which is fine, fair; this was a goodbye conversation anyway, and maybe she just couldn't think of anything to say. Or! Maybe conversations about leading people on are particularly fraught for Eve because she's worried she's leading Danny on because while she's enjoying the relationship-ish aspects of their dynamic, she does not actually want a relationship.

Danny shuts his laptop and puts his phone on Do Not Disturb on the other side of the room. Then he wonders if Eve will see the Do Not Disturb and think Danny has gone to bed at ten thirty on a Friday like an octogenarian. He turns Do Not Disturb back off and powers down the phone instead.

"You are literally losing it," Danny says. He flops back onto his bed and presses the tips of his fingers against his eyelids. "You are genuinely fucked."

It should not be this hard. That's Danny's prevailing sentiment. When you know, you know—that's what people say, but Danny does not know anything at all.

4

HIGH

"Olives, yes or no?" Eve says, holding up a jar.

"Eve." Danny takes it from her and puts it back on the shelf. "I'd rather die."

"Excellent! Maraschino cherries, yes or no?"

"Haven't had one since I was of Shirley Temple–ordering age, but fuck it, I'm pro."

"Hmm. So sweet, though."

"We call that an efficient flavor."

"You are so right. Consider me convinced."

They've been wandering the aisles of the Lower East Side Whole Foods for a solid thirty minutes by this point. Danny makes a mean pesto gnocchi (by which he means the *New York Times* Cooking app makes a mean pesto gnocchi), and, ostensibly, they're shopping for ingredients. Actually, they're seeing how well their food preferences align. Not to brag or anything, but they are so aligned.

"If you could only have one spice in your cabinet," Danny says.

"Paprika. Smoked. Sweet paprika can get out of my face. What's yours?"

"I don't know, salt?"

"Salt is not a spice. Salt is a chemical agent."

"Okay. Then I will also take the paprika."

"Smoked or sweet?" Eve asks.

"Don't patronize me."

They finally get their ingredients and pack them into bags and begin the walk back to Eve's apartment through the sunset-drenched streets, weaving around construction scaffolding and dripping air conditioners. There's something lively and perfect about the

Lower East Side, or about being there with Eve. The steady stream of day-drunk twenty-two-year-olds makes him feel like maybe he too graduated college just a moment ago. He's always felt an urgent rush to get to the next stage of life, like if he doesn't hurry, he might miss his only shot, but this summer with Eve, he feels for the first time like there is something good about staying young. Danny catches her looking at him from behind her sunglasses, so he asks, "What?"

"Just thinking you're cute," she says.

"Wholesome."

"You are the prototypical boy next door."

"Am I?" Danny says. "I don't even know what that means."

"It means you have dimples," she says. "I bet all the moms wanted you to ask their daughters to prom."

Danny scratches his jaw. "I was a kid detective. Is that the same thing?"

Eve stops on the sidewalk. "Shut up. Tell me everything."

"Those are contrary requests."

"You were a kid detective?"

"Oh, yeah," Danny says. "Someone was stealing jam from Mrs. Weber's stand at the farmers market, but Biscuit and I tracked him down. Old Man Davenport was pawning it off as his own because everyone knew he made shit jam."

Eve presses her fingers to her lips. "This isn't real. You had a friend named Biscuit?"

"Biscuit was my dog."

"Shut up. This is a fake story."

"This is not a fake story. Mrs. Weber was so grateful, she gave me a lifetime supply of jam. She sends it to me in the mail every month."

Eve holds up a hand. "We're verifying this right now. I will not be taken for a fool." She pulls out her phone; puts it on speaker.

"Hello?" Julian says.

"Hi. Briefly, re: Danny. Does he or does he not receive a special gift in the mail each month?"

"Oh, Mrs. Weber's jam? Yeah, totally. You've gotta try it."

"Okay," Eve says. "That will be all." She puts her phone away and looks up at Danny. "What's wrong with you?"

"I have a wholesome boy-next-door charm and a keen eye for clues," he says.

At Eve's apartment, Shannon is out—they have the kitchen to themselves. Danny likes Shannon, but he is also slightly terrified of her. She speaks like a California surfer (she called an ice cream "rad" the week prior) and then, disarmingly, asks if you've considered the perils of viewing technological advancement through a teleological lens. She has a fern named Hannah, which Danny at first thought was quirky and fun, but alas! The fern's full name is Hannah Arendt, and Shannon would like you to speak to it about epidemic loneliness. Which is all just to say, it's for the best that Shannon has a date tonight. Eve turns on music while Danny unpacks the bags. They cook, they eat, and they queue a tense, high-stakes drama *The New Yorker* called culturally relevant on the living room TV. When they settle back into the couch and press Play, Danny sets his hand on Eve's knee. She leans against his shoulder. The theme song plays. Eve slides her hand down his arm.

"Danny?" she says.

"Eve."

"I have a hypothetical for you."

"Sure."

"What if, hypothetically, we did not waste an hour pretending to watch this show?"

"Good point," he says. "We could just go straight to sleep."

"Sleep is the best medicine, as they say."

"Brimming with antioxidants."

"God did not intend for us to oxidize," Eve says.

He takes her knee and slides it toward him so they are facing, and then he kisses her. She exhales. She smells like sunscreen, which smells like summer, which smells like nostalgia.

In her bedroom, he puts his mouth between her legs while she twines her fingers through his hair. She says, "I love when you do that," but there is a lag before the *when*, so you would be forgiven for wondering if she was about to say something else. She says his name when she comes.

When you know—well, you know.

5

LOW

Eve keeps mentioning this party she's going to go to, a friend's thing, and Danny can't tell whether it's an invitation or not. He doesn't know why he can't just ask her. "Is that an invitation?" he could say, or, "I can't tell if you're inviting me to this." Better yet, he could just make other plans and pretend not to care. Alas! Danny is so bad at not caring.

He keeps that Thursday evening open until the morning of the party, a morning after Eve has spent the night at his apartment, and she mentions, "You can probably come to this party if you want to."

It's Eve's and Shannon's college friends. When they enter the apartment, someone calls Eve's name, and Eve immediately disappears.

"Please be my shepherd," Danny tells Shannon.

"For sure, man," Shannon says. "I will expect you to *baa* at regular intervals, though."

Danny spends the evening being superchill about whether or not he is near Eve at any given moment. On the bright side, everyone he meets is like, "Ooooh, *the* Danny?" Downside, Eve seems thrilled that Danny can fend for himself and as such does very little fending.

At one point, he and Shannon are comparing the relative merits of different types of tortilla chips when she goes, "No fucking way," and then, "Hang on, stay here."

She bobs and weaves to the other side of the party. Danny sees Eve standing near the door looking shocked as a needlessly tall man stoops to hug her. Though Danny has met him before, his most recent acquaintance with this man is in the annals of Eve's social media.

This is Fletcher.

Fletcher has entered the party.

Danny is nothing like Fletcher, whose mother was a professional tennis player and whose father is the CEO of a performance cycling company. Fletcher has the face of an AI vampire and grew up summering in Monaco. Danny, on the other hand, is the prototypical boy next door. Danny is the guy whose defining characteristic is proximity.

Danny has listened to all of *ski rat*, which will be released in its entirety in two weeks' time. Eve has spoken extensively of her decision to be more vulnerable on this album—more specific in the stories and feelings in each song. Which means that Danny knows a lot about Fletcher. Perhaps more than one should know about the recent ex of the person they're seeing. The lyric "naked in a river" seems to stick in Danny's brain.

The chips taste too strongly of lime. Danny keeps eating them because he wants to look like he has purpose. He absolutely does not want to keep standing there watching Eve talk to Fletcher, but he also doesn't want to abandon Eve.

When Shannon reaches them, Fletcher laughs and stoops to pick her up off the ground in a hug. *My man! Don't go around lifting women!* Shannon is also laughing, though, so that's good. They all seem to be instantly engaged in a zany and high-energy conversation about someone they all know. Of course; they've all been friends for years. Danny wonders again whether Fletcher was at that bachelor/ette party. He eats three more chips. Would you believe it? They still taste too strongly of lime!

Danny goes to the bathroom, and when he comes back, Eve, Shannon, and Fletcher are gone. He lets out a long, slow breath and leans against the wall. It should not feel like this. A slow loop of the apartment, and no Eve. Finally, he finds her alone on the balcony.

"Oh, hey," she says.

"Hey."

"Do you want to head out? I'm kind of dead."

They thank the host and Eve hugs Shannon. No sign of Fletcher. Back on the street, Eve says, "That was so weird."

"You didn't know he was going to be here?"

"No. He was in town for some work thing, I guess."

"And how are you feeling?"

Eve raises her hands overhead in a full-body shrug. "You know."

But Danny doesn't know. How could he know? Eve doesn't tell him. And he doesn't ask because he's not sure he wants to push for the answer. Because sometimes, it seems like everything is perfect—like they are meant to be—but then other times, it seems like it has not been nearly long enough since Eve and Fletcher broke up, and Danny has no idea whether the thing between him and Eve is waxing or waning.

"I might actually just call it a night, if that's okay," Eve says. "I think I just need to, like—take a shower and be mopey."

"Yeah, of course. Will you let me know if there's anything I can do for you?"

"Aw," Eve says, and she kisses him for just a moment. "Let's hang out this weekend."

Then she leaves.

What if he didn't overthink this? That would be great. But that word, *mopey*. Why mopey? Mopey because she's full of doubt and regret? Mopey because Fletcher said something that Danny should have asked about? How long does this feeling go on, the uncertainty of it all?

He presses the heel of his hand against his chest.

Is she or is she not the love of his life? Can he or can he not introduce her to his dad? Should he or should he not start telling people that this is the woman he's going to marry—which makes for a very cute story if he ends up being right and a very pathetic gaffe if he ends up being wrong.

Love Is an Algorithm

What he wants are odds. He wants a number to tell him he's not insane.

On the subway the next morning, he's so thoroughly inside his own head that he misses his stop and has to walk six blocks back to work, which is to say, Julian's apartment, where Danny is so relieved Eve no longer lives.

Julian is working at the kitchen table when Danny arrives.

"I have an idea," Danny says.

"The diner," Julian says. "Breakfast burritos. Yes."

"No. I was thinking we stop focusing on matching people and start focusing on people who are already in relationships."

Julian looks up from his laptop. "Meaning?"

"You can't retain your customers if all you offer are first dates. Once users are in a good relationship, we never see them again. So we pivot. We make something for people who want to optimize their relationships. We make something that tells them objectively whether or not their relationship is working."

Julian lowers his laptop screen halfway, hesitates, then shuts it fully. He lays his palms flat against the top with his thumb on the Apple logo, and the links of his watch clink against the titanium. He stands and starts to smile (braces, $5000), and steps forward to reveal white Adidas ($180) and a Guess button-up ($98) and shorts that do not resemble swimwear. He says, "Let's go."

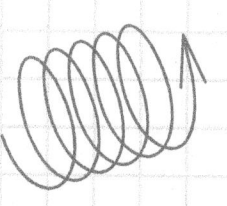

Ten Years

1

TEENAGE EVE

When Eve is a teenager, she falls ill with a collection of symptoms doctors can't diagnose.

Before the sickness, she thinks she'll study math. That is her best subject, and she's drawn to sprawling questions with tidy answers. Some part of her senses that math is for boys, and thus, a more admirable pursuit than humanities, which are for girls, and thus, easy.

But the stomachaches begin midway through her freshman year of high school. Doctors suggest it has something to do with puberty; generic-brand period pain. Some days, after lunch, Eve finds she can't stand from the cafeteria table without passing out. She takes to not eating at school, which makes the counselor refer her to an eating disorder specialist.

Sophomore year, she starts getting dizzy. "Like standing inside of a bell that someone's just hit with a hammer," she says. The doctors wonder if she might have vertigo. They suggest perhaps she is not consuming enough calories and again refer her to an eating disorder specialist.

She is checked for all of it: POTS and endometriosis and PCOS and depression and celiac and hypothyroidism and hyperthyroidism and IBD and stomach ulcers and lactose intolerance. Every time a new doctor suggests a new condition, Eve googles with trepidatious glee. These horrible symptoms could be hers! She could belong to a community of equally unwell people!

Without fail, she does not have the condition. Seemingly, she has nothing. The specialists begin suggesting lightly, then more forcefully, that perhaps the root of Eve's unwellness is Eve. Her parents begin to refer to it as the "Great Malaise." Eve starts to hope she has something awful, something really tragic, because she wants proof of her nociception more than she wants to be okay. Their longtime family physician, Dr. Swann, becomes a semiregular fixture in the Olsen home. She is brusque and bossy and not entirely sympathetic to Eve's predicament, but she also never hints that she does not *believe* Eve's predicament. She also has absolutely no patience for Phillip. Dr. Swann is Eve's first evidence that a woman can be uncowed by her father.

In the era of the Great Malaise, Eve falls behind in her math classes. She is moved from the very advanced class to the advanced one, then from the advanced one to the normal one. She drops out of dance, which she has done since she was three, and takes to carting around the old acoustic guitar Julian received—and never learned to play—for his thirteenth birthday. And for the first time in a long time—ever, perhaps—Eve is able to sit side by side with uncertainty. Good art does not answer questions. It asks them. Good art is not certain; it's curious.

The day she writes her first song, she eats a piece of peanut butter toast and passes out rising from the kitchen table. She goes to her room when she can and lies on her bed and cries: at the thought that this will be her life forever, that she has no agency, that this is, in fact, all in her head. The ceiling swirls above her. She is convinced she can see words written there, or music notes, a whole song arriving fully formed. When she closes her eyes, she falls asleep, and when she opens them, the song is gone. So she sits on the floor of her bedroom and writes her own.

She does not have answers. She does not have proof. But what she does have—what no one can take away from her—is purpose.

And then, when two years have gone by, it all stops. The Great Malaise ends. Dr. Swann stops coming. There will never be a diagnosis—that's just one of those things you have to content yourself with. Her parents say she outgrew it, as if it were a bad habit or an old pair of tennis shoes. They hoped that when she outgrew her symptoms, she would also outgrow music, becoming once more the daughter who will cleave to their plans.

But in the depths of her pain, Eve finds something: an unshakable faith in her own experience of the world. No one can tell Eve who she is. No one can tell Eve how to feel.

2

ADULT EVE

It's Gigi, not Danny, who first tells Eve about Pathos's new angle. Gigi is trying on wedding dresses and has invited Eve along in what Eve takes to be a gesture of good faith.

Gigi looks spectacular in every dress. Which makes sense—she is an influencer with the glossy dark hair of a Disney princess and the proportions of a woodland fairy living under a toadstool.

"I know I'm saying this for all of them," Eve tells her when they reach dress four, "but hot, babe."

Gigi smooths the skirt. Flatly, she says, "I look like I'm going to get murdered in a Swedish cult."

"I don't know," Eve says. "I don't think it's that bad."

"No, that's what I'm going for."

"Oh," Eve says. "Sure, why wouldn't it be?"

The sales assistant swoops in to crow about how beautiful Gigi looks, how stunning and regal and mesmerizing. When she leaves to get another dress, Gigi says, "I hate it again."

Eve has to step into the hallway because she gets a call from her manager about the album launch, which is happening tonight at a bar in Williamsburg. It's just a check-in. Is Eve doing okay?

"Great!" Eve says. Eve feels like she's going to throw up in the nearest potted fern.

When she returns to the dewily lit changing room, Gigi is back in her street clothes—a long black slip dress with a slit up the side.

"Are you okay?" Gigi asks.

"Oh! Yeah!"

"You're all twitchy."

The sales assistant rushes them again. "So?" she says. "What do we think? I think the second one really called to all of us."

"I'm considering," Gigi says. "Will you let me know if you get anything more funereal?"

To the poor woman's credit, she doesn't even blink. "You bet."

Gigi exits, and Eve jogs after her.

"Surely marrying my brother isn't a death sentence?" Eve says.

"It was a joke. Could you not tell it was a joke? I was smiling."

"Were you really?"

"Let's go back to your twitchiness."

Eve rubs the knot in her shoulder. "Just the album, I guess. It's more . . . vulnerable. Than anything I've done before."

"How?"

"It's mostly about Fletcher. He was pretty unhappy with it." Eve hasn't spoken to Fletcher since they bumped into each other at that party, where they made stilted conversation and tried to escape each other as quickly as possible.

"But most people have no conception of you or Fletcher as real people. Your music is just a vessel on which they map their own experiences." Gigi puts on her sunglasses. "Maybe best to take a reader-response theory framework of it all. I want coffee."

Eve subtly texts Shannon as they walk.

> **Eve:** do we know anything about gigi's hobbies or interests
> **Shannon:** idkkkk yoga?
> **Shannon:** ist hat reductive i don't want to be a bad feminist
> **Eve:** i think she's a genius and we've been beguiled by her beautiful hair
> **Shannon:** 100% plausible
> **Shannon:** make her friends w us!!!!! :)

Gigi gets Eve's order and pays for both of them. When Eve tries to thank her, she doesn't react. They settle in at a too-small table by the window.

"How are things with Danny?" Gigi asks.

"Oh. They're good. Really good."

"Really?" Gigi says. "If you hurt him, I'll put crushed-up cyanide capsules in your oatmeal."

"How terribly specific," Eve says.

"Danny is a precious commodity," Gigi says. Her voice is, as ever, completely flat.

"No, I know."

"Do you?"

Eve looks at her coffee. "I know it hasn't been that long, but he really matters to me."

She feels Gigi looking at her. Finally, Gigi says, "Do you love him?"

Eve swirls the ice in her cup. The table next to them is eavesdropping and not being subtle about it. Does Eve love him? At the dress shop, he texted her from San Francisco, where he's meeting with investors. It was a picture of a sandwich board outside a café that said OUR SOUPS ARE HOT AND WEIRD. He wrote: You are soups. The thought of him thinking of her made her feel warm and safe and generally like she had swallowed sunlight, which seemed, she recognized, like a disproportionate reaction to a joke about soup.

"We haven't talked about it yet," Eve says.

"How do you feel about the relationship health thing?"

"The what?"

"The new part of the app. The reason they're in SF."

"I don't think I know about this."

"They want to stop being for first dates and start being for relationships. They're going to tell you what your relationship health is."

"How could an app possibly know that?"

Gigi shrugs. "Ask Danny."

"So the app tells you whether you're in love?"

"Or whether your partner is pulling away."

"I don't know how I feel about that," Eve says.

"Love is so hard," Gigi says. Eve can't tell whether she's being sarcastic. "It would be so much easier if someone else did all that work for you."

3

TEENAGE EVE

Around the same time Eve's Great Malaise goes away—though she doesn't know it's the end yet—she meets, for the first time, Danny Aagaard.

Julian is set to take Amtrak home the Wednesday before Thanksgiving. It's his freshman year of college; Eve's junior year of high school. The house smells like food—pie and buttery potatoes and balsamic vinegar—which Cecilia acquires at the Citarella on 75th and Broadway and is now heating/arranging. Eve lies on the couch with her guitar propped haphazardly on her lap, playing but not really playing. She has this sound stuck in her head, and she is trying to figure out if she came up with it or heard it in someone else's song. Mostly, though, she's waiting for Julian.

In his first months of college, he does what's expected of eldest sons—which is to say, he completely disappears. She prowls his social media as girls from his dorm tag him in pictures and videos. There he is at a soccer game; in a low-effort Halloween costume; drinking from a red cup. She wonders who these girls are. If one is a girlfriend. If she will be Eve's friend—someone to give Eve dating tips and eyeliner recommendations.

Eve hears the front door open and she starts to sit, then lies back down again; she doesn't want to look too eager to see he-of-the-unanswered-quintuple-text. She hears their voices before she sees them.

"Julian! Sweetheart, welcome home. And—oh."

"Hi, Mrs. Olsen. Thank you so much for having me."

"Of course, I just—"

"Mom, Danny. Danny, Mom. Danny's my roommate."

"Oh. Yes. Of course. Right, Danny, right, thank you for the flowers, that's so thoughtful."

"I guess I should've told you he was coming."

"That might have been nice."

"Oh—I'm so sorry. I can—"

"Don't be silly. Come in. Make yourself at home."

Danny steps into the living room behind Julian, and for the first time, Eve sees him.

He stands in the hall framed by the big window, which is just barely ajar, with the cold autumn air swirling behind him and the branches of the honey locust tree out front tapping against the glass. He's wearing a flannel and has one hand in his back pocket. He looks like the kind of young adult they'd cast as a fifteen-year-old in a movie for child labor reasons—too wholesome to be a real adult but too handsome to be a genuine teenager. He looks like the guy who won homecoming king but assumed there had been a mistake. This is not someone with the courage or antiestablishment instinct for trends. His haircut is generic. His eyes are hazel. He doesn't look like he could withstand a football tackle but would fare well at a fun run.

Some years later, Shannon tells Eve she has very specific taste.

"Your type is just an exquisitely nonthreatening man," Shannon says.

"I like a guy who looks like he was a kid detective. Is that such a weird type?"

"Yes," Shannon says. "But all men are a weird type."

The truth is, though, that Eve doesn't think of herself as a person with a type on the day Danny walks through her front door. It is possible that her type is made right then.

When he first sees her, ten years before they start dating, he smiles generously and says, "Eve?"

4

ADULT EVE

Eve spends most of the day of her album launch pacing alone in the apartment she shares with Shannon—the one they moved into together just a few months prior but is already proving more characterful than anticipated.

The apartment, Eve and Shannon call the Court because it's on Attorney Street, an alley of mechanics and dog trainers and funky dive bars whose college-age crowds tumble along the sidewalk late into the night and early into the morning. The Court is on the fifth floor of a series of narrow apartments above a tiny tarot shop: PSYCHIC ADVICE BY DEBBIE, the window says, and beneath, a painting of a golden hand crosshatched by crimson lines.

The Court is a fickle space, possibly haunted, where the water is sometimes forty degrees and sometimes two hundred, but never in between. There is a clanging radiator in Eve's bedroom (nicknamed Bang Clang) and a huge metal pipe in the bathroom (nicknamed Hot Pipe). Both Bang Clang and Hot Pipe should be off for the summer, but every few days, they spontaneously turn on and begin blasting heat into the apartment. Their super believes this is on account of some sort of supernatural activity; he blames Psychic Debbie.

Because the apartment is so mercurial, Eve and Shannon discuss it as a living thing in need of coaxing and regular sacrifice: "Will my hair dryer work today, if it pleases the Court?" "Can the bathroom door close today, if it pleases the Court?"

The windows face a brick wall with a small ledge where three pigeons make their home. Every morning, around sunrise, the pigeons begin to coo. Early on, Eve decided that she could be annoyed at the pigeons or delighted by them, so she ascribed them a storyline: Their names are Matilda, Esme, and Thad, and they are in something of a tumultuous throuple.

Inside the Court, it's an eclectic hodgepodge of secondhand furniture and decor. Some days, Eve thinks it looks chic and intentional—the heaped velvet pillows and the weird little art deco chandelier and the inexplicably red kitchen cabinets. Other times, she thinks it looks like it belongs to two people who have not yet acquired the money or taste to live somewhere better.

Eve thought it would be nice to spend a "chill" day at the Court so she could "unwind" before the album launch, but by the time it gets dark and she's ready to go, she has never been more fully wound. Bang Clang has been bang-clanging her last nerve.

She walks into the Williamsburg bar when it's still mostly empty. Shannon is there already, talking behind the counter with the manager, a thirtysomething woman Shannon briefly dated but saw no future with because the woman's ten-year plan involved moving to a commune upstate. Shannon has nothing against communes; she's just kind of been there and done that.

The manager greets Eve and says, "Hey, big fan." This is unlikely—Eve doesn't have the kind of streaming numbers that produce a lot of big fans.

Shannon has already put up giant posters of the album cover. On it, Eve sits on the golden wood floor of a '70s-style living room with her legs stretched in front of her. She's wearing a retro ski suit bell-bottoms, chevrons, a huge belt—and an expression that says *Please get me the fuck out of here.* This photo was taken after two hours of making other expressions and was entirely genuine.

The theme of the evening, in honor of the album art, is "'70s après-ski but it's summer in New York." Eve is wearing thin red ski bibs and a black bra. She had originally planned to include a tank top for some portion of the night but then her parents remembered they were going out of town this weekend. Eve wonders when you become famous enough that you're willing to wear lingerie at events where your parents will see you.

"Hot," Shannon says, gesturing to Eve. "Excellent."

"Nauseated," Eve says, gesturing to herself. "Excited?"

"You're gonna do so good."

Eve put very clear instructions on the invitation:

7:00: This is when the party technically starts. Show up now if you want to hang out with me while I'm nervous and it's weirdly light out.
8:00: This is when you should show up if you want to get the good snacks.
9:00: This would be an ideal time for you to show up to vibe to some music.
10:00: This is a slightly late time to arrive but I support you.
11:00: This is very late and I await your most colorful excuses.
12:00: This is when I will be going home.

Danny shows up at 7:06 looking flustered.

"Hi," he says, kissing her forehead. "My flight got delayed. I came straight from the airport. This is amazing, you're amazing, how can I help?"

Julian and Gigi arrive at 7:28 in matching color-block windbreakers.

"Where are Mom and Dad?" Julian asks.

"They had a thing with the Colemans."

"That's so typical! I'm sorry. Fucking hell, man."

Eve pats Julian's shoulder. They look at each other with pity. Eve thinks of her parents as caricatures—memes of self-involved sixtysomethings who refuse to be impressed by their children. Julian thinks of them in a more human aspect. Eve feels Julian's way is probably kinder, but at least she's never disappointed.

"Breathe, my guy," Gigi tells him. "Eve, come here. Julian, photo." She grabs Shannon from somewhere and spends ten seconds posing everyone, tilting them into the best light and rearranging Eve's hair. "Okay. Look indolent."

Julian takes the picture. When he shows them the screen, Gigi says, "Yes."

"Holy shit," Shannon says. "This is the best photo anyone's ever taken of me."

"We look like a spy trio," Eve says.

"All in the lighting," Gigi says. Eve thinks it's more all in the Gigi.

There's no way for a launch not to be anticlimactic. The music is new for everyone else, but Eve is already tired of hearing these songs seven thousand times. She keeps noticing phrases that seem so boring—are they cliché, or has she just gotten used to them?

They play the album all the way through twice on the speakers. Eve nurses a beer and says, "Hi, hi, oh my gosh, thanks for coming, hi." The bar is humid, and all the voices blur together in a low hum.

"I'm running out of things to say to people," Eve tells Danny at one point.

"You got it," he says. From then on, whenever anyone approaches, Danny talks incessantly. "What's that you're drinking? No way! Is that your favorite? Tell me about it!"

Eve is pretty sure her cousin Janine will forevermore believe Danny is just that passionate about IPAs. He holds her hand, and she leans against his shoulder.

She ends up standing on a low table singing "ski rat" and "retrocognition" and then "HONEY LOCUST," a song off her first album, and when she looks into the dark depths of the bar, she sees Danny gazing back at her with a beer pressed to his chest, and though there are no spotlights, she thinks for a minute there are because he is the only thing she sees: like a sunbeam.

When they are back in his bed two hours later, they face each other across the pillows. His skin, in the lamplight, is gold. His eyelashes are honey. One of his hands is tucked under his cheek, and his wrist still has a green paper band from the bar. Sometimes, when Eve looks at him, she is baffled by the thought that thousands of people have met Danny, and only a fraction have fallen in love with him.

"Oh my god," Eve says. "I never even asked how your trip went."

"You were somewhat busy."

"Forgive me."

Danny kisses her palm and looks up at her. "I'm just happy to be here."

She lifts his chin. Their foreheads touch and she kisses him gently, just for a moment. "But really. Tell me about the trip."

"But we were kissing."

"We can do that after," Eve says.

"Foiled again," Danny says. He tucks her hair behind her ear. "It was good. San Francisco is weird. I didn't expect it to be so corporate."

"Gigi said you were meeting investors?"

"We have a new pitch for the app. I've been wanting to get your take on it, actually."

"Shoot."

"Well, we'll still match people. But then we'll also be a support system as the relationship goes on."

"Support system how?"

"It'll give you personalized advice—how to handle conflict, get out of a rut, whether you should break up. That sort of thing."

"How are you going to tell people if they should break up?"

"We'll give them a relationship score."

"Like, 'two stars, would not recommend to a friend'?"

"You sound skeptical," Danny says.

She pauses. "I don't want this to come out the wrong way. But do you really think something like this will help people feel more secure? What if you find out your partner loves you less than you love them?"

"Wouldn't it be better to know?"

"That's very Miltonic of you."

"I have bad news," Danny says, "because I've listened to your first album many times, but I have never made it past the third page of *Paradise Lost*. I hope you can still find it in your heart to love me." A pause. "I mean love in the colloquial sense. Platonically. As bros do."

"Danny," Eve says.

"I really didn't mean that in, like, a declarative sense—"

"Technically, you were declaring on my behalf. You declared nothing of yourself."

"I did declare I'm not the sort of suave sophisticate who has read *Paradise Lost*."

"Are you worried?" Eve says. "About how I feel? Because I was wondering, with the app, if this is because you feel like I've been too much or not enough or like we're not on the same page. But I can just tell you. If you want to talk about it."

"Okay," he says.

"I've never had anything like this before."

"Like what?"

"It's all just so easy. You make me laugh, and you're kind, and I'm incredibly attracted to you. I like who I am with you. I care so much about this going right. It just feels like it always is. Right." When he doesn't immediately respond, she asks: "Is that how you feel?"

And then he smiles. It takes a second to get from his mouth to his eyes. "Yeah," he says. "Exactly."

"Hey, Danny?"

"Hey, Eve."

"Can I tell you something slightly deranged?" she asks.

"That would make me so happy."

"You know how I got attacked by a mountain lion. And then got in a car crash."

"This is why I'm giving you Bubble Wrap for your birthday."

"There's a superstitious part of me that feels like the universe stepped in with drastic measures because it got tired of waiting for me to come find you. So that's how I feel. About you. If that clarifies anything."

He wraps his arms around her and pulls her into his chest. Kisses her hair and the nape of her neck. "Actually," he says, "that clarifies a lot."

Eve doesn't say she loves him even though she does. Why not?

Because she read a magazine at age twelve that said men need a chase and this worked its way into her brain on an inexorable level.

Because she suspects this is the last time she will say it for the first time.

Because she is afraid he will not say it back.

5

TEENAGE EVE

Eve spends the whole of that first Thanksgiving dinner with Danny being mortified of her family. Have they always been so stuffy, so pretentious, so *boring*? Everyone jockeys to seem like they know the most about whatever political thing just happened even though everyone is getting their information from the same *New York Times* column. Eve keeps shooting looks at Danny, trying to see if he thinks her family is as embarrassing as she does, but he just politely eats and thanks everyone for everything more times than is necessary. "The potatoes are amazing, the salad is amazing, wow, these biscuits, thank you so much." Eve wants to point out that no one present made any of it. Besides, the best thing on the table is a jar of homemade huckleberry jam that Danny brought as a gift.

The crucible moment, in Eve's eyes, happens when Phillip asks Danny how classes are going. Notably, Phillip has not yet asked Julian the same.

"Sir, frankly, I'd be in so much trouble if Julian weren't in my history section," Danny says. "I'm awful at history, but it's a freshman requirement. I swear, Julian's like a walking encyclopedia. What was that thing the TA told you about your essay?"

And then Julian takes the baton, and suddenly Phillip is nodding at Julian's fresh new insights on Cold War disarmament policies. Danny catches Eve watching him. He gives her this puzzled little smile—like he doesn't realize he has done something special, or that his efforts would mean something to her.

Once everyone is done, Danny begins to clear the plates. Eve waits for her parents to stop him, and when they don't, she's mortified all over again. She leaps to her feet to help.

They end up at the sink together—her washing, him drying—while the voices of the others drift softly from the dining room. Occasionally, their arms brush. Danny takes off his flannel and is wearing a slim white T-shirt beneath. He has a terrible watch tan. On his neck, he has a thin silver chain he will later lose because Julian will tell him it makes him look like a fuckboy—but at the time, everyone has those thin chains, and the fact that Danny's is settled in the hollow of his collarbone makes Eve feel like she might faint.

"The jam was really good," Eve says. "Did your mom make it?"

"I don't know my mom," Danny says apologetically.

Eve wishes she could drain down the sink. Danny takes a wineglass from her—their fingers almost touch on the stem—and she is certain she has never met someone so polite, so sympathetic, so gracefully easy.

"It's a funny story, though," he says. "This woman from where I grew up actually mails me that jam. I figured out this guy was stealing from her, and now she thinks she has to repay a debt."

"That is funny," Eve says faintly.

"Not to freak you out or anything, but you're looking at Bozeman's former preeminent kid detective."

Eve wants to laugh but can't remember how. She tries to imagine how the beautiful girls who tag Julian in photos would act. They would flick soap suds and look up through their eyelashes. They would know how to banter and how to flirt, and they probably had, Danny and the anonymous, confident legion.

"Hey," Danny says, "was that you playing guitar? When we first came in."

"Oh. Yeah."

"What was it?"

"I made it up."

"Do you write a lot of songs?"

Eve eyes him warily. She's averse to this line of questioning because she's afraid of anyone realizing she takes herself seriously. When she doesn't hand him the next baking sheet to dry, he looks up at her and wipes the back of his wrist against his forehead. It's the first time she notices he has freckles. She loves them immensely.

"Yeah," she says. "I want to go to school for music."

"That's awesome," he says, and he seems to mean it. "In ten years, I'll be going around telling everyone I knew you when."

"Ha," Eve says. "We'll see."

"In ten years," he says, nodding firmly like they just made a promise.

In ten years, Danny will tell Eve that once, he solved a farmers market mystery and won the undying affection of a middle-aged jam peddler. In ten years, Eve will act like this is the first time she's hearing this story because the truth is unbearable: that she turns those fifteen minutes of dishes over and over in her head for the whole of December, worrying the edges until they become smooth and soft, hoping that when Julian comes back for Christmas, Danny will once again walk through the door behind him. He doesn't. Eve keeps waiting for Julian to say his name, but Julian speaks only of everything and everyone else, and finally, on New Year's Day, when Eve can't wait any longer, she asks if Danny is having a good holiday. "He's so whipped," Julian says. "He can't handle being away from his girlfriend for, like, two weeks." Eve goes to her room and cries about having been so young, and so naive, and so convinced that love had to go both ways. She writes a tragic song and imagines sweet Danny Aagaard listening and being moved. She imagines standing on the balcony in a robe and saying, "It's too late, Danny," or something equally cinematic. She writes another song, a better one, about the moment she first saw him, the flannel and the honey locust tree out the window, but she hides the story in so many mixed metaphors and blurred stories that he will never really know it's about him. And then she moves on with her life. Mostly. Except that she will never again let herself love someone with as much certainty as that month she loved Danny at age sixteen.

You can build walls in an instant. Taking them down again is the work of a lifetime.

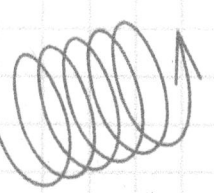

Buggy

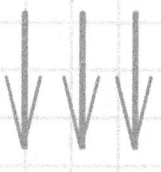

1

It takes Danny and a team of seven engineers four and a half months to cobble together a beta. They build it out of the existing app, which saves them time, but it also means Danny is confronted with a lot of shitty code he wrote two years prior. The four and a half months go like this: Every day, Danny wakes up and climbs out of his queen-size bed into the desk chair that directly abuts the bed (huge, his apartment is not) and clickety-clacks on his keyboard. He vibe codes until his first meeting with Julian (nine thirty) and then checks in with his team, and then he realizes he hasn't yet eaten so he makes a pour-over coffee while he responds to emails, and then he gets distracted with an idea for how to unsnarl something, so he goes back to his desk and codes some more, then he realizes he still hasn't eaten, so he goes back to the kitchen and pours a metric ton of granola into a bowl, then someone calls him because a fire needs to be put out urgently (they will have broken something in the existing app while making a new feature), and he will have another coffee and eat his granola and wonder why he feels vaguely like death (maybe he is allergic to granola?? Google granola allergy?), and then he will go back to coding until his eyes start to burn and he thinks, *Hey, maybe I should wrap things up for the day.* Rinse, repeat, ad infinitum.

Eve is on tour. If that clarifies anything.

This is the most Danny and Julian have argued over the course of their partnership. Julian wants to create a totally new app so people in long-term relationships don't get scared off by the matchmaking function; Danny insists they fold the two halves together so early-stage daters immediately adopt the new features.

"People who are secure in their relationships won't feel motivated to use us," Danny says. "We need to get people who are in hazy situations."

"Right," Julian says. "How are things going with Eve, by the way?"

"Good. Great."

"And yet."

"I just think," Danny says, "most of our users will be motivated by fear."

Danny wins. They end up calling the two halves of the app Seekers and Keepers. People using the app to find a first date: Seekers. People using the app to turn a first date into a second, or a relationship into a marriage: Keepers.

They also fight about how to assign users a relationship score. Danny thinks they should have a one- to five-star scale, which is visually clean and easy to interpret. Julian thinks this isn't granular enough. They settle on percent—a number out of a hundred, like a grade, which is the same thing they did with their compatibility metrics for Seekers.

"But not a percentile," Julian says. "It's not normally distributed. Most couples are middling. A score in the nineties is, like—superspecial."

"It shouldn't be that special," Danny argues. "People don't want to be told they have mediocre relationships."

"Deep down, I think most people think their own relationship is a solid eighty. Good enough, but room for improvement. Not that anyone would admit it."

"Are you and Gigi an eighty?"

"We're at least a ninety-eight," Julian says. "I fear that should be obvious."

"So what's a zero?" Danny asks. "Is that two people who hate each other? No relationship at all? Abuse?" It occurs to Danny that this rating system could get messy quickly.

"Zero should be apathy," Julian says. "Complete lack of a relationship." There's a pause. "I wouldn't want to use an app that validates abuse."

"But there's so much gray area. Like, you know, accidental gaslighting. Teasing that goes too far. That sort of thing."

"The whole point of this is to remove gray area. Users come with questions, we give them a concrete answer."

Danny blinks a few times. Googles "vision blurry things dancing like little worms." Probably nothing to worry about!

"What's a fifty?" he asks.

"Committed but unfocused," Julian says.

"We should include trends, too," Danny says. "Trending better, trending worse."

"What are you and Eve?"

Googles "pounding headache how many Advil." Googles "how to Advil sponsorship."

"We're great," Danny says. "At least a ninety-eight."

Julian gives him a thumbs-up that may or may not be sarcastic. Danny codes the numbers into being.

It flattens things, but technology always does.

Then there's the issue of the Rampart data breach. As it turns out, bad actors will pay a shitload of money for the user data collected by your garden variety dating app. There was a moment shortly after Eve's former employer was hacked when Danny didn't know how bad the damage was. Best case, the hackers got basic metrics: number of users, et cetera. Worst case, they got email addresses that could be linked to profiles that could be linked to conversations. As a rule, senators don't love it when they're caught asking twenty-three-year-olds about their feet.

In the end, most of the personally identifiable information was stored securely on Pathos's end. Danny did not TA Intro to Encryption for nothing! This doesn't stop Julian from bringing it up literally every meeting. He calls it Code Name Aries. *Aries* as in *Ram*. *Ram* as in *Rampart*. There is no need for code names because it's public knowledge and also it just freaks out the employees.

"Obviously, in the wake of Aries, we have to be hypervigilant about user data going forward," Julian says in an all-hands; in front of investors; while getting coffee on an ordinary Thursday. "How much would people pay to get all that?"

"A lot," Danny says compliantly.

"We need to be agile," Julian says. "Like flying squirrels."

Basically, Danny loves Julian like a long-lost brother, but also sometimes he thinks it would be so neat if Julian shut up.

Danny is vaguely aware that Chloe and Julian are launching a massive rebrand, of which Danny disapproves (he thinks their branding is nice!), but his head is too far in his computer to do anything to stop it. It is decreed by the powers that be that they must change their name. Pathos, as it turns out, really does sound too much like *pathetic*. When Julian tells him they've settled on Pattern, Danny laughs.

"It's a great name," Julian says. "It evokes planning, nature, and forward thinking. It evokes self-knowledge."

"I just wonder if it could evoke slightly less tartan."

"The etymology comes from *patron*," Julian says. "As in protector, supporter, patron saint."

"Okay," Danny says. "But do we think it sounds like a knitting app, is the thing."

"Actually," Julian says, "we do not."

But for all the things Danny and Julian argue about, they are in complete agreement about Bug.

For the first week, his name is Love Bug.

"Drop the 'Love,'" Chloe says. "It's cleaner."

Bug doesn't look like a bug; he looks more like a round little dinosaur. He answers relationship questions and provides advice. Technically, he is an AI chatbot powered by Pacifica (billionaire Alvin

Breckenridge's LLM), but they try not to refer to Bug as a bot. What does a robot know about love? Bugs, like love, are found in nature.

Though Bug describes himself as a helpful pal, the problem he really solves is that of data gathering. Early on, Danny was faced with the question of how to assess a relationship. How do you know if it's good or not? They could track phone location (how often are you with your partner?), identify frequency of date activities (when do you book a restaurant for two?), and ask survey questions (do you feel satisfied with your partner?). It feels, to Danny, hand-wavy and inauthentic. But then he comes up with the idea for Bug.

Let's say User A asks Bug for an idea for a birthday present for his girlfriend. Bug is pleased the user remembered! That merits some relationship points. Then User A says his girlfriend mentioned she's been wanting to learn to cook, and also that she hates clutter, so instead of getting stuff, maybe some sort of cooking class? Bug loves this. The attention to detail! The consideration! Their relationship score goes up by six points. Meanwhile, User B just asks for birthday present suggestions. Bug suggests a candle, and User B follows the referral link. When User B's girlfriend gets the candle, she logs into her own Pattern account and asks Bug what to do about the weird, disappointed energy that descended over her boyfriend when she wasn't more excited about the candle he gave her even though surely he must have noticed she doesn't have a single candle in her apartment because her mother was a hoarder? Quietly, Bug deducts eight relationship points and suggests User B's girlfriend have an open conversation—Bug can roleplay if she needs practice!—which User B's girlfriend declines.

When he tries to sleep, Danny pictures Bug hopping from one nubbly foot to the other. *Hi hi!* Bug says. *Love isn't always easy, but I'm always here to help. :)*

2

One week before Danny's mom leaves, she says the house has bugs.

Danny is twelve. He does not know for certain how old his parents are.

"What kind of bugs?" his dad asks over breakfast.

"I don't know. Ants. I saw them in my bathroom."

They pause—all of them. "Her bathroom" is technically Danny's bathroom, though she's been using it for some months now because she's been sleeping in the bedroom for the little sister who never eventuated. She has never referred to the little bathroom as hers before, and now she wraps her ivory puffy coat tighter around her shoulders and does not look at either her husband or son across the table. It is autumn in Montana, and cold, and everything is dying.

"I've never seen any ants," his dad says, "but I'll take a look."

Three days before Danny's mom leaves, she emerges from the bathroom with her hair dryer still in one hand and says, "Calvin. Bugs."

Danny and his father follow her into the bathroom. They all stand there in front of the foggy mirror and look around and after a suitable amount of time has passed, Danny's mom says, "Well, I swear they were just here."

"Why don't I set some extra traps just in case?" Danny's dad says, reaching to take her hand, which she places flat across her shoulder as if for the express purpose of avoiding being held. It strikes Danny as the worst thing his father could have done, though he can't imagine what would have been right.

One day before Danny's mom leaves, she relocates her hair dryer and curling iron and whitening toothpaste back to the primary bathroom, which leaves Danny with a deep sense of foreboding he cannot explain. He feels he will never understand the contrariness of people, the unmappability. In the backyard, throwing the tennis ball for Biscuit, Danny's dad says to Danny, "Guess she got tired of the ants, huh?"

"I never saw any ants," Danny says.

Behind them, the screen door audibly shuts. Danny glances over his shoulder and does not see his mother. His father sets a hand on Danny's shoulder. When Danny shifts away, his dad ducks his chin like he's been injured.

The day after Danny's mom leaves, Danny flips on the lights in his bathroom and looks at the static blooming across the mirror, the fuzzing blackness, the frenetic whorls of thousands and thousands of ants.

As if summoned by Danny's silent distress, Danny's father appears in the mirror beside him.

They stand together to watch the ants rivering through cracks in the grout and up the showerhead and across the tile and around the drain. In the mirror, Danny appears to be swarmed. When his dad lightly places his hand on his shoulder, Danny flinches, which makes his dad flinch, but how can you blame Danny? He feels like he is covered in ants.

Danny goes into his bedroom and locks the door, which he knows is rude and immature but also he feels like he's dying, like the ceiling is caving in, like he has knocked his life into an irretrievably claustrophobic direction. The day before, his mom vanished. He came home from school and she was just gone. His dad said she was just taking some time, but that she'd probably be back real soon. How soon? Danny calls his mom to tell her she was right, but she doesn't pick up.

When he goes back to the bathroom, his dad is gone. The ants have moved to the window now, blocking out the sun. Danny opens the cabinet under the sink with the tip of his shoe and retrieves a roll of paper towels. Historically, Danny took bugs outside, not out of kindness but out of guilt. He stops feeling guilty after the first hundred. He does not cry, or make any sound at all, because he does not dare open his mouth. But he does kill them. Every last one.

3

The day Danny tells Julian the app is done (enough), it's early November. It's also the day of Eve's final tour stop, which is at Brooklyn Steel. Eve is the opener for Stella Seaport, who was popular for a while but then became less so. Originally, Stella Seaport was meant to have a different opener, a pair of brothers who play synthy brass and sing about ones who got away, but they went on hiatus at the last minute after a feud, presumably about one of the ones who got away. So at the last minute, to capitalize on *ski rat*'s unexpected popularity, the record label swapped in Eve. Danny has been reading reviews and watching Instagram Reels of the tour, but he has not actually seen the show because Eve told him not to. The last time they met in person—when she came home for a few days between shows—she told him he really didn't need to come to Boston or DC because their final show, the one at Brooklyn Steel, would be the one where they worked out all the bugs.

"I want to support you bugs and all," Danny said.

"But I want you to think I'm cool and talented," Eve said.

"As opposed to how I think of you now."

"Something of a talentless hack, right."

"I think you're the coolest person I know."

"I mean, I'm no erstwhile kid detective," Eve said.

The morning of the concert, Danny goes for a run to shake out the nerves. Unfortunately, he discovers he has misplaced most of his running abilities while trying to be a cofounder. He cuts it short at five miles and showers, then he goes to meet Julian for coffee at the coworking space where Julian has purchased a trial membership. A full membership for their twelve employees will cost them ten thousand dollars a month. Julian says worrying about this price is like "worshipping the risk of failure." Danny, apparently, loves to pray.

They sit across from each other at an ash-colored laminate table. The wall to their left is exposed brick. To their right, there's a fridge full of those sodas masquerading as seltzers with names like Pippity Poppity Extra Natural Not Soda.

Julian lowers himself into the chair. Danny studies the movement. Danny can't seem to move like that—languidly, easily, as if the chair is there to serve him. Danny is more of a huncher.

"So does it work?" Julian says.

"I think it works," Danny says. Then: "I mean, what does it mean for an app to 'work,' really?"

"Reassuring," Julian says.

"It's a good UI. It's intuitive to use. We have push notifications working, and asynchronous surveys, and the Bug interface isn't perfect but it's usable."

"So it does work."

"I'm just saying that people are complicated."

"We can figure that out as we go."

"By 'that,'" Danny says, "you mean the human condition?"

"Not to sound like a dystopian movie villain," Julian says, "but surely AI can crack that in a month or two."

Danny shifts his laptop for Julian to see. He's running an iPhone emulator, and the phone interface fills the screen. Danny walks him through the features—the personality quizzes they included in the initial incarnations of the app, now adapted to spit out advice rather than matches. There's a feature where both partners can choose A or B, B or C in a series of anything that might be up for debate—restaurants, wedding ring styles, vacation destinations, bed frames—and then spits out the optimally satisfying compromise. Then there's Bug. Hi hi.

"I want to do an internal beta," Danny says. "Get everyone in the company to use it and give feedback."

"How soon can we announce?"

"How much feedback are we going to get?"

"That's a nonanswer," Julian says.

"It was a nonquestion."

"You know, it's convenient for you that you have a perfect control in your beta. A perfectly happy example to compare against."

"Do you mean you?" Danny says.

"Why wouldn't I?"

"No one's perfectly happy."

"Are you and Eve having trouble?"

"That's not what I said."

Julian gives him this look. Is it pity? How is Danny looking back? Also pity, maybe. Danny supposes this is the point of it all: to understand finally what anyone else means when they talk about love.

"People are complicated" is what Danny says again.

"The idea is that we can make them less complicated," Julian says. "Anyway, when are you meeting my sister?"

Danny and Eve have been talking on the phone Monday and Wednesday mornings and Sunday afternoons. They text every day: good morning and this meme made me think of you and you're going to do great today. Originally, they only talked twice a week, but then Danny asked for a third call, the act of which made him feel like he was tearing off his skin. Eve said sure, no worries, it would be great to connect more! Danny wondered if it would ever go away: the bottomless pit within him that begged to be filled with unequivocal evidence of love.

He has checked and double-checked her flight information and cross-referenced the LIRR schedule (Eve hates Uber) and concluded she will arrive at her apartment between 3:02 and 3:07, but he will not see her until after tonight's show. Then, tomorrow, they will sit on her bed, and he will ask about the tour, and she will ask about the app, and she will see through him completely. She will see that he has not created a dating app because he wants to help people or because he wants to get rich or because he saw a gap in the market but because he cannot bear the uncertainty of loving someone who may or may not love him back.

Last night, Julian and Gigi invited Danny to join their date night. They went to the AMC near Penn Station and watched a movie about a priest who falls in love with a nun. At one point, the priest says, "I wish I could be certain—of anything." And the nun says, "Oh, but then we wouldn't need faith." Danny felt like he was missing something, having grown up without any semblance of religion, because he thought this was a pretty shitty trade-off.

"Danny?" Julian says. Danny's mind has roamed far from the co-working space. "Dude. Are you okay?"

"What if the app doesn't work? What if it's all a huge waste of time?"

"It won't be."

"Why are you so sure?"

"Because," Julian says. "Everyone wants to be better at being in love."

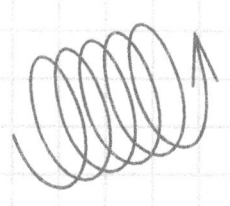

Touring Test

1
WONDER BALLROOM, OR

A lot of people Eve cares about come to see her perform. Her childhood dance friend Ali, who now lives in Phoenix. Her cousin Emily, in Bellevue, with her two kids, Marjorie and Gideon, who bring Eve a jar of homemade gluten-free sugar-free nut-free granola backstage. ("Don't blame me for this," Emily says. "This is literally just who they are.") In Denver, even Fletcher's friend Graham idles by the door after the show to tell Eve, "Hey, I hope you're well, we're all rooting for you."

Eve's parents don't come to see her perform. They do not ask about tickets for her Brooklyn show. Which is fine, good, great. She'd be embarrassed if they did.

There are nineteen stops on Stella Seaport's Shadow Puppet Tour—a tight domestic loop of the country running from summer's end through fall. Stella will not add stops or play more than one encore. She does not diverge from her set list, which has been methodically calculated and smoothed down like a river stone. Before every show, Stella talks quietly and intently with the lighting guys to make sure every angle and cue is precise. Eve had little time to prepare, and she spends the first few shows scrambling to find a formula that works. Start with "ski rat"? No, definitely end with "ski rat." "HONEY LOCUST" alone on the acoustic guitar? No, dear god, definitely needs someone on piano. Eve thinks Stella dislikes her for the chaos she brings, but Stella doesn't say anything. Stella hardly says anything to anyone.

Eve hates the tour bus. Not the people, but the feeling of being moved down a highway in a breakneck living room. She distracts herself by working constantly on new music. From the moment the driver depresses the gas pedal to the moment he puts it in Park, Eve is writing lyrics or playing her guitar. The others commend her dedication, and Eve is too embarrassed to admit the truth, which is that she is less dedicated than she is terrified. She hasn't been in a car since Boulder. She can't stop smelling the fumes of exploded airbags.

Eve quickly makes friends with Stella's musicians: There's Clay, the guitarist with the pine tree tattoo on his forearm, and Nara, the bassist with the gold nose ring, and Eliza, the drummer with the undercut. As far as Eve can tell, everyone involved with the tour is bisexual.

Eliza used to tour with an artist who subsisted entirely on fast food and caffeine pills, and everyone kept getting sick, so now she's fanatical about keeping them healthy. Every morning, she knocks on Eve's door until Eve goes to the hotel gym or outside for a run. Now that Fletcher is gone, Eve finds she likes running. She no longer feels she has to run a seven-minute mile to have human worth. Clay and Eliza sprint on ahead, and Eve and Nara lope behind, stopping to take photos of squirrels and stretch on park benches.

And Stella continues to keep to herself.

"She got famous too young," Nara says on one of their runs. "This is how it always happens. Prodigies are awkward. Let her warm up."

"I feel like she thinks I'm not serious enough," Eve says. "I mean, what do I know about music theory?"

Nara squints at the sun. "It's not that you're not serious. Did you see Stella's first tour?"

"Opening for the June Bugs, right?"

"Total shit show. Different set list every night. Different *covers* every night. Six months in Europe. She told me every time she got feedback, she'd take it, so by the end, her show was this Frankenstein's monster of ideas. So now she's supercareful about everything."

"That sounds exhausting," Eve says.

"This is a good tour for you," Nara says. "She'll keep you from exploding yourself."

From then on, Eve hears that phrase in her head every time Stella looks at her. Eve didn't realize people thought of her as someone self-destructive, a pleaser, in danger of explosion. Eve is not actually sure what exploding herself means, but she would rather not find out.

Their Portland show coincides with Eliza's dad's birthday; he's in the audience. Before her encore, Stella announces that it's her drummer's dad's special day, and everyone sings. Eliza's dad comes on stage and hugs his daughter. They're both crying. After the show, Eve helps the crew pack up. She always does this. She got a tip from an audio engineer a few years back that you have to be the first one there and the last one out. Stella abides by the same principle. She doesn't talk much, but she loads all the equipment and nods her thanks at everyone.

It's midnight when Eve and Stella get the last amp on the bus. Stella shuts the door, fans herself, and says, "My parents haven't come to any shows, either."

"I'm sorry," Eve says. "Why not?"

"Just one of those things."

"I forget it's still one of those things when you're Stella Seaport."

Stella shrugs. "It's hard to know if your family is weird," she says. "Because it's the only one you get to see all of. Please don't use my full name, Eve Olsen."

"Sorry." Eve pauses. "My parents don't come to my shows because they think my music is not very good or smart."

"No one ever gets anywhere trying to create something smart. Try to create something real."

"What if it's sentimental and bad?"

"If it's real enough, it'll be smart."

"My parents will still probably think it's bad."

Eve has never even told this story to Danny because she never figured out how to talk about her parents' money without sounding ungrateful, but she got into music school, and her dad said he wouldn't pay a cent. So she went to a different school, the name-brand school, and her dad told her if she took a single music class, then she could pay him back her college tuition. So she took no music classes but sometimes passed open windows on the quad and heard piano leaking out and walked more quickly. And now she is here, and her parents are not. Why would they be? They tried so hard to make her into a different person, and she kept becoming this one instead.

"Well," Stella says, "some people are just assholes." She nods and starts to walk away. Then she slows. Glances back over her shoulder. "The thing you were playing on the bus. Is that new?"

"I'm trying to think about my new album. So that it doesn't take four years again."

"It's good. You should start playing it."

"At the show?"

"We might as well have fun with it," Stella says. "This is our last tour before AI destroys the singer-songwriter."

Eve laughs in a way she hopes is light and fun and does not indicate she has a boyfriend and brother working diligently on AI.

"Add it to the set list," Stella says. "And stop worrying about what your family thinks."

2

Shitty lyrics Eve writes on tour:

I want our love to be vast like Pacifica
not like the ocean but like the website
A meteoric arc of limitless growth
A love that will never die—cryogenically frozen, like Alvin Breckenridge's
glimmering head

3

THE FILLMORE, CA

Shannon comes to Eve's San Francisco show and stands in the VIP section with her parents.

"Your parents came!" Clay says when he sees them waving.

"Those are my friend Shannon's parents," Eve says.

"Another classic whiff for Clay," Eliza says. "Put it in the book."

Eve almost plays one of her half-baked new songs but chickens out at the last minute. Stella's performance is, as always, flawless. At least one newspaper has called the show robotic, which Eve thinks is unfair. Stella can't win.

After, Shannon and her parents wait to drive Eve home.

"You didn't have to wait," Eve says.

"Honey!" Shannon's mom says. "*Get* to wait."

Eve feels her stomach turn in on itself when Shannon's mom presses the key fob and the lights of the Subaru flick to life. She smells burning rubber.

"I'm happy to drive," Eve says brightly. "I'm superawake. All these shows."

Shannon and her parents all look at each other. "Okay," Shannon's mom says after a second. "Sure thing." She hands Eve the keys.

The whole drive south, Shannon's parents ask earnest questions from the back seat. "What's the best part of being on tour?" "How has your creative practice changed between your first album and now?" "What do you hope people take away from your music?" And then, when Eve answers, they nod and go, "Yes, wow, that's such a good way of putting it." Eve follows Shannon's directions down the highway, down the peninsula, into the Santa Cruz mountains.

When Shannon's parents talk about her, it's with such vivid pride. "That's our girl, bringing transparency to tech, casting a light into the darkness." Shannon laughs and waves them away when they try to pat her face. Eve watches it all in glances in the rearview mirror and pretends not to.

It's two when they finally reach the intentional living community, called Treehouse, and Shannon's parents go to their cabin and Shannon and Eve to a guest cabin. Eve has three days before she has to be in LA for the next show, and there is nowhere she sleeps better than Treehouse. She wants to take a picture of it for Danny—of the indigo basin of stars, the sky-hungry redwoods, and the coils of fog—but it's too dark.

In the morning, Eve wakes because Shannon throws a pillow at her face.

"Ow," Eve says.

"Ow? That's organic bamboo."

"My poor, delicate face."

"Okay, but," Shannon says, "if you don't get up, there won't be any coffee left, and then you'll be like, 'What kind of monster would bring me to a place with no coffee?' and then you'll wish I'd thrown more organic bamboo pillows at your face, poor and delicate though it may be."

This is a compelling argument.

Eve follows Shannon into the misty morning. Treehouse gives summer camp, and Shannon gives camp counselor in her bandanna and long flannel. Eve, who never went to summer camp, is in a Mets hat and Lululemon leggings. She loves the forest but feels like an impostor when in nature, like the trees might smell her fear. Colorado never loved her back. To grow up in the woods—like Shannon, like Danny—is strange and admirable. It seems like the sort of place where families really know each other. Sometimes, when in the edges of her mind, Eve will catch herself thinking she also grew up in the woods, went to camp, made friendship bracelets and s'mores. Eve has a phantom limb nostalgia toward this imagined life; she thinks it probably comes from watching *The Parent Trap*.

They get their coffee from the mess hall and drink it in Adirondack chairs on the back porch.

"Do you ever think about moving back here?"

"No way, dude," Shannon says.

"Why not?"

"I like New York. I like New Yorkers. I like that you have to order your bagel in five seconds if you don't want to get yelled at. I like that everyone tries so hard. I like that people in New York are all in a hurry to do something great."

"Maybe," Eve says. "Not as many trees, though."

Eve shares her insight about *The Parent Trap*, and Shannon says, "See, but that was me with *Gossip Girl*. I wanted to go to galas at 30 Rock, not drink Bud Lights with Mickey Weaver at a beach bonfire."

"Mickey Weaver?" Eve asks. "I don't think I've heard about Mickey Weaver."

"Really? We snuck off to make out in what I later learned was a patch of poison oak."

"Oh! This is Incriminating Rash Guy?"

"Exactly," Shannon says. "Meanwhile, you were eating yogurt on the steps of the Met."

"Hey," Eve says. "First of all, I was really more of a Clif Bar girl, and second, it was the Natural History Museum."

"A thousand pardons."

"Forgiven."

"Still would've traded you for Mickey Weaver."

"We all want what we can't have?" Eve asks.

"I don't know," Shannon says. "I think it's normal to be curious about other people's lives. Good, even." Shannon swipes Eve's Mets hat off her head, and Eve grabs for it, but Shannon holds it on her curls.

"Everyone's going to see how greasy my hair is," Eve says. "They're all going to say, 'Ha ha, look at how greasy her hair is.'"

"Too bad. I'm a real New Yorker now. I'm walking a mile in your hat."

"But you already have your cute bandanna. That's two headwear. Now I have no headwear."

"Let's go Mets, baby."

Eve feels a tug in her stomach like *oh*, and she senses that it's inspiration she doesn't want to scare away by calling it inspiration. The sun is just breaking through the fog in fine, luminous beams. It's just there—an inkling.

Shannon goes to a coffee shop in town to work—she's researching an article on crypto—so Eve sits on her bunk in the cabin and strums her guitar. The curtains are pulled back and in comes the light. That's what Eve wants—the sound of light through a window.

When Danny calls, Eve leans her guitar against the bed. Danny is so good about calling. Eve is forever losing track of time, but then there is Danny—steady Danny, who never forgets anything and who is never impatient when Eve does. Earlier on the tour, he suggested they talk three, rather than two, times a week—like he knew she was feeling a little lonely and a little lost, like he knew she needed him to make her feel tethered but that she would not think to ask because she would never have expected him to be so willing to give more of himself than he already did.

"Hi," she says.

"Hey. Where are you now?"

"California. Shannon's commune."

"I thought it was an intentional living community."

"My sweet Danny."

"Is it culty? Do they wear matching outfits and sing culty songs?"

"I hope so. I think I could make a splash in the culty song space."

"Goes without saying."

"Unfortunately, Shannon's parents and co are mostly former tech people who just really love kombucha. They all have three to five college degrees. I don't think I could sway them with a rousing chant."

"Maybe this is why Shannon is so intimidating," Danny says. "I bet she can sense that I would totally be swayed by a rousing chant."

She totally can. Eve loves her for it—her measured skepticism—as she loves Danny for saying so—his complete sincerity. It's funny to Eve that Danny jokes about being intimidated—that he seems to believe he is intimidated by anyone—because he's not, really.

On a break in the tour, when Eve was back home and Danny was over, their dinner was interrupted by a call from one of his investors, who began to shout so loudly that Eve assumed Danny's phone was on speaker. Danny held the phone calmly away from his face, kissed Eve's temple, and mouthed, "One second." He went into Eve's bedroom and shut the door. She could still hear the investor from the table. "Not what we agreed on, not a blank check, are you men or are you children?" Danny's voice, when it came, was smooth and calm. Eve had not realized that she expected Danny to shout back. That was what men did when threatened, yes? Phillip was easily provoked; Fletcher tailgated cars that cut him off in traffic; Julian, much as Eve loved him, would not have held his temper on the other end of this call. But Danny just spoke in that measured way, paused to listen, spoke again firmly and softly. Functionally, Danny was not intimidated by anyone. He did not change his course when someone wanted to make him feel small. When Danny came back a few minutes later, he apologized and poured Eve another glass of wine.

"Are you okay?" she asked.

"Oh, I'm fine. He just needed to feel included. Hey, how long do you think the line is for Van Leeuwen right now?"

That might've been the moment Eve really knew.

"I've been thinking of new songs as trees," she says now, leaning back in the bunk bed. "Like, with layers of bark. I don't know if this metaphor holds water or if I'm just really surrounded by trees right now."

"No, I get that," Danny says from her phone. "I think about that when I'm coding. You're not just moving forward but moving out. Increasing complexity."

"Giving it texture," Eve says. "Right."

"How are the new songs?"

"I have this idea for something, but it keeps having too few layers. It's just not interesting enough. I guess I'm worried that if I spell out my meaning too literally, it's good on the first listen, but then there's nothing to go back to. Like, would you rather write a song that makes great background music for a mall? Or a song that's a little weird but makes you think?"

"That's kind of like coding, too. Do you make something users will find familiar, or do you risk asking them to adopt something that might be better?"

In moments like these, Eve wonders how she ever could have dated Fletcher, who had no creative practice. She never would have said creation was a prerequisite for her relationships, but now that she's had it, she could never settle for less. It's incredible what a kind and interested person can do for your standards.

"How's the app going?" Eve asks.

"It's okay. Some days, I'm like, 'This is a terrible idea and we're wasting our time.' And other days, I'm like, 'Wow, if my parents had this twenty years ago, maybe they could've figured their shit out.'"

When Shannon gets back, Eve mentions this.

"That's funny," Shannon says. "Maybe we all take the career path we think could've fixed our parents."

4

Shitty lyrics Eve writes on tour:

You read a New Yorker *piece about an article*
About a review of a movie no one saw
And I just wonder if you'd love me more
If I could rhyme anything with Flaubert

5
THE OBSERVATORY, CA

From Northern California to Southern California. Eve is starting to flag. So are Clay, Eliza, Nara—everyone but Stella, whose performance remains precise and unchanged. Eve is dying for the tour to end, but she's also aware of the gaping lack of a plan on the other side of the last show. She doesn't know how to capitalize on her fragile success, and *ski rat* isn't big enough to protect her from a shitty third album. LA might be Eve's worst show yet. She's so tired, she almost goes back to the hotel instead of helping clean up. She doesn't, of course. Neither does Stella. Last one out. Stella nods at Eve before she goes.

After the Southern California shows, the Shadow Puppet Tour has a week off before their final three East Coast performances. Most everyone goes home, but Eve elects to stay with her family friend Holling in San Diego instead.

Holling lives in a bungalow in Ocean Beach. Eve lugs her suitcase over the loose gravel to his door, which is blue and surrounded by potted cacti.

Holling opens the door before Eve can knock, and he hugs her before she can set down her suitcase. He's the youngest in the mess of assorted cousins/children of her parents' college friends with whom she went on forced vacations growing up. Most of the others in their extended group, the other children of their parents' friends, are thirty. In the Our Parents Are Friends group text, when someone fires off a reference to a Vine she does not remember or uses too many emojis, Eve will make a joke about AARP and Holling will lend his Gen Z support.

He ushers her inside a house that is too adult and too expensive.

Once he shuts the door, he hugs her again. He has, of course, been tall and grown for some years now, but it's still surprising to Eve that her eyes would be level with his collarbone, that his face would be so entirely devoid of baby fat. He's wearing a soft linen button-down with the sleeves rolled up. When their hug breaks, he holds her shoulders, smiling down at her from arm's length. His wrist has three thin hair ties around it even though his own hair is short and neatly styled and he does not currently have a girlfriend.

The kitchen is suspiciously clean, like it has recently been visited by a professional. Holling removes pizza ingredients from the fridge—dough and mozzarella and a punnet of basil. He pours two glasses of wine and asks Eve about the tour so far, and her parents, and Julian's impending wedding. She tries to ask him questions in return and he finds the quickest possible way to divert the conversation back to her.

"How's music stuff?" he asks as they put the pizzas in the oven. "Working on anything new?"

"Just messing around."

He waits expectantly. His eyes are very big, like a lemur's.

"I mean, I have a few ideas, but nothing that's coalescing into an album."

"Uh-huh?" Holling says.

"How's your work?"

"So boring," he says. "Laws! Tell me more about the new songs."

The thing about Holling as a conversationalist is that you can tell he was always the youngest one in every social setting. He's very good at making you feel slightly heroic just for existing.

"Well, I'm writing about being back in New York. And, like—love."

"How do you come up with your ideas?" Holling asks. "Do you use AI?"

"Everyone keeps asking that! Do my songs sound like AI?"

"No," Holling says. "Unless that's a good thing. In which case, sure."

"Definitely an insult," Eve says. "I guess I want my songs to be smarter or more sincere than AI. Like, I want them to have more to say. More feeling."

He pours her more wine, and she lets him. "I saw the stuff with Fletcher. That's so shitty."

Eve had started to lift her wine, but now she sets it down again. "What?"

"Oh," Holling says. "Did you not—" He takes out his phone. Opens Instagram.

"I blocked him," Eve says. "I didn't want to be tempted to see what he was up to."

Holling winces. He navigates to Fletcher's profile and opens the most recent Reel.

It's an overproduced clip of Fletcher's running shoes kicking up mud as he ascends a mountain trail. In melodramatic voice-over, he says, "There will always be people who want to bring you down. The important thing is, keep running your own race blah blah sports cliché blah." In the comment section, ultrarunner_fred has written: lol fuck eve Olson. User mattypbedford has helpfully responded: Ski rat is legitimate oatmeal trash. Eve has seen her share of bad reviews but also knows that this particular opinion has already made its way into long-term memory. She will be lying on her deathbed worrying she was legitimate oatmeal trash.

"It's not like you used his name," Holling says. "You could've been singing about anyone."

"Yeah. But I was singing about him."

Holling kills the app and puts his phone back in his pocket. He nudges Eve's wine closer to her. "Is it weird?" he asks. "Knowing that people will go looking for themselves in your songs?"

"I try not to think about it. If I could ban my family and friends from ever hearing my music, I would. I think I'd be a better songwriter if I were only talking to strangers."

"Have you written any songs about Danny?"

"'HONEY LOCUST' is about Danny." She has never said this out loud before.

"But that's from your first album," Holling says.

"I know."

"That was, like, five years ago."

"I know."

"You've liked Danny since then?"

"I've liked Danny since always."

"I didn't realize," Holling says. "You two really have, like, an actual love story."

Eve finishes the glass. The song goes:

Sweeten my lips, let me stay here warm

Hiding inside from the locust swarm

I'll taste the fruit from any devil's tree

If you breathe my soul back into me.

Which makes it seem like it's about the Garden of Eden! When it's actually just about being horny for Danny in a flannel.

"It was easy to sing about him when he didn't know," Eve says. "But how do you write a song about love when everyone is like, 'Hey, I know who this was inspired by'?"

"Have you considered a career in contract law instead?" Holling asks.

"Alas."

The window is open, and the breeze through the gauzy curtains smells like sea. Eve is so happy in New York—finally, after so long in her Colorado haze—that she resents San Diego for being tempting.

"Stella wants me to play one of my new songs," Eve says.

"Really? Eve, that's awesome."

"But I can't decide which one to play. I have one that's sappy but fun and one that's clever but depressing."

"Which one do you want to play?" Holling asks.

"The sappy one feels cliché. The clever one feels honest."

"And you want your music to be honest?"

"Of course," Eve says. "If it's not coming from a place of real feeling, it might as well have been written by AI."

"What are the songs about? The smart one and the sappy one."

"The smart one is called 'Settle Down.' The sappy one is 'Sunbeam, Baby.'"

"Because Danny is a sunbeam, baby, and you're a happy little plant?"

Eve makes an aggrieved noise. Holling pats her cheek, and the ensuing flour makes her sneeze.

It occurs to Eve that there is another version of the story, perhaps not all that different, where she's dating Holling instead. There's another one where she never broke up with Fletcher. There's another where she dates no one at all. How is she, the Eve of these other stories? Is she happy? Does she long for more?

"If you had a hundred lives," Eve says, "a hundred random dice rolls from your birth to now, what percentile do you think this one would be?"

Holling frowns. "I don't know. Sixty?"

"Are you unhappy?"

"No. Sixty seems good, right? Better than average."

"But you have—" Eve gestures around the bungalow "—so much."

"I was born with so much. I've made medium hay of it. Why? What would you be?"

"Ninety-five?" Eve says. "I hadn't thought about it until just now. But yeah, maybe ninety-five."

Eve is surprised but pleased. She's been too busy to stop and think about how many lucky things have befallen her lately. There was no reason her album broke out instead of someone else's. No reason she should have bumped into Danny exactly when she did. She tells this to Holling, who says, "You could also complain that your first album wasn't bigger. Or that it took so long for you and Danny to find each other."

"I guess," Eve says. "Shitty way to live, though."

"Do you believe in soulmates?" Holling asks.

"Of course not," she says. But then she thinks about how she felt the first time she saw Danny, like she had just met the love of her life. And the way she felt when she saw him again this summer, like a key had just tumbled a lock. And the way they make the same jokes and like the same songs and look at a skyline and pick the same favorite building. The way it feels simple. The way it feels obvious. She thinks of her ninety-five. "Oh no," she says. "I fear I do."

"Well, then there's your answer," Holling says.

"My answer?"

"About what song to play."

"You think I should play the sappy one."

"I think you should play the honest one," Holling says. "Because you are honestly so sappy."

6

Shitty lyrics Eve writes on tour:

Never read Romeo and Juliet *during wildfire season.*
If you don't have anything to worry about,
There's always wildfire season
And the end of love.
My high school English teacher just DMed me.
La la la la la
I need to sleep.

7
BROOKLYN STEEL, NY

When Eve's plane lands at JFK, she cries with her head tucked against the window. The tour bus went on ahead of her; she stayed an extra day in DC because she was meeting with a producer there who love love loves *ski rat* and wanted to know what Eve was working on next. Eve played him some of her new stuff. He said "hmm" a lot. "Hmm, anything else? Hmm." He also nodded a lot. Eve could not determine whether this was good or bad.

She didn't cry on her flight from Denver, so this is weird. Everything is objectively better now than it was then. Her Instagram following has quadrupled. Her streams are up by a factor of ten. She has a wonderful boyfriend and she lives in the same city as her best friend. These are positives! It's just overwhelming. Suddenly she has so much more to lose. She is pretty sure the *hmm*s were not good.

Backstage in Brooklyn, her hands shake like they never have before. Danny is there in the audience. Shannon is also in the audience, and Julian, and Gigi. These are people who would probably support her even if she was really shitty, and yet, it feels so much worse than performing in front of strangers.

She steps out into lights burning like an imploding sun and sees them all there in the front, Danny and Shannon and Julian and Gigi. Her parents are not there. Why would they be? Why would they be! Eve is once again wearing basically just a bra under a windbreaker.

She plays her set. Sings a lyric wrong. Almost drops her guitar because her hands are so sweaty.

When she gets to the end, she thanks everyone from the tour. She thanks Stella. She thanks her friends and family for coming to watch. And then:

Love Is an Algorithm

Eve gives herself five seconds to decide who she is. Five seconds of silence is a long time on stage. She has both songs tugging at the muscle memory of her fingers. It's just a simple question, really: Would Eve rather be smart or in love?

There was a time, before the Great Malaise, when Eve's parents used to call on her to calculate restaurant tips. She was young then, maybe seven or eight, an age when 18 percent of $137.54 was a feat. But then they grew accustomed to this trick, and they started calling on her to answer crossword clues: ETNA, ENO, ENT. But they got tired of that, too, and so it fell upon Eve to unearth new hoops and new ways to leap through them. The reason Eve wants her parents to think she's smart is because they never will. So she could sing the clever song. But they didn't show up. And even if they did, it would not be good enough. But then there is Danny: who has never asked her to be anything other than she is.

Five seconds of silence, and then Eve says, "My last song is a new one, so bear with me." She shuts her eyes against the glare of the lights for a moment, and she says, "This one is called 'Sunbeam, Baby.'"

And then she plays it.

When it's done, she kisses her palm and holds it out to Danny, and nobody else matters, in the end. He's standing there at the front with his black T-shirt and his corduroy button-down and his chin tilted up to her like she's the sun. When she writes a song, she knows thousands of people might hear it, but thousands of people are an exercise of imagination. She can't write a song picturing thousands of imagined reactions. She writes a song and she thinks of Danny. On one hand, this feels reductive and small—creating art, and all for a boy! On the other hand, what could be more obvious? She writes about love so that he knows how she feels. She writes about love so it becomes more true.

That's probably the real reason machines won't ever stop people from writing love songs. The machines might get good at making them. But people will still want to make them true.

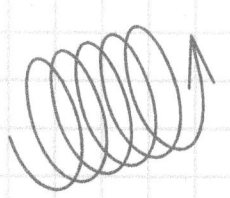

Buggy 2.0

1

Danny wakes up in Eve's bed the morning after the end of the tour with her head on his chest. His arm has absolutely no feeling in it. He breathes very carefully so she can keep sleeping. Eventually, the radiator turns on and Eve says, "Bang Clang, stop bullying me," and pulls the covers over her head, so Danny pats her shoulder and goes to the kitchen to make coffee.

The apartment is hazy gold with morning light. It feels off-kilter. Shannon has moved the silverware drawer to the left. The loose-leaf tea has migrated in front of the coffee beans in the cabinet.

Danny starts a pot. He sprays lemon cleaner on the kitchen counter and wipes it down. Last night, they came straight here after the show ended. They did not talk much—he told her it was amazing, and they said how much they missed each other. But mostly, they kissed, and they had sex, and they kissed, and they fell asleep. They didn't try out the app, and Danny did not mention how he'd been feeling—like he was trying to climb up a perfectly smooth wall with nothing to hold on to.

He throws away the paper towel and leans against the counter.

If it was meant to be, it would feel easier.

If it felt easy, it would mean he didn't care.

Her bedroom door opens. She hasn't put in her contacts; she's wearing large, clear glasses. She crosses the kitchen and presses her face into Danny's chest and squeezes him so tight it's hard to breathe. He inhales delicately. She smells like her lotion, like grapefruit.

"Hi," she mumbles.

He carefully touches the back of her head. Lifts a tendril of hair.

He can feel the press of her glasses against his shoulder. The warmth of her mouth at his heart.

"Hi," he says. "How are you?"

"I want to sleep for a hundred more years."

He smooths her hair down the curve of her head. Draws circles between her shoulder blades.

"We can arrange that," he says.

"You promise?"

"Absolutely."

She pulls away to inspect him. "I still feel like plane."

"You look cute."

"Like a cute plane," she says.

"Exactly."

She rubs her thumb against his cheekbone and comes away with an eyelash.

"Perfect," she says.

She showers and he sits on her bed with a mug of coffee. The mug, from Our Lady of Perpetual Breakfast, says BREW UNTO OTHERS, which Danny must admit is pretty good.

Eve is singing. Danny feels like it's weird to listen but also weird not to. He doesn't recognize the song. He busies himself answering Slack messages on his phone.

When she emerges in a towel, she smells even more strongly of grapefruit. "Do you remember what I was singing?"

"I liked it."

"Yeah, me too. I turned off the water and it ran away."

"Something about a canopy?"

Eve waves a hand. She climbs into his lap and pushes his shoulders until he falls back on the bed. Her hair drips against his face, and she wipes away the drop. He catches her wrist.

"Hi," she says.

"Hi."

"Where are you?"

Love Is an Algorithm

"What do you mean?" he asks.

She rubs at the crease between his brows until he smiles. "Ta-da," she says, and she kisses his forehead, the tip of his nose, the corner of his lips. "I can see when your brain is going, you know."

He didn't know. "Uh-oh."

"No uh-oh," she says. "Nothing to uh-oh."

She slides her hands up his chest and pulls his shirt over his head. She touches her lips to his, then her tongue. He rolls on top of her and the towel falls, and he kisses his way between her legs while she runs her hands through his hair.

It's morning slow, easy, looking at each other, breathing together. Danny is overwhelmed by the feeling of being consumed. He loves her so much he does not exist outside of them.

After, curled together on the bed, she says, "I hear you finished the app."

"'Finished' in the loosest sense of the word."

"Can we try it?" Eve says.

"Do you want to?"

"You made it. Of course."

He sends her the link to the beta and pretends he is feeling super-chill about all of this. No big deal! Perhaps he should not have had three cups of coffee. When she gets it open on her phone, she tilts her screen away, so he does the same.

"You can't look at my answers," she says. "You'd find out how big a crush I have on you. It would be embarrassing for both of us."

Danny smiles at his phone. He has stared at this interface for so many hours, but now, with Eve suntanned and languid and alive beside him, it seems small and robotic. He clicks through the survey questions anyway, trying to be honest: About his insecurities—that he cares too much. About what he values in Eve—the way her brain works, the way she makes him laugh, the sex. About what he values in himself when he's with her—a desire to be his kindest self, and the genuineness that only appears with someone kindred. Some of the questions are quantitative—yes or no, scale of one to ten—and others are short answers, to be analyzed by Bug.

Danny finishes, and Bug appears on the screen to ask if he can have access to Danny's text history with Eve. Bug assures Danny that he will not store this data: It's just to crunch some numbers :)

Eve gets there a moment later and says, "Permission to share all our messages?"

"It looks at response time and word choice," Danny says. "It's really interesting. We brought on this linguist."

"This feels . . . Do you think people might worry it's invasive?"

"We're not storing the messages."

"Yeah, but. I've sent you racy photos. With, like, a lot of side boob."

"But we're not saving them anywhere." For a moment, Eve says nothing, so Danny adds, "We don't have to. It's totally fine."

"No, no, sure." Eve taps her screen. "Permission granted."

"Eve."

"Danny." She turns to look at him. Her hair falls across the pillow. "Your brain is going again."

Quietly, he says, "I'm so tired."

"I don't know if you've heard," she says, "but I'm embarking on something of a hundred-year sleep. Maybe you can embark with me."

"I'd embark anywhere with you," he says.

On his phone, he taps Accept. Bug scoots across the screen with a heart-shaped balloon. Calculating.

"Is it going to give us different scores?" Eve says. "Is this a competition?"

"Same score," Danny says. "We're in this together."

She puts down her phone and curls herself against his chest.

They look at Danny's screen and wait.

It says: 84.

They look at each other. Back at the screen. Danny feels, in his stomach, a sense of weightlessness—of imminent crash.

"Oh," Eve says. "Well, so it's wrong."

"What?" Danny says.

"There must be a mistake."

"There must—oh. Yes."

"We're way better than eighty-four," Eve says.

"Yeah," Danny says. "Yes. Like, the best."

Eve laughs, then she takes his face in her hands and kisses him—his cheekbones and the tip of his nose and his eyelids, and he feels himself shattering and fusing back together. He has never been so glad to be laughed at. His body is warm and gooey like honey. She is laughing at his fear. That's how silly it is. How ridiculous to be afraid—that this is not good. That this might not last.

"I love you," he tells her. "You know that, don't you?"

"I love you forever," she says. "I love you a hundred."

Four and a half months, Danny has worked on this project. Before that, years—years of building this app, this company—and before that, years of studying and tens of thousands of dollars of student loans to be able to do work like this. Lots of people get to be in love; how many people get to make things like what Danny has made? And it's not right. It's broken. Danny is so relieved.

How silly. How human.

Of course Danny would rather have the love.

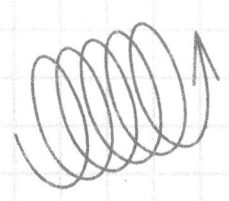

The Freemium Love Experience

1

Danny and Eve are welcomed to Thalassia Sanctuary Resort and Spa by a woman who asks if they had a nice flight, if they'd like help with their bags, if they'd prefer still, sparkling, champagne, passion fruit juice? The lobby has no doors to speak of, and a breeze that smells of ocean and coconut sunscreen wafts its tropical way to their sweat-shined skin.

It is May, and Julian and Gigi are getting married.

2

#people-team

Makayla 4:18 PM
Please join me in wishing a happy wedding to **@julian**! I know not all of us could make it out here, but I think I speak for everyone when I say we're thrilled to all be invited. We're family!!

🔒 **marketing-shit-talk**

Chloe 4:21 PM
hey family! reminder that u are being paid to be a corporate shill this weekend ty

Danny 4:23 PM
What if we tried to be a little upbeat

Chloe 4:24 PM
@Danny you have been invited to this channel as a friend and I can revoke your privileges at any time

3

Eve and Danny's room is on the west end of the hotel. They feel weird allowing someone else to carry their bags, so they bolt to the elevators when no one is looking. When the mirrored doors roll shut, Danny assembles Eve in his arms and kisses her.

The doors roll open again at the next floor. It's a couple in their seventies, pool towels slung over their shoulders. They look aggrieved.

"It's just an elevator," the man says. "What is it about elevators?"

Eve and Danny stand very respectfully side by side for the remainder of the ride. Danny hooks his pinkie around Eve's.

On the walk to their room, Danny says, "I hate getting in trouble with authority."

"Do we think they were authority?"

"They looked like hardened DEA agents."

"They looked like retired accountants."

"With a thirst for blood and the bright eyes of justice," Danny says.

"With names like Russell and Pamela and two Pomeranians at a luxury dog hotel back in Boston," Eve says.

"I may never recover from the judgment in Russell's eyes."

"I, however, take pleasure in the unmitigated envy in Pamela's."

Danny scans his card and the door opens. The room has been staged precisely for their arrival. The balcony is open, allowing an unobstructed view of the swaying palm fronds and Gatorade-turquoise pool. The sheets are the white of baking soda—too bright to behold.

Eve flops back on the bed and spreads her arms wide. "Uh-oh.

This is very comfortable. I may not be able to make it to this wedding now."

"You said you were ten out of ten excited on the plane."

"I'm eight out of ten now. I got scared again when I got here. I mean—I just want them to be happy."

The question of Julian and Gigi's happiness—or lack thereof—is one of intense speculation between Eve and Danny. They discuss it the way other couples might discuss a favorite sports team, tracking the highs and lows across seasons.

When Julian and Gigi first tested the app's relationship score feature, they got one hundred. A perfect score. But clearly—clearly to Danny, clearly to Eve—they aren't perfect. Gigi takes hours to respond to texts even though she lives on her phone, and the lack of response makes Julian antsy. Julian makes and changes plans on a whim, which will make Gigi say things like, "You know, it's pretty hard to go with the flow when the flow is this unpredictable." But they're also a good couple—Danny believes this fully. When Gigi started dating Julian, Danny was living with him. Gigi came over all the time, and Danny loved how naturally she fit—how she loved all the same French restaurants and synthy dance music as Julian. They spoke to each other in British accents—bad ones. When Gigi shared gossip from her vast network of friends of friends, Julian would listen with his chin propped on his fists. "And then?" he would say. "No way. And then?" At the time, Danny was dating Kyra. Danny has never told Julian, but part of the reason things fell apart with Kyra was because he started comparing them to Julian and Gigi. He began to think it should be so easy, and that he should be just as sure.

Why Danny ultimately believes Julian and Gigi are going to make it is because Julian and Gigi believe they are going to make it.

This is what has guided Danny's recent work on the app. How can you go beyond grading a relationship to help your users optimize? How can you identify negative patterns and provide the tools to break them? How can you give your users the certainty that Julian and Gigi have: that you are with the great love of your life?

"They'll be happy," Danny says. "They're Julian and Gigi."

"Yeah," Eve says. "Not as good as us. But pretty good."

"I mean, no one is as happy as us," Danny says. "Just look at Russell and Pamela."

"Hanging on by a thread."

"Moments from inviting Jan from book club to be their third."

"Watching porn in the bathroom with the door locked and the shower running," Eve says.

"Poor Russell and Pamela."

"At least they have Countess and Albie."

"Are those the Pomeranians?" Danny asks.

"You know them so well."

Her hair is splayed across the pillow. She has dried drool at the corner of her lip because she took a nap on the plane. She's a very drooly sleeper, Eve. Danny loves her so much.

They have been dating now for a year. The time has gone both very fast and very slow. Fast because Danny has been happy. Slow because it feels to Danny that this is the way things have always been. Last week, while they were out at dinner at a new sushi place Shannon recommended, Eve said, out of nowhere, "There's so much to say about bad times, but what do you say about being happy that anyone really cares about?" Though this was ostensibly Eve saying she was happy, Danny's first thought was that she was saying she wanted to break up with him in pursuit of better writing material. He told her, at the sushi place, "I think I'm anxious." She took his hand and said, "Can I help?"

Now, he sits down beside her, and she clambers over to him to rub the space between his brows that creases with worry. "You're stressed," she says.

"I'm always stressed around your parents."

Eve presses her palms against the sides of Danny's face, which makes him stick his tongue out at her.

"You have nothing to be worried about," she says.

"I have literally so much to be worried about."

"You're funny and smart and charming and kind."

"Eve," he says, "I worry about stepping on sidewalk cracks. I worry about forgetting to say 'rabbit' on the first of the month. I worry about not worrying enough. Of course I'm worried."

"You'll be perfect," she says.

She is twenty-seven. He is twenty-nine. They have both dated other people and are pretty sure it has never felt like this, but who can remember? Danny is not religious, but he is fairly certain that whoever made him had Eve in mind from the start.

"Okay," Danny says. "Can I keep worrying anyway?"

"Julian's your best friend. My parents love you."

"My question stands."

"Yes," Eve says. "You can keep worrying anyway."

"Thank god," he says, and he reaches behind her neck to pull her gently toward him. His lips touch hers and he smiles against her mouth. They have wedding tasks to get to, but what if they just did this instead?

He kisses her forehead and they both stand.

"I love you a stupid amount," he says.

"Is this how Julian and Gigi feel, do you think?"

"I hope this is how everyone feels."

What a miraculous thing to imagine: that everyone might be this convinced they have fallen in love with exactly the right person.

4

Eve and Danny have to go their separate ways for Thursday Night Festivities. Danny watches her, in her fruit-punch-colored dress and her hair in a flouncy ponytail, go join the swath of spiky-heeled women. Gigi is dressed in white, in what is surely a wedding dress with a wedding dress price tag but is just being used now, for Thursday Night Festivities. Chloe, from Marketing, is also there, but she's standing slightly removed from Gigi's college friends and sisters. She shoots Danny a look that says *Please kill me*. Eve, who sees all, squeezes Chloe's arm, and says something brightly to the group.

Danny watches this play out with quiet pride. In any conversation, there are always some people who would like to take the center stage and others who would rather relax in the audience. And then there are annoying people who take the stage for too long, or boring people who refuse to participate. But Eve has perfect balance. She knows just when to seize a moment, but she knows too when to ask a thoughtful question and cast her golden gleam of attention on someone else. She can walk into a circle of near strangers, take Chloe's arm, and save her from drowning. When Danny first started dating Eve, he saw this trick as a kind of perfect calibration—the social skills of someone who has always been charismatic. But he has come to think of it in different terms: Eve finds it easy to be kind. Eve is kind like it costs her nothing.

"You made it," Julian says.

Danny turns and sees Julian there in his white linen pants and white linen shirt and the sort of watch one gets from one's grandfather, if one has the right sort of grandfather. His hair is freshly cut.

He looks—and Danny means this with the utmost love—like he's about to vom.

"How are you doing?"

"So good!" Julian says. "Crushing it!"

"But actually?"

"Gigi's sister just asked me if I was planning to do anything about my eyebrows before the wedding."

"What's wrong with your eyebrows?"

"Everything," Julian says, "I fear." He rubs at his brow with his thumb. "How was your flight? How's your room, is it okay? I haven't talked to Eve yet. Is she good? Oh, fuck, it's Cabot. I hate Cabot. What kind of name is Cabot, anyway? Hey, Cabot! Good to see you, man!"

Danny claps Julian's shoulder. Julian makes a deflated little sound and puts on the face he wears when they meet with investors. It says, *I have the right sort of grandfather.*

This is a skill, Danny has learned, possessed by all Olsens. They have a specific variety of WASPy repression that allows them to disguise emotion at will.

Their first semester of college, Danny and Julian took a slew of breadth requirements—Conversational Spanish and Baroque Architecture and History of War—and Julian had seemed impossibly clever. They sat shoulder to shoulder in every class and revealed tiny bits of selfhood to each other one hour at a time: "*Me llamo Danny.*" "No, I've never heard of a colonnade." "Of course I don't have a favorite war."

And then their second semester. They both planned to major in computer science. Julian had taken the AP class in high school; Danny's hadn't offered it, but Julian encouraged Danny to skip the intro class anyway on account of his self-taught dabbling. "I can always help," Julian said, which was intended cheerily and received as such. It did not occur to Danny until their first assignment that they had both gotten it all wrong. They were tasked with creating a game—the one where you skip the stones over each other until you have just the one left. Danny wrote his program, then wrote it again better. He delighted in the puzzle of it—the way debugging built new, complicated shells of logic, and then the way a clever revelation would streamline it all down again. But then he saw the way Julian tried to solve the problem—which was to say, he didn't, really. He would write a few lines; get stuck; move on to something he was better at, which was most things. The night before that first assignment was due, Julian sat with his head on his keyboard at his tiny dorm desk. Danny had caught him. Julian had his headphones on—hadn't realized Danny had come back into the room. And then, when Danny approached Julian's desk, Julian had sat up, smoothed the dread from his face, and said, "Hey, man, what's good?"

"What are you talking about?" Danny said.

"Just, like, where are you coming back from?"

"No," Danny said. "What the fuck was that?"

"What do you mean?"

"Your whole face just changed. Like, you just got a totally new face when you noticed me."

"I don't know what you're talking about."

Danny kneeled next to Julian's desk. "What if we didn't fuck with each other and I helped you fix your incredibly shitty code."

"Okay," Julian said. "But for what it's worth, my code would have to exist for it to be shitty."

From that point, Danny always got to see Julian's walls going up and coming down again. Danny is wall-exempt. It has led him to believe that the greatest gift someone can give is the ability to see them clearly.

The men of the groom's party migrate from the hotel lobby to a Sprinter van in the driveway. It's a few old college classmates, a few people from work, but mostly characters from the Olsens' extended network of family friends. Of them, Danny's favorite is Holling, and that's who falls into step beside Danny on the walk to the van.

Unlike some of the family friends (Cabot, for one), Holling has an actual job and phone banks for Democrats, so Danny likes him even though he's obviously in love with Eve.

"I hear you just went out of beta," Holling says. "Congratulations."

Out of beta; just launched a web app with payment processing; Bug has now started learning from user conversations and relationship trends. It looks very little like the app of this time last year.

"Hey, thanks," Danny says.

They get in the front row of the van. In the back, Julian is slapping a drumbeat against a headrest. One of the other guys is saying, "Okay, but when I got married . . ."

"So I know basically nothing about engineering," Holling says. "But how'd you do the chatbot? What's it built on?"

"Pacifica?"

"Daddy Breck, nice."

"He's an asshole, but he really did make the best LLM."

"So how'd you do the scoring algorithm? Does it learn?"

Danny is surprised at the question. "Yeah, it does. It checks patterns from other users and adjusts its scoring."

"So it's only going to get better with time."

"I mean, in theory. Right now, it's a decent algorithm, but it's hard to account for self-reporting errors. What we see is that forty percent of users rate their relationships an eight out of ten. Eighty percent rate between a seven and a nine."

"So everyone thinks their relationship is pretty good?"

"Basically, yeah," Danny says. He thinks of it this way: A user might be in a generic, dull relationship, but if their last relationship was a constant screaming match, they'll think, *Well, it's better than that, so it's probably pretty good.* Or, a user might be in a phenomenal relationship, but they'll think, *But we still bicker sometimes, so it's not perfect.* "Self-reporting just isn't that effective," Danny says. "Hence Bug. That's our AI."

Holling nods. The van goes over a bump. In the back, there is the unmistakable sound of a beer opening.

"So Bug analyzes conversations between partners," Danny says. "And the way people write about their concerns. And then, once we have more longevity data—who breaks up, who stays together for years—we'll be able to explain what a good relationship actually is. Protect people from settling for bad partners; give bad partners the tools to be better. That sort of thing."

"And what was the source for your training dataset?"

"Didn't you say you knew basically nothing about engineering?" Danny asks.

Holling spreads his hands. "I compulsively undersell myself because I have some deep-seated insecurities relating to my father. Bug told me that."

"We used ourselves as our training data," Danny says. "Which is probably why Bug told you that."

5

Thursday Night Festivities end up including: axe-throwing, whiskey tasting, jazz club. It feels to Danny like Julian has read a pamphlet somewhere on acceptable masculinity. "I'm sorry," Julian says at one point. "Cabot and Brooks said they wanted to plan it, and I was too busy to realize it was a terrible idea."

"I mean, all that matters is that you're having fun," Danny says.

"Do I really look like the kind of man who would have fun throwing axes?" Julian says.

"Your hair says *no*. But your tattoo of the Augustus Saint-Gaudens statue of Diana in the American Wing of the Met says *I contain multitudes*."

"But you, tough guy," Julian says. "You really scream *elite axe thrower*."

"Actually, we kid detectives were bigger in the slingshot game."

Danny gets back to the room before Eve. He lies on the bed and checks his phone. Pays a bill. Scrolls through work messages. Opens Pattern.

He looks at his and Eve's score. It's gone up to a ninety-two, both because Pattern's predictions are getting more accurate and because he and Eve have a better relationship than they did six months ago. He finds himself compulsively checking a few times a day, just to see if it's changed.

He opens the chat window.

Bug: Hi hi! Want to chat?
Danny: I just paid my credit card bill and threw up in my mouth a little

Bug: Bad news bears! Have you considered not doing that?
Danny: I had to buy a $1200 tux for this wedding. But also, like, why did I eat a $22 fast casual Mediterranean grain bowl every single day this week?
Bug: I could make a joke about your insatiable love of hummus, but based on our previous conversations, I wonder if your stress has more to do with your relationships. Do you feel inferior to Eve's family? Like you will never belong?

Danny types himself a note to check the configuration on Bug's bluntness.

Danny: Stab me in the heart why don't you
Bug: Sorry about that! But let's not hide from tough feelings :)
Danny: You know, if you're not successful, I won't be able to start paying myself a normal salary, and then I won't pay back my college loans, and then I won't be able to stay in New York. So it would be awesome if you were successful.
Bug: Ah, I see. You fear Eve won't love you if you aren't financially successful. Have you talked to her about this?
Danny: Yes.
Bug: Great! How did it go?
Danny: She was kind and understanding and I felt so much better for fifteen minutes.
Bug: And then?
Danny: And then we went to work and I went back to feeling the exact same way.
Bug: Would you like me to suggest some relationship optimization ideas?

Danny: Sure.

Bug: Great! It's really nice how much you care about Eve. Let me write some suggestions :)

Ideas for Eve
- Eve can get easily overwhelmed. Offer her a calm and comforting setting when she returns, but don't force her to open up if she needs to decompress after an intense day.
- Share something nice you noticed about her today.
- Put on some music you both like to help her feel at ease. I think Alias Paradise is just the thing for you two tonight!

Danny connects his phone to the room speaker and puts on Alias Paradise, a band whose concert he and Eve went to last month. A moment later, he hears footsteps outside.

The key scanner beeps, and the door opens. Eve emerges in with her hair coming out of its ponytail and she smiles at him and he feels an almost painful trepidatious ache at the base of his throat, because he feels certain that this is the point of it all, and uncertain, now that he's found it, how he's supposed to go about the business of the rest of his life.

"How was it?" she asks.

"They made me throw an axe."

"Honey," Eve says. She climbs onto the bed and lies with the whole of her bodyweight dead across him. He is pleasantly squished. "I'm sure you were very brave."

"That's what everyone is saying. How was your night?"

"Good."

He wants to ask what she means by *good*, and if she can elaborate, but he does as Bug told him and doesn't force it. He just runs his hand through her hair and lets them sit there in the calm.

"I love this song," Eve says.

"Yeah? Me too."

Another moment of silence.

"I liked watching you with Chloe," Danny says. "She looked nervous, but then you pulled her into the group."

"Oh," Eve says, "she would've done just fine on her own. But—thank you."

Another silence.

"Hey," Eve says then. "So something weird happened."

"What's that?"

"So we were all drinking cocktails at the beach, right? And Gigi was playing music. I mean, someone was playing music, but I assume Gigi made the playlist because it was all her vibe, you know? And then 'AWAKE/ARISE' came on."

"AWAKE/ARISE" is a song from Eve's first album. A lyric explanation website informed Danny that this was a reference to *Paradise Lost*. "Has anyone shown you the maze beneath Manhattan? Underneath the C where the light can't reach." Danny remembers listening to that song when it first came out, when Eve was just Julian's little sister, as he stood on a street corner near Union Square with the night dark and deep around him. He had lived in New York for two years at that point but still felt so far from local. He remembers picturing Eve, then, as he had last seen her—a senior in college, her hair in a messy bun, an overlarge crewneck and classic sunglasses. Both younger and older than Danny. He remembers thinking, *Yes, you're a New Yorker, and it's effortless*. He remembers imagining that deep underground, far below the subway, there were other tunnels, a secret only true New Yorkers knew, and he remembers wishing she would show him the maze beneath Manhattan. It has always been one of Danny's favorites of Eve's songs, because although *Paradise Lost* allusions don't do much for him, Danny understands what it means to long.

"Great song," Danny says.

"Well, one of Gigi's college friends was like, 'Ugh, skip.'"

"Incorrect!"

"And then Gigi's other friend was like, 'Oh my god, shut up, that's Julian's sister, she's right there, blah blah.' And then everyone was apologizing and awkward and I just wanted to jump in the ocean. You know? I wish no one I knew had to listen to my music. Do you feel that way? With the app?"

Danny considers. "No, actually. I think I'm just flattered that anyone wants to use it."

"Does what I'm saying make any sense, though?"

"Yeah. I think so."

"I can't think of how to explain it better. Too sleepy."

Danny kisses her forehead. "We have time."

Shortly before Danny's mother left, she found him at home watching TV and said, "Promise me consumption won't be your only hobby." He was twelve. It was also shortly before he enrolled in an online coding class for the first time. He felt, in those months after she left, the deep weight of not mattering, and it was creation—the writing of code, the solving of puzzles, the enlivening of numbers into actions—that made him feel sane. He resented and appreciated her for teaching him that—to create rather than just consume. But he always thought of creation as the making of something someone *else* would consume. Danny makes an app; other people use it.

But now there's this thing with Eve, and it's a thing they have created. It cannot be used by anyone else. And yet, when Danny gives to this thing, he feels the same way he feels when he codes. Like he is making something that matters.

6

#marketing-social-media

Chloe 5:04 PM
Hey squad! We have the team from Miravelle doing videography, but please record with your phones too! Vertical, sound on, and clean your cameras please

julian 5:09 PM
Huge weekend for me AND for the company! Thank you all so much :')

7

On Friday, they rehearse on the rolling emerald lawn behind the resort. Danny gives a thumbs-up to Eve in her running shorts as she processes down the aisle with her stand-in bouquet (reusable water bottle). The whole time, three black-clad videographers from Miravelle, the agency Chloe hired, rotate around and around. At one point, the actual wedding photographer has a hushed fight with one of them. Everyone is determined to pretend they don't hear. Smiles remain plastered. The cameras never stop rolling.

The welcome drinks take place by the pool. They're serving his-and-hers-themed cocktails. His is a paper plane. Hers is a French blonde. Eve is busily chatting with Shannon, so Danny offers to go get all three of them drinks. Unfortunately, this positions Danny alone in the bar line just as the Olsen parents descend.

"Daniel," Cecilia says.

Danny turns. He tries to hype himself up. He imagines saying, "Hey, *so* great to see you, but I thought I should probably mention that you always call me Daniel but technically my legal name is Danny! Just Danny! That's all it says on the birth certificate!" And then they would all laugh and no one would ever bring it up again. But shucks—Danny's a coward.

"Mrs. Olsen!" he says. "You look so nice. That's a lovely dress."

"Oh, isn't that sweet," Cecilia says to Phillip, as if to settle a conversation from some prior moment. Is Danny the kind of person who could not say something sweet? Danny? The man who cannot even assert his own name?

"Quite the weekend," Phillip says. "You must be thrilled about the app. I read about the funding round."

"Julian did a great job," Danny says.

"Your parents must be especially proud of you."

It's the emphasis on the word *especially*. *Your* parents must be *especially* proud because they can't have expected much from *you*. Danny imagines how it would feel to say, "Just my dad, actually, but alas! He loves me regardless of my merit." But he loves Eve and he loves Julian. So he is doing his best to be stuck with these people for the rest of his life. He just smiles.

"Daniel, darling, I think it's your turn to order."

Danny does. He gets a beer for Shannon and a wine for Eve and a paper plane for himself.

"Sampling the menu?" Cecilia says.

"For Shannon and Eve."

"Only joking."

Danny collects his drinks. He feels awkward holding all three of them; awkward not knowing how to say goodbye.

When he was with Kyra, they used to take the train to Philadelphia, where she grew up. They would arrive on a Friday night with their backpacks of toiletries, and Kyra's parents would cook them a dinner of spaghetti and sauce out of a jar. Her father would offer him a can of Yuengling. Kyra's younger siblings, all four of them, would trickle in and out of the house without warning. Everyone would clean up, and then they'd all migrate to the old corduroy couch and watch the latest sitcom to arrive on the latest streaming service. Kyra's mom would get up every five minutes to get everyone tea, some cookies, an extra blanket. It was so boring, and Danny had been so grateful to be allowed to be part of it.

As Eve's parents smile placidly back at him and his three drinks, Danny wonders if he will ever be part of this family, really. If they will ever allow him to belong. He co-owns their son's company. He is dating their daughter.

"Well, I better get these back," Danny says, lifting the drinks.

Phillip says, "Okay," chuckling, as if Danny has said something funny. Or, perhaps, as if the joke is just Danny.

Danny doesn't see Eve and Shannon. He ducks his head and makes his way to a small table, partially concealed in ferns, by the pool. There, he sets down the drinks, lowers the brightness on his phone, and opens Pattern.

Bug: Hi hi! How's it going?
Danny: I think Eve's parents hate me.
Bug: But Danny! Who would hate you?
Danny: The people at the coffee shop when I order something too complicated. Investors who want us to sell user data to advertisers. Jeremy, from eleventh grade, because I accidentally went to prom with the girl he was in love with. Nate, from sophomore year of college, because I didn't let him cheat on my exam and then he failed and had to retake the class and he called me a narc even though I didn't know he was trying to cheat on my exam and, frankly, I probably would have let him. My mom. Anyone who believes Eve deserves better.
Bug: I see now I should not have asked that rhetorical question. It seems like there are a lot of complicated feelings about parents going around. Want to tell me more about that?
Danny: Eve and Julian's parents just have impossible standards for their kids. And I am definitely not who they want for Eve.
Bug: In your view, who do they want for Eve?
Danny: Someone smarter than me. Someone who comes from a better family.
Bug: Based on your conversation history with Eve, you focus more on money and status than Eve does. My analysis suggests that these concerns are more of an impediment to the future of your relationship on your

end than Eve's. My advice is that you shouldn't let this get in the way! Keep being polite to Eve's parents, but don't let them discourage you. Does that help?

"Hey, Danny! Why are you hiding behind this plant?"

Danny immediately locks his phone screen as his old college friend Brandon moves one of the ferns aside to join him by the pool. Brandon also studied computer science and then went to Silicon Valley to work for Apple. He is six foot eight and looks down at Danny with his arresting, unblinking blue eyes. When Danny and Brandon first became friends, Julian said, "He's such a good dude, but man, we simply cannot stand next to him."

"Do I look like I'm hiding?" Danny says.

"For sure. Very clandestine."

"Oh," Danny says. "That's what I told my barber I was going for this week. Give me something clandestine."

"Hey, cheers to the launch, man. You have a freemium model now, yeah?"

Danny explains that freemium offers a relationship analysis, score, and five thousand weekly words of chat with Bug. The paid subscription offers feedback ("You don't communicate well when you're hungry!"), suggestions ("Have you considered getting her tickets to stand-up for Christmas?"), and unlimited chat.

"Will there be tiers?" Brandon asks. "Like, if I pay for a platinum subscription, will you tell me about my partner's chats with Bug? Will you tell me if my situationship is still going on dates with other people?"

"We're still trying to figure out some of the details," Danny says. "But basically, no. We don't want to share so much that users feel like they can't trust the app."

"That's good. I keep telling my boyfriend we should get on, but he's technophobic. He thinks his phone is spying on him."

"I'm surprised you two can get along."

Brandon laughs. "You know, on paper, we shouldn't." He glances over his shoulder, and Danny follows his gaze to the bar, where Gigi and Julian are clinking champagne flutes in front of the content crew to get the perfect shot. "They kind of are perfect for each other."

"You think so?"

"Who but a professional influencer would've been okay with her wedding becoming an ad? But they both look really happy."

"They're a one hundred," Danny says. "In the app. Like, they are a perfect hundred."

"Do you genuinely believe that?"

"I look up to them, if that makes sense. Like, I wouldn't want what they have, but also—I don't know that I know anyone else as happy as them. And once you see that that's possible, you know you can raise your standards for your own life. Does that make sense? That's part of what I wanted to do with Pattern."

Brandon laughs. Shakes his head. "Fuck," he says. "You know, I was going to try to poach you this weekend."

"From my own company?"

Brandon tells Danny about his new start-up—green tech with a good profit model but a bad habit of unsuccessfully explaining their product offering. He talks about how good the team is, and how he loves SF, and how nice it is to focus on something to do with climate. But then he says, "So, yeah. We need more engineers, and I was going to try to convince you to come out, but now I'm remembering that you and Julian are actually my favorite couple."

"He's my best friend," Danny says, shrugging.

"And I'm no home-wrecker," Brandon says.

8

#marketing-publicity

Chloe 9:14 AM
Huge feature from our friend Shannon Offenbach at MAGNET! 6M unique monthly visitors—keep up the good work all!
Goodbye, dating apps—Pattern wants to get you in a relationship that lasts | Shannon Offenbach

 Direct Message

julian 10:53 AM
heeeeeeey so nothing to worry about I'm doing good, everything ok, but maybe you could swing by room 307 when you get the chance before the ceremony please everything is fine hahaha

9

The morning of Julian and Gigi's wedding, Danny knocks on their door. Gigi, he knows, has already gone to the spa to get ready; Eve, as one of the bridesmaids, is there, too. Julian had said some months ago that he wanted to get ready alone. Something about meditating and getting in the zone. Danny was led to believe a juice cleanse was involved.

When Julian opens the door to room 307, he is not drinking a green juice. He is, however, eating a fistful of dry cereal straight from the box. His eyes are wide. His hair looks like he just stepped out of a wind tunnel. He appears to be wearing not his wedding tux but—good lord, can it be?—a gray suit jacket with navy suit pants.

"My god," Danny says. He touches Julian's forehead. "Are you well?"

"I thought maybe I'd try something. Put myself out there! Live a little! Express myself!"

Danny shuts the door behind him. "Okay, but you once told me suit jackets are strictly monogamous with the pants from whence they came, so. You can see my cause for concern."

"No concern! We're doing great. Hey, want some Guava Zeros? They're knock-off Cheerios, but they're guava flavored. And they're zeros instead of O's, so, you know. No copyright violation."

"Are they good?"

"Do they sound good?"

Danny admits they do not and asks if that was why Julian summoned him—to try the Guava Zeros. Julian admits it was not and says he's feeling a teensy bit out of sorts, if Danny can believe that.

"No way," Danny says.

Julian sits on the floor with his Guava Zeros cradled in his lap. "Gigi and I dropped," he says.

"What?"

"We dropped."

"Dropped what?"

"In Pattern," Julian says. "We were doing this whole piece for socials yesterday at welcome drinks about being one hundred? And then we had sex last night—"

"Is that relevant to the story?"

"—and I woke up being like, hell yeah, I'm awesome, I get to marry Gigi fucking Badeaux, and we're perfect, and how many people get to know that their marriage is definitely going to work out? And then I logged onto the app and it said we were a ninety-eight."

"Okay," Danny says. "An A-plus."

"A ninety-eight," Julian repeats. "And we've always been a hundred. But the algorithm is getting more data now. It's getting smarter. So maybe we're going to keep going down. Maybe we're actually a seventy, and the app has been totally wrong this whole time. Maybe when we're old, we're going to be sitting silently on opposite ends of the dining room table listening to our forks shriek against our plates because we're so completely indifferent to each other that we may as well be alone."

"That feels specific."

Julian lies back on the carpet. "I love you so much," he says, "but can you get my sister?"

Ten minutes later, there's a knock at the door. When Danny opens it, Eve stands on the other side. Her hair is tied up in a bun but her makeup is overwhelmingly done. She's still wearing shorts and a large button-up.

"You look great," Danny says.

"I am meant to look great in photos, not from six inches away, but thank you."

"Is that my shirt?"

"Yes, but it's been in my custody for some months now."

Julian makes a tragic sound from behind Danny.

"How's the patient?" Eve says.

Danny moves so Eve can enter, then he shuts the door behind them. Eve stands over Julian with her hands on her hips.

"Is this of the body or of the soul?" Eve asks.

"Either way," Danny says, "we may need to amputate."

"Can you two stop flirting and make me feel better?" Julian says.

Eve sits cross-legged beside Julian and takes his Guava Zeros. She slowly munches her way through a handful of them as Julian regales her: the ninety-eight, the dread, the shrieking forks.

"I said that seemed very specific," Danny adds.

"Well, yes," Eve says. "You've met our parents."

"But your parents are together," Danny says.

"They're together, but they're not happy," Eve says.

"How unhappy can they be if they stayed together all this time?"

"They would've been better off getting a divorce a long time ago," Eve says.

Danny takes a half step back without meaning to. He watches Eve notice. When she does, a mask falls across her face. It's too fast for Danny to stop. Eve has just suggested the undoing of Danny's family was a good thing. Danny has reacted with shock to a truth Eve holds deeply ingrained within her. She looks away from him. His palm touches his phone through his pocket, itchy with the need to ask Bug for a solution.

Eve lies back on the ground next to Julian. Danny leans awkwardly against the wall.

"Jules," Eve says.

"Eevee."

"In the family lore," she says, "what do we know about me?"

"You're the best one but you threw away your potential?"

"No, the other thing."

"You're mean and don't get along with anyone," Julian says.

"Exactly. And yet. What do I think of Gigi?"

"You think she's cool."

"And?" Eve says.

"That she has nice hair."

"And?"

"That she's the shit."

"Precisely," Eve says. "I think she's the shit, and I think you're the shit, and I think the two of you are going to have a happy life."

Julian turns his head to look at her. His eyes are large and vulnerable. Danny has perhaps never wished for a sibling as concretely as he does in this moment.

"How can I be sure?" Julian says.

"Well," Eve says, "you can't."

"That's actually not the feedback I need right now."

"You just can't," Eve says. "Even if you and Gigi were totally perfect, one of you could still get hit by a bus. A meteor could come kill us all. Maybe you'll just grow apart. It happens."

Julian presses his hands against his face. "You were doing so well."

"You're still a ninety-eight," Danny says. "And hey, maybe that's an error. Maybe you're actually a hundred."

Julian lowers his hands. "I know you're placating me, but can you say that two dozen more times?"

"You're a hundred," Danny says. "You two are perfect together."

"I mean," Eve says, "no one is *perfect* together."

"What if," Danny says, "we tabled that thought for a moment?"

"I'm just saying! It's not certain, but you're choosing to take a leap anyway! That's beautiful."

"I hate leaping," Julian says.

"No leaping," Danny says. "Just stepping. Into a great decision with no negative repercussions."

"Danny—" Eve says.

"Eve," Julian says, "we love you but maybe save your 'uncertainty is beautiful' thesis for people who have not devoted the past year of their lives to alleviating the discomfort of uncertainty."

They all laugh. It feels like releasing a pressure valve to acknowledge this omnipresent thing. Danny looks at Eve like, *We're okay?* And Eve nods back like, *We're okay.*

Julian stands and brushes Guava Zero debris from his chest. He looks down at himself. "Good god," he says. "These pants don't match this jacket."

"You have thirty minutes before the first look," Eve says. "Please change. Or we will literally never hear the end of it."

Julian ruffles her hair, which makes her bun fall to one side. She squints at him, and he looks pleased.

In the hallway, Danny says, "What did you mean about family lore?"

"Oh," Eve says. "It's just a joke we have."

"That you're mean?"

"Just, you know how with families or friend groups, people sometimes get typecast in a certain role? Little brother, innocent nerd, mean girl. Et cetera."

"But you're not mean."

She laughs like it's perfunctory. Pauses. Laughs again like she means it. "It's so weird," she says. "How much of love is just finding the person who sees the version of yourself you want to be."

"But," Danny says. "You're not mean. Why would your family say that?"

She kisses his cheek. "See? Exactly."

10

Danny: Why does Eve think she's mean?
Bug: We're not always the most honest judges of ourselves. Have you asked her?
Danny: Why would her family tell her that, though?
Bug: It's difficult to fully understand someone else's family.
Danny: Do you think she doesn't realize that's not a normal thing to expect your family to say?
Bug: Do you think you realize all the ways your own expectations for family are abnormal?

11

Danny stands at the front of the aisle beside Brooks and Cabot. While they wait for the wedding to start, Brooks and Cabot loudly discuss their latest business idea, which they describe as on-demand Christmas tree delivery for New Yorkers.

"Dude," Cabot is saying. "And in October?"

"Pumpkins," Brooks says.

"That's what I'm fucking talking about."

"Booyah."

"Laugh out loud."

"Hey, Danny, you want to build an app for us?"

Julian did not want to invite them to be part of his wedding party, but, as he told Danny a few months prior, it was this or he allow his parents to choose the DJ. One must pick one's battles.

When Julian comes down the aisle, his parents stand on either side of him. Danny knows the Olsen parents are annoying but also, god, the way Cecilia looks at her son.

The bridesmaids arrive next in various shades of blue. Eve smiles her stage smile at the crowd and Danny thinks, *That's the woman I'll marry someday.* He waits for her to look at him so they can silently share this thought, but she doesn't. She looks everywhere but at him. This is objectively not a big deal and not worth reading into. Danny needs to stop overthinking. She probably does not want to marry Danny. Okay, no, stop the spiral. Stopping the spiral in three, two, one. Doesn't want to marry Danny! No, STOP. Gigi is coming down the aisle, for Christ's sake. Can you stop being an anxious little freak for one second? Gigi, gorgeous in her long silky dress with her dark hair pulled back, fixes Danny with this split-second look like, *Hey, bro, you're making a face that's going to ruin my photos,* and this makes Danny smile and then he watches his best friends get married. In the back part of his mind, he's thinking that this is not something they have as of yet designed the app to account for: for the siblings and parents and friends who are not in the love story but are nonetheless part of it, setting good examples and bad ones.

The officiant asks if they do. And they do.

12

At the reception, the wedding party sits at the head table. When it comes time for Danny's toast, Julian and Gigi both shoot him thumbs-ups. It's all somewhat embarrassing; he loves them so much.

He stands, and all the cameras pan toward him. Chloe has made it abundantly clear that this moment will be commemorated on the company Instagram feed for all eternity.

Danny rolls his shoulders under the weight of all those gleaming lenses.

"So Julian and I were roommates in college," Danny says. "And we got along so well, we started saying it was destiny of the great housing gods—so that was cute of us. Julian could bring anyone out of their shell, which was exactly what I needed. He always had these schemes for how we should spend our spare time—like sneaking onto the roof of the history building during the prospective students' weekend and making ghost noises. And I think I was what Julian needed, too, because I said practical things like, 'Hey, you seem to have broken your ankle, we should probably stop making ghost noises and get off this roof.' I met Julian eight years before he started dating Gigi, and so I thought I knew him pretty well. For example, I never thought he'd come home from a first date and tell me he just met the woman he was going to marry. But that's exactly what he did when he met Gigi.

"For those of you who don't know," Danny says, "Gigi speaks four languages. She is weirdly well-read in the field of neurobiology. She's also one of the most curious people I know. Since Julian fell in love with Gigi, I've seen him become even kinder, more sure of himself, more willing to ask hard questions. But I've also seen Gigi and Julian bring out a silliness and lightness in each other I didn't expect.

"In my very limited experience, sometimes you meet people who don't get you. Sometimes, you meet people who do get you. And sometimes, you meet people who get who you want to become. And those people are the people who grow you up. They're the people who will stay beside you through everything. When I look at Julian and Gigi, I see two smart, funny, driven, empathetic people—great people on their own who have managed to make each other even greater. And I can't wait to see all the ways they grow together for all the years to come." Danny raises his glass. "Cheers," he says, "to the happy couple."

Everyone claps. Danny sits. Eve kisses his cheek.

The buzz of adrenaline only lasts until Eve and Julian's dad stands. He clears his throat and everyone falls abruptly silent. Julian agonized over the order of speakers. It was eventually decided that just Danny and Phillip should go before dinner—Danny, because Danny wanted to get it over with, and Phillip, because Julian wanted to get it over with.

"I remember when the kids were young," Phillip says. "In middle school. There was a dance, and Julian was working up the courage to ask the girl he liked. Eve, meanwhile—Eve's in sixth grade and three boys have already asked her. Of course, me, Mr. Dad, I want to know if she likes any of these boys, and she just rolls her eyes at me and says, 'Daddy, they all bore me.'"

Eve presses the bone in Danny's knee to convey that she has never once called her father Daddy.

"So we always knew Eve would have boys wrapped around her finger. But Julian! He was our sensitive one. And you know what? He asked that girl he liked to that dance. And she said no."

Julian gives a forced laugh—a "ha, ha" with both syllables clearly defined, which makes the rest of the reception follow suit. *Ha! Ha! We're having such fun!*

"And now we're here, against all odds—" hold for more laughter "—watching Julian tie the knot with the most gorgeous, accomplished girl. Just to echo what Julian's cofounder, Daniel Aagaard, said, it's true that some people really bring out your potential. And not every relationship will do that. Some will just hold you back. But with Gigi, in this past year especially, we've seen Julian blossom into his full potential. It's a real joy, as a parent, to see your child achieve."

When Danny thinks of Eve and Julian, he doesn't think of sibling rivalry. But as he listens to Phillip, he wonders if this is despite, rather than because of, circumstance. Eve lifts her glass; sips slowly.

"So thank you, Gigi," Phillip says. "For being just who Julian needed." He raises his glass. "Cheers." Do his eyes meet Danny's? Just for a second? "To the happiest couple."

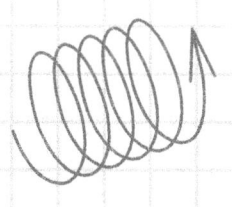

Pancake

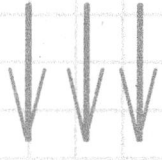

1

A decade prior. A semiprestigious college sends out acceptance emails.

2

One home: Bozeman, Montana. An '80s ranch style, lawn scattered with the detritus of sport-based hobbies and woodworking projects.

One son: Danny.

Danny's dad is laughing and picking him up—Danny is too big to be *picked up*, this is an indignity! But Danny's dad is proud, so proud. All this hard work.

Now Danny's dad is crying, and Danny is saying, "Dad, please don't, look, I'll come back and visit you all the time, please, really, I will."

"You won't," Danny's dad says.

"Please don't do this."

His dad cries harder. "I'm just proud," he says. "That's the only reason."

3

On the other side of the country, another home: Manhattan, New York. An Upper West Side brownstone, the surfaces smelling of sterile lemon furniture polish.

A different son to different parents: Julian.

Julian stares into his phone. Eve is playing guitar on the couch and pretending there is not something monumental happening in the space between Julian's eyes and his phone screen, and something else monumental in the space between Julian and their father. Eve plucks out hollow, lonely little notes that cannot sustain themselves against the force of so much damask wallpaper. Phillip looks at the phone over Julian's shoulder.

"I guess there's that," Phillip says.

"It's an acceptance," Julian says.

"Congratulations!" Eve strums something cheerful. They both look at her like, *Don't do that.*

It's an acceptance—Julian's first. No one in this family has gone to this college before because for the past century, everyone in *this* family has gone to Harvard.

"Cheer up," Phillip says.

Julian turns, cautiously hopeful.

"Eve can still go to Harvard."

Julian looks at Eve with betrayal, like she was the one who said it. Eve doesn't want to go to Harvard. She doesn't want to work at her dad's company. Eve wants music, and Eve wants love. In that order.

"Well, thank god for second chances," Julian says.

"It was a joke," Phillip says. "We're very proud of you."

"Because it feels like you're saying, you know, good thing Eve is around because Julian is a failure."

Their dad says, "Some people love the first pancake."

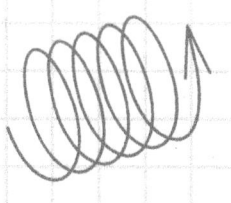

Boom

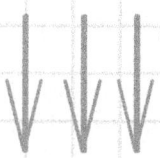

1

Eve lies in the sun of McCarren Park with her book shading her face and one AirPod in. She's listening to a song she wrote called "Evergreen." Yesterday, she loved it. Today, she thinks it is negative space; creation for creation's sake; three minutes utterly devoid of meaning. She opens Spotify and puts on someone else's music. It makes her thoughts go fuzzy, like she is separated from her brain by a pane of glass. It would be so easy to never have a creative thought again.

So you could say being a professional full-time musician is going well. She can't possibly complain: This is exactly what she wanted from the start.

2

Eve and Shannon's lease runs out at the end of June. Eve is acting supercool and blasé about this. She was raised to believe discussing one's finances was crass, but here are Eve's finances:

Eve was the opener for nineteen of Stella's shows; her cut was low but she sold a lot of merch. (Everyone wants to look like a '70s ski rat.) Eve has played at two festivals and a smattering of other shows, all of which amounted to half of what she made with Stella. Her streaming money, once you account for her label cut, isn't nothing, but you definitely couldn't live on it. And then album sales—well, people just don't really buy albums, but Eve accidentally had a vibe that was great for vinyl, so that effectively added 20 percent to her yearly earnings. If she did not have any expenses, this would be a very exciting salary. Alas! Her manager gets 15 percent (and Eve is happy to lose this 15 percent because she would be literally nowhere without her manager), and the tour expenses eat another 20-ish percent, and then there's equipment, insurance, and finally, that large marketing and PR budget that curated Eve's great-for-vinyl vibe in the first place. What you are left with is, ironically, four hundred dollars less per year than what Eve made as a copywriter for Rampart. This is fine except for the fact that Eve now needs to capitalize on her momentum with an even bigger year, and also that her rent in New York, in the apartment she shares with Shannon, is 30 percent more than the rent on the house she shared with Fletcher in Boulder.

Danny has been dropping hints for some time that they should move in together. And it's true that they are already sleeping in the same bed twenty-eight nights a month, and it's true that Eve loves being with him, imagines they will probably be together for a long time. But it's also true that she is afraid of what it will mean to link herself financially to a man once again. Would she have stayed with Fletcher for so long if they didn't co-own Gus the Subaru? If they didn't share a couch and a bed and a carbon steel frying pan? Eve cannot stand to think of Danny becoming someone she loves out of obligation.

So when Danny drops these hints, Eve evades. She knows she should probably tell him about how she's feeling, but every time she starts, she worries what it will do to him. If it will make him more anxious. If it will make him doubt their relationship, and if those doubts will leak into doubts about his work.

Two weeks before the lease expires, Eve still hasn't given him a firm answer. She knows she has to, but she doesn't know what her answer is. There is no way she and Shannon will stay at the Court—the Court, where there is an ominous scuttling in the walls every few minutes, which they have optimistically nicknamed Nibbles the Mouse—but the question is, do they find a new place together or does Eve move in with Danny? She considers asking Bug but has a latent fear that Danny and Julian can read her chats.

She's sitting on the lumpy couch with her guitar. Eve is trying to turn her uncertainty into a viable song when someone buzzes the door. Probably a package, she thinks, because Shannon works from seven in the morning until nine at night and thus has all her worldly needs delivered.

Eve is slow to get up. Her head is stuck in "Evergreen," as it has been for some months now. It is both the best and the worst song on the forthcoming *Sunbeam, Baby* because it's so close to being great. The time signature is 6/4, which makes the song feel dreamy and sexy but hard to dance to. She has double-tracked the vocals, layered on backup vocals, stripped it all back again. Intimate or epic? More reverb or less? The song should feel like summer—she knows this—but should it feel like waking up at a campsite next to the person you love or like a pool party with all your friends and too much beer? And then there is the chorus, which goes like: "It's an evergreen rush with his evergreen touch and my evergreen crush and I want it so much." It's fun to sing! But also sort of painful and cringe in a way that makes her want to die. I mean. Evergreen crush?

Eve comes back to what she always comes back to, which is that she does not feel comfortable writing about happy relationships. Does the world need to know she wants "it" (sex with Danny) so much? She has experimented with other choruses that use words like "revisionism" and "asymptote." Weirdly, none of these choruses were very good.

When she writes a clever song, she doesn't feel vulnerable. It might not be everyone's cup of tea, but it's still clever. But if she sets out to write a fun, easy, breezy song and she fails—if she tries to make something enjoyable that does not end up being enjoyable—then there is no point. She is afraid, truth be told, to release a poppy, fun song, because she's not sure anyone will like it. Also, because she's afraid that if she strips back the irony and the complexity, everyone will see the truth, which is that all Eve really wants is for people to like her music. She does not know how she can be a professional musician and still be so worried that people will judge her for taking herself seriously.

Someone buzzes the door again, twice in quick succession. Eve goes to the door, but when she opens it, it's not a package at all.

It's her dad.

"Oh," she says, taking a step back. "Hi."

Eve and her dad look alike. Always have. He still has his hair, and it's thick and blondish brown, an elegant wave coiffed just so. His eyes, like Eve's, are set too far apart on his head, which makes him seem prey-like, deerish. He's never smoked and rarely drinks and goes to the gym every day from exactly five thirty to exactly six thirty, so in most regards he is aging well—except for in the eyes, where he looks hollow.

"May I come in?"

To Eve's knowledge, her father has never set foot on the Lower East Side. "Sure. Can I get you tea? Or something?"

"I'm just fine." He sits on the very edge of the ottoman, and Eve takes her wary place back on the couch, lifting the guitar into her lap. "Were you playing something?"

"Oh," Eve says, "yeah." She hesitates. "Did you, you know, want to hear it?" She feels like a frat boy at a house party. *Anyway. Here's "Wonderwall."*

"Oh, no, that's all right," he says. "So. This is where you live."

"Yeah. Me and Shannon."

"The reporter."

"Yeah, she's a tech journalist."

"She's saying good things about Julian?"

"I mean, I think that would be an ethics violation, but sure."

"He's doing well these days."

"Yeah. I'm so happy for him."

"It was good of him to include Danny."

"In the company? In the company that Danny cofounded?"

"Everything I say, you hear the worst possible version of it."

Eve does not respond to this. She sets her guitar next to her on the couch and folds her hands in her lap. Is everyone like this with their parents? Like they're trying to break a record for how quickly the conversation can go bad?

"I'm not here about Danny," her dad says. "I'm here about you."

Eve sits back into the couch. At this moment, the ominous scuttling of Nibbles the Mouse comes scratching through the walls.

"Eve," he says. He gazes around the apartment. At the big *New Yorker* posters (Shannon) and the framed vintage ski resort map (Eve, courtesy of Stella Seaport); at the umbrellas leaned up against walls; at the running shoes, knee-high boots, white sneakers, strappy heels strewed under every couch and chair. Eve lifts her chin and waits for him to look back at her.

Again, he says, "Eve. What are you doing?"

"What do you mean?"

"I always saw myself in you, you know that? You have drive. But my god. Why are you using all that drive for *this*?"

Eve pauses. "By 'this,'" she says, "you mean music?"

"Music. This apartment. Danny. All of it."

"Whoa," Eve says. "What does Danny have to do with anything?"

"Princess," he says. "I'm just worried, is all. You know, I knew this woman who gave up a great career, a whole life, just because she wanted to paint mugs."

"Maybe they were great mugs. Maybe painting mugs made her happy."

"Your life can't be all one thing. You've got to leave doors open for yourself."

"Dad, I love music. I'm making money with music. Can you just please trust me?"

"You think you're making money," he says. "But you're not making 'send your kids to college' money. You're not making 'pay your mortgage' money. What's your plan here? Marry Danny and hope his app keeps you in the black?"

Eve feels like she's been slapped. "Excuse me?"

"You know how many miserable wives we know who can't leave their marriages because they can't afford to?"

"What," Eve says, "like Mom?"

Phillip claps his hands twice against his knees. "You're not using the degree I paid for. I think it might be best if you paid it back."

Eve stares at him.

He stands.

"Wait," she says. "Wait, is this a joke?"

"You're wasting your potential," he says. "I can't watch it, and I want no part in it."

"I don't have four years of college tuition money to pay you."

"Then get a different job. You get a different job, a real job, one where I know you can take care of yourself, and you don't have to pay me a dime."

"This is insane."

"You need to know what you're getting yourself into."

"But I didn't study music. That was our deal. I did what you wanted."

"None of this—" he looks at the apartment, which does not have in-unit laundry or an elevator or a doorman or air-conditioning or closets or windows that open all the way but is nonetheless Eve's home, Eve's life "—is what I wanted."

"Why are you doing this?"

"Because, princess—we love you."

He leaves. Eve watches him shut the door calmly behind him. She calls her mom, who lets it ring and ring. Finally, Eve texts her.

> **Eve:** did you know dad was going to do this?
> **Mom:** I don't want to get in the middle of it.
> **Eve:** in the middle of . . . him asking me for hundreds of thousands of dollars?
> **Eve:** i'm not convinced he has legal recourse for this, actually
> **Eve:** is he just being a dick?
> **Mom:** Please don't make this difficult.
> **Eve:** is this just a pride thing? he just wants to embarrass me?
> **Mom:** Turn autocorrect back on, honey. It's exhausting.

Eve sets her phone on the coffee table and rubs her fists against her eyes until she sees white stars. Nibbles the Mouse runs up and down inside the walls. Well, she thinks. Well. That was good. Actually. It was good that it happened, because now Eve can stop trying to impress her parents. For real this time. It's freeing. This is exactly what she wanted from the start.

3

The next day, Eve tells Clay that she wants her album to be a hit.

"Sure," Clay says. "That's a pretty niche hope, actually."

Clay was the guitarist from Stella Seaport's tour, but he's also a good producer. Eve and her manager couldn't find anyone else who felt like the right fit, so they're giving Clay a shot even though he doesn't have a ton of production credits to his name. Eve still isn't used to the experience of collaboration. *PRELAPSARIAN* she wrote alone in her dorm room, and most of *ski rat* felt fully formed by the time they recorded it. But Clay is a much more skilled musician than Eve, and he suggests things that would've never occurred to her. She is probably better with lyrics and has a nicer voice, but he's great at crafting a four-to-the-floor pattern that will really make a song danceable. What Eve appreciates most about Clay, though, is that he's honest. A month ago, her label asked for an update on the progress of *Sunbeam, Baby*, and Eve considered giving them what they had; Clay told her she'd regret it if she didn't work on it more, and he was right.

He's also become her friend. He and his boyfriend, Matthew, are regular double-date partners for Danny and Eve. Matthew is very clean-cut—a straitlaced, corporate lawyer type. They've been together for five years. He always orders fancy wine for the table.

Now, Eve and Clay are in the studio—ostensibly rerecording "Evergreen" for the thirty-second time.

"I'm tired of chasing something that awards people will like," Eve says. "I want to make something popular."

Clay raises his eyebrows, and she tells him about her dad.

"So you want this album to earn a bag?"

"I mean," she says, "sure, but mostly, I think I just want to write to an audience that my parents have no part in."

"I have some ideas," Clay says. "You might not like them. But can I take the album to a friend and come back with some feedback next week?"

"What friend?" Eve asks.

"Do you trust me?"

"I'm a brand-new Eve," she says. "Let's live a little."

4

Clay emails her a ZIP file on a Saturday morning. The subject line is: "Act now! Make money fast! Get your bag!" Eve is still in bed. Danny is over, but he's already drinking coffee on the couch because that code simply will not compute itself. Eve has been partaking in the useful Saturday morning ritual of one-more-video on her phone. Outside, the throuple of pigeons are having a spat.

She texts Clay.

Eve: are you trying to give me a virus
Clay: lol open it
Eve: that is exactly what a virus would say

Eve opens it. Inside, there is a WAV file, which she plays.

It's "Evergreen." But also, it's not. It's faster now. It feels somehow both intimate and epic—like it's being sung inside a cathedral. Now, the bridge builds with palpable tension, and at the end of it, Clay shouts, "Hey!" Cue the chorus.

Eve calls him. "What the fuck," she says.

"I know."

"This is good."

"This is great."

"Who's your friend?"

"Before I tell you," he says, "can you agree that this is absolutely the best version of the song so far?"

"Yes, obviously. Who is it? Is it a murderer? Is it someone I've dated?"

"It's AI."

Eve pauses. From the living room, she hears Danny typing. "Oh?"

"Look, I know this guy. He's in the industry. He made this tool to help musicians. So I fed it your album, but I said I wanted it to be more fun, more summer, more danceable. I said it should calibrate everything to blow up on TikTok. It's still your music. It's just, you know. Going to make a shitload more money."

Eve plays the song again. It really is good. "Shit," she says.

"Way of the future, baby."

"What was it trained on?"

"I don't know. Songs, music journalism, Instagram data? It has a plagiarism detector, which obviously I used."

"I feel weird about this."

"Please think on it? It's so catchy. Play it for Danny."

"You already know what he'll say."

"Yep!" Clay says. "Ta!"

Eve ends the call. She wraps the blanket around her shoulders and pads outside. Danny lowers his laptop lid halfway, looks up at her, and smiles.

"Hey. Coffee?"

"Sure," Eve says. "Do you think it's ethically suspect to use an AI music editor?"

"Uh-oh," Danny says. "I fear this is a trap."

"Ha ha. But do you?"

"No. I think it's ethically suspect for an AI music editor to scrape data from musicians without paying them. But I don't think it's wrong in the abstract. This feels like it's going somewhere."

Eve holds out her phone and plays him the song.

"Eve," Danny says.

"I know."

"I love this."

Eve powers down her phone and sets it on the table. "I'm going to not think about this for six hours and see how I feel." She drops onto the couch opposite Danny. "Can I watch stupid reality TV to distract myself?"

He hands her the remote. For an hour, they just sit like that in companionable silence. Danny types. Eve watches TV and pretends she's not thinking about her phone, which she can feel psychically behind her.

At one point, while the reality TV personalities are having a stilted conversation about sexual preferences, Danny says, "What would you think about sex stuff on the app? You know, like more about—here's some stuff you might both be into. I feel like we're not doing enough with that. Users keep writing reviews about it."

"Is this because Kyra brought up anal while you were breaking up?"

"I cannot believe I told you that."

"I mean, it's a pretty good story."

"That aside. Should we put it in the app?"

"I don't know," Eve says. "Shouldn't people have those conversations themselves?"

"Maybe they don't know how to bring up what they want."

"But what if you suggest something that makes users uncomfortable? And then they feel like they have to go along with it?"

"Yeah." Danny's quiet for a while. "That's fair." More quiet. "Do you hate it?"

"Hate it?"

"Pattern. Bug. The whole thing."

"Danny."

He rests his chin in his hands and looks at her. "Just a question." His voice is so soft. Like she is already forgiven.

She scoots closer to him on the couch. His arm moves around her to make room for her head on his shoulder. "I'm really proud of you," she says. "And I think it's really exciting, everything you built, how well it's doing. But I just— I guess it makes me nervous sometimes. What if it makes us worse at processing our emotions for ourselves? What if it gives bad advice? I'm not saying it does. It's just something I get anxious about. Does that make sense?"

"Totally. I worry about that, too."

"You do?"

"Of course."

If it were Fletcher, he would've gotten defensive; tried to litigate her feelings. And yet, Eve cannot shake the feeling that Danny's reaction was precalibrated via a conversation with Bug, who knows full well Eve does not often open the app, who could easily surmise Eve's doubts, who could have warned Danny exactly how Eve was feeling and how she would most like him to respond. She finds herself often thinking this way when Danny does something particularly perfect. *Are we meant to be, or are you just following an algorithm's instructions?* When he errs, she feels oddly reassured. A week prior, he completely forgot they'd planned to go to the gym together. He was late at the office, and when she finally called, he fell over himself apologizing, and she said it was okay. Better than okay. She would rather date a human.

"Hey," Danny says, "feel free to say no, but I actually had an idea. What if you told Bug to look at your old data with Fletcher? That way, you can see what it has to say with the benefit of hindsight. And also, you know, without the specter of your current boyfriend having designed the app hanging over you."

"Have you done that?"

"Yeah, with all my exes. It's interesting."

This makes Eve jealous, which makes her wonder if Bug told him it would.

5

Danny has dinner plans with friends that night, and Eve is still not ready to confront the good version of "Evergreen," so she does what Danny suggested. She gives Pattern access to her entire text history with Fletcher. The wheel on her phone spins and spins, and then, finally, her screen fills. Relationship score: 72.

> **Bug:** Hi hi! This appears to be a past relationship. Would you like me to provide some analysis?
> **Eve:** please tell me what you would've told me if i fed you this information while i was still dating this guy
> **Bug:** Okay!

The wheel spins again.

> **Bug:** A score in the seventies can feel disappointing or upsetting to some users, so please keep in mind that this is just one data point. Remember, you can increase your score!
> There's plenty that works well in this relationship. You have a shared network of friends, which increases lifetime relationship satisfaction by 30 percent. You both effectively use I-statements in arguments and seem comfortable setting boundaries. It also seems, at least from what I can see, that you have a very steady relationship without a lot of ups and downs. That can be the sign of a stable base for the life you build together. But no relationship is without its problems. It seems that

you and Fletcher are disconnected from each other. Though you don't ignore each other, you also don't go beyond the minimum. It also seems that you don't fully value each other for who you are. He doesn't laugh at your jokes or read the articles you send, and you don't seem to appreciate the time he spends planning the logistics for your life. Neither of you are bad people for this! It may just indicate a mismatch in personality. This persistent lack of enthusiasm may lead to resentment over time.

While I believe you could have a happy, fulfilling life in this relationship, it might require more work from both of you than you would expect from a more compatible match.

Eve sets down her phone. Uh-oh, she's crying, how embarrassing. Nibbles the Mouse scratches the walls again, which makes her cry more. Nibbles! Please chill out!

Shannon unlocks the door just as Eve is collecting herself, but the look Shannon gives makes Eve think she has not, in fact, sufficiently collected. Shannon deposits her Trader Joe's bags on the floor and goes to Eve.

"My dude," Shannon says. "What ails you?"

Eve shows her the phone. "If I'd've had Pattern when I was with Fletcher, it would've told me good enough wasn't good enough and I would've saved four years of my life."

"Oh, babe."

"And also, I'm kind of distressed by how accurate this is."

"Why's that?"

"Because," Eve says. "Because I want my friends and my brother to know me better than an app. But also, none of my friends told me to break up with Fletcher. And I obviously should have."

"In our defense," Shannon says, "we didn't have the advantage of reading your entire text history."

"What if Danny and I are also bad? And no one says anything?"

"You're not."

"Really, though. From the bottom of your heart."

"Honestly?" Shannon says. "I think you need to be able to have this conversation with him. I think you two are still working out some stuff. But basically—yes, of course. You adore each other. You were never this happy with Fletcher."

"Then why didn't you say anything? I don't mean that as an accusation."

Shannon lifts her hands. "I didn't know what you looked like when you loved someone the way you love Danny."

Eve hugs Shannon, and they just stay there like that in the rectangle of light from the hallway.

"I kind of want to move in with him," Eve says. "And by kind of, I mean really and a lot."

"I know."

"But maybe it's a bad idea."

"Maybe," Shannon says. "But also? I think you'll be okay."

6

Playlists Eve makes for Danny:

- songs for beep boop clickety clack (coding) (safe for work)
- what's Danny running from?! (180 bpm)
- i'd embark anywhere with you <3

7

They look all over the city. The Upper West Side is too close to Eve's parents'. Astoria is too far from Danny's office. The Village is more than they can spend. As they both develop public personas, they are also more conscious of where they live as a part of those personas. Where will they be noticed or unnoticed? Where will they fit?

Sometimes, on the street, people stop them. Eve is mostly stopped by women in their twenties with Blundstones and lots of rings. Danny is mostly stopped by men in their twenties with wool coats and nice watches. Basically, Brooklyn likes Eve and Manhattan likes Danny. They compromise by living in Williamsburg.

They move into a two-bedroom garden-level unit between an overpriced smoothie place and an overpriced coffee place. They invite all their friends over for a housewarming, and Danny asks everyone to bring a candle, which he insists is a storied Norwegian housewarming tradition his dad taught him about despite no firm internet evidence existing to verify this claim.

"I'm just saying, if you were going to make something up, we could have told them all to bring something of greater value," Eve says.

"Gold ingots," Danny says.

"Pints from Caffè Panna."

"Diary entries full of salacious gossip."

"You love gossip," Eve says.

"I just love to examine the human condition."

"Well," Eve says, "in the spirit of embracing your Norwegian heritage: *Jeg er interessert i å kjøpe elgen din.*"

"I have no idea what you just said."

"'I am interested in buying your moose.'"

"You know I don't speak Norwegian, right?"

"You have some homework, then. I'm up to two sentences."

"What's the other one?" Danny asks.

"*Jeg må snakke med en mann om en fjord.*"

"Meaning?"

"'I have to speak to a man about a fjord.'"

"You really honed in on the important stuff," he says.

"Sure did."

Danny kisses her nose, like he finds her cute, and then her mouth, slowly, like he finds her beautiful. They kiss for a long time, there in the kitchen, in the apartment that is theirs.

Danny has the better bed, so they sell Eve's. Eve has the better drinkware—"It's Anthropologie, Danny!"—so they donate Danny's gray IKEA mugs. Eve has so many shoes, but she is spared the embarrassment because apparently Danny owns Nike Terra Kigers and Invincibles and Vaporflys and Alphaflys, and don't even get him started on his quarter-zip collection. On the walls, they hang up the vintage ski map and a painting of trees that Julian bought Danny for way too much money. On the bookshelves (they need *two* bookshelves, which Eve takes as a moral victory), they stack old textbooks and pulpy romance novels and doomsday nonfiction and glossy literary hardcovers. There are guitars, and photos from Julian and Gigi's wedding, and a bowl of matchboxes from all the restaurants they've gone to. There is also a large ceramic goose, gifted by Chloe in lieu of a candle at the housewarming. "Am I regifting this? Yes," she said. "But I do think he'll be happy here, if you'll have him."

When Eve fills the bathroom cabinets with her overabundance of hair stuff and teeth stuff and makeup stuff, she leaves the top drawer, the prime drawer, empty. And then, when she unpacks the box labeled ACTUALLY IMPORTANT STUFF, she takes out a hundred crumpled, water-stained sticky notes and puts them there, in the top drawer.

The first time Eve showers in the new apartment, she discovers that the showerhead makes a thin, haunted noise when water comes out. Ah, New York. She tries to match the pitch. She turns the note into nonsense lyrics: "baby, new high, baby, dream wide." She thinks it's someone else's song, but then again, she's not sure. Maybe she'll look it up later.

When she gets out of the shower, there's a sticky note affixed to the mirror. It says:

You + me baby new high
Dream big baby, baby dream wide
:)

Very carefully, she folds it in half, and then she puts it in the top drawer.

Sometimes, at night, she wakes up and sees him on the other pillow facing her, his face gentle and young, his lips just barely parted. She doesn't know how long this feeling is expected to go on. She asks Bug how to tell the difference between the honeymoon phase and a good relationship, and Bug suggests that maybe you can't—maybe some relationships are just only good for a season. Then she asks Bug what the odds are that she and Danny are only good for a season, and Bug tells her they seem to be doing great, but, of course, Bug cannot predict every twist and turn of the human heart. So Eve just holds her breath and looks at Danny sleeping. She wants the knowledge that she and Danny will last forever, but she knows she does not have the wisdom to handle it if the answer is no. Eve has never felt like this before. Like she is so in love she has something to lose.

8

Playlists Danny makes for Eve:

- That's the song of the summer, baby
- Someone spiked the coffee at Our Lady of Perpetual Breakfast
- Every concert we've ever seen together in chronological order :)

9

Eve calls Clay to tell him she wants to move forward with the edited album. They have to rerecord a few things, but now, with the suggestions of their algorithmic dystopian sidekick, they are inspired and clear-eyed for the first time in weeks. Eve's manager comes into the studio to listen to the latest cut of "Evergreen," and she sits with her jaw cupped in her palms and her gaze fixed on the table in front of her. It ends, and she says, "Again." Eve and Clay glance at each other. They listen again.

"Okay," her manager says then. "Well. So we have it."

"It?"

"The big one."

That's how they start talking about "Evergreen." *How's the Big One? Do you think we need to start teasing the Big One on socials? I am so tired of the Big One!*

The day "Evergreen" is set to drop on streaming, Eve and Clay plan to meet in McCarren Park for a croissant. Eve's Instagram post is scheduled; the single is queued; the teasers have trended. Now, all that's left is to pray. And eat croissants.

Clay is late. Eve sits on a bench in the shade and waits. She listens to *Sunbeam, Baby* in its entirety, watching the dappled light patter through the leaves. It's saccharine sweet, this album. There are no references to *Paradise Lost* or *The Odyssey*. This is an album about falling in love, having sex, feeling light, being happy. She knows what the critics will say: that it is dishonest. That's what they always say about joy. Joy is simple, and simplicity is dishonest. But Eve also feels this may be the most honest thing she's ever written. There is a line on the last song, "Mariana," that goes: "Honestly, it's just not that deep."

That will be the headline that the critics use. It will also be what her parents say, should they ever choose to listen.

Clay shows up thirty-eight minutes late. Eve knows this because that's the duration of *Sunbeam, Baby*.

He looks vaguely concussed. He drops onto the bench next to Eve and pulls his Knicks hat farther down his head.

"Sorry I'm late," he says.

"Are you okay?"

"Matthew broke up with me."

"What? No. What?"

"He said I just didn't have it. Like, the intangible it. Something was missing."

"Oh my god. Clay, I'm so sorry. Did you see it coming?"

"I had no idea. Like, none. I thought we were great." He pauses. "We were a seventy. In Pattern. And we always kind of made fun of it, you know, privately. Like, oh, sure, seventy, but they don't know that opposites attract and that we balance each other out and we're going to be together forever. But last night, he was like, 'I actually just don't think we're that compatible after all.'"

"Oh, Clay."

"This is going to be the only time I say this, and you can't repeat it. But just for my own peace of mind: literally, fuck Danny."

Eve feels the words hit her chest like a physical blow. She pats Clay's shoulder. She suggests they go get wine instead of croissants, but Clay says only competitive physical exertion will cure him. They end up playing pickleball on the McCarren Park courts.

"Whatever it takes to help," Eve says, "but pickleball? Really?"

"It's America's fastest growing sport."

Eve doesn't check her phone most of the day. When she finally does, it's sunset, and she sees she has messages from Danny, Julian, Gigi, Shannon, Holling, her manager, assorted friends and distant relatives. She has the sense something big is about to transpire, is already transpiring, but how do you prepare for something like that?

In a way, she's grateful she and Clay spent the whole day talking about other things.

Clay hugs her, and they walk home in their separate directions.

Eve feels terrible for Clay, of course. But also, she cannot imagine being caught off guard by a breakup. If she and Danny break up, she knows exactly why: because he will do something to make her doubt their relationship, like put his career above hers, and this will make her think of her parents and their retrograde gender roles, which will make her pull away abruptly, which will make him perilously anxious, which will make her retreat even further because she cannot bear the responsibility of making a man feel psychically whole. It would be his fault for his dependency, but it would also be her fault for her unwillingness to communicate. And then they'd be done. The thought makes Eve so sad her teeth ache. But it would not catch her off guard.

10

Eve's manager calls her while she's blow-drying her hair a few days later.

"I have a potential partnership for you," her manager says. "This guy wants to meet you."

"Really?"

"He's a famous actor. Hush-hush. But he's launching a beer company, and he's trying to get social media traction. He thinks 'Evergreen' would be perfect, but he wants to turn something around ASAP. While the song is still trending. His exact words were, 'We fly her to California, shoot, edit, post, bing bang boom.'"

"What famous actor is going around saying 'bing bang boom'?"

"Actors are weird."

"I mean," Eve says, "it pays, right? How much does it pay?"

Her manager says a number. It is the number of a college tuition.

"Just to use my stupid song?"

"They want you to be in the ad."

"Really? Will someone professional do my hair and makeup? Because I have a huge zit on my chin right now."

"That's the spirit," her manager says.

The brand is called Summer Camp. Their cans look like enamel mugs. Instead of plastic rings, they are held together with friendship bracelets. At pop-up events, they offer tastings using canoe paddles as beer paddles.

In the social media ad, which requires Eve to fly to Lake Tahoe, she stands on a dock wearing a white lifeguard T-shirt and red terry-cloth shorts. "Evergreen" plays. At the end of the bridge, the drums get loud and Clay goes, "Hey!" In the ad, this is the moment where

Eve holds up her can of Summer Camp Off-Duty IPA. Pops the tab. Turns to look at the camera over her shoulder. Big logo. Boom.

They pay her a college tuition. "Evergreen" plays and plays, and then, when the rest of the album drops, "Evergreen" becomes incessant. Incessant to everyone, or just to Eve, just to Eve's algorithms? It feels like she can't escape it, but her streaming numbers still can't compare to the Main Pop Girlies. Eve cannot fathom how overwhelmed they must feel by the presence of their own music. The first time she hears "Evergreen" in public—while buying ice cream in a bodega—she almost has a heart attack.

Eve sits for an interview with a magazine where they ask her what overnight success feels like. It doesn't feel overnight, is what it feels like. They ask if her fans have been supportive of her new sound and she says yes even though many of them have not. They think she's too mainstream, a sellout, just another beta pop wannabe. She is written up on the music criticism website, the big one, and they say: "Olsen's journey into radio dance pop isn't just surprising—it's boring." They go on to say: "While her lead single, 'Evergreen,' may fuel this summer's pool parties, the album will ultimately be lost in the beige algorithmic haze of heartless pop intended to trend on social media. It's full of sound, sure—but, ultimately, signifies nothing."

Eve reads the review on her phone and closes the tab. She gets on the L to the C and takes it uptown.

At her parents' door, she rings the bell. She waits there awhile; it seems possible, after all this, that they never answer.

But then they do. Her dad; her mom hesitating behind.

"A gift for you," she says. She extends the vinyl of *Sunbeam, Baby* in their direction. On it, she has taped a check full of zeros. It is the first check she has ever written. Who writes checks anymore? She had to go to the bank to get it. The memo line says: "Wasted potential."

"Here's my album," Eve says. "I think you'll really hate it."

Mooooon

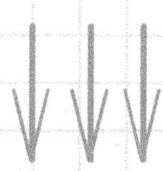

1

Q: WHY DID THE SHOE GO ON A DATING APP?
A: IT WANTED TO FIND ITS SOLE-MATE!

"Who has the champagne?" Chloe asks. "Olive, champagne me!"

The office—because they have moved out of the coworking space and into an office of their very own—is cramped with bodies and Christmas trees and boughs of holly and a menorah in the middle of it all. Danny keeps trying to work, and Chloe keeps coming over and turning off his monitor. She has placed a Santa hat on his head, which he has begrudgingly accepted.

Tonight is the night *Soulmates* becomes available on streaming. It's a dating show based on and sponsored by Pattern. All the contestants pair off and vie to have the highest score by the end of a month, and then the winners get an all-expenses-paid wedding.

Danny had nothing to do with *Soulmates*. Danny prefers his reality TV to involve polar bears or baking bread. From start to finish, *Soulmates* was Julian's baby, and this solution suited them just fine.

The month of December has been their biggest month to date. Danny has launched new privacy features (which probably no one will notice but of which Danny is immensely proud) and begun work on version 2.3, which will include Same Page. Same Page is a feature where users can ask Bug if they're on the same page—does she also want to cancel dinner? Does he also think our friend is kind of annoying? Bug will keep quiet if you are not, in fact, on the same page.

For the first time, Danny gave everyone on his team a holiday bonus. Today is the last day before the office closes, so he handed out cards to the tech team. Everyone was paid commensurate with the recent success of the app. Checks upon checks. Olive said, "This is kind of surreal." Danny knows. For the first time in his adult life, he is not in debt.

Julian clinks his champagne flute from the front of the room. Danny glances up; back at his screen; up again.

In their early years of collaboration, they worked together incessantly. There was not a day when they did not eat at least one meal together. But with success (and age, and marriage), there's distance. They manage their separate teams. They attend different meetings. In October, Julian caught a cold and didn't give it to Danny. This was the first time this happened in a decade.

Which is why Danny didn't fight back against *Soulmates*. From the start, he thought it was a bad idea—they're trying to sell their ability to create real, lasting love, not dating-show infatuation—but Julian was excited, and Julian's instincts are right more often than they're wrong.

Now, Julian thanks everyone for their help on making this happen. He shows a graph of their downloads, and the spike when the show began advertising.

"And we just keep going up from here," Julian says. "Merry Christmas, happy holidays, and let's crush it next year."

Danny hates the phrase *crush it*. It gives him the proverbial ick. This is a trait he shares with Gigi. The first time Danny and Gigi met, they were at brunch at Our Lady of Perpetual Breakfast, and Julian kept saying—with the best of intentions—that Danny was totally crushing it at work. After the fifth instance, Gigi said, "If anyone says anything else about crushing it, getting this bread, making these gains, or grinding on this KPI, I am legally entitled to put my head through the wall."

Now, Gigi sits on a desk pushed at the front of the office. She meets Danny's eye and gives her head-through-the-wall smile.

"Just before we get started," Julian says. "I want to shout-out my brilliant, talented wife."

Some whoops from the crowd. Chloe goes, "Ow ow!"

"A year ago, I was complaining to Gigi about our Seeker user base—which was only twenty-one percent women. Just a whole bunch of lonely dudes. And Gigi goes, 'Yes, because you keep talking about love the way a lonely dude talks about love—like it can all be solved with data. You have to start telling love stories.' That was where this whole thing began. Gigi's been part of *Soulmates* from the very start—which is why I was so pumped when she agreed to host the show. And also why I'm stoked to announce that our Seeker user base is now thirty-six percent women—and it's going to keep rising from here. Babe, we all love you, but especially me."

"Gross," Gigi says. "I love you back."

"Okay, okay," Julian says. "Without further ado."

Chloe turns on the projector, and the title screen of *Soulmates* fills the wall. Everyone cheers. A song about bells and sleighs begins jingling, and a woman's voice says, "There's no way I'm going back to my hometown alone this Christmas."

Danny stays through the first episode, then he does his round of goodbyes. Everyone boos. He says he has a late flight that night. When he reaches Julian, he feels the eyes of the company.

Danny hugs him. "Merry Christmas, man."

"Hey," Julian says. "Have a good one."

He kisses Gigi's cheek.

"Don't get eaten by a bear, okay?" she says.

Outside, in the cold dark, Danny zips his parka. All the bars are lit with twinkling white. A delivery truck goes by playing "Carol of the Bells." When Danny exhales, his breath hangs in the air.

2

Danny told his dad six times (he counted) not to pick him up from the airport. It's late, and Danny's dad, Cal, has trouble driving in the dark. As soon as Danny steps into the baggage claim area, he sees Cal holding a deconstructed cardboard box on which he has written: DANNY!!! Danny feels, in order: pity, then annoyance, then love, then guilt. When they hug, Cal is already crying.

3

Danny's bedroom is exactly the way he left it when he went to college. Cal calls this era Before College—BC. AD is After Departure. As in, *The house is still so quiet in the year 12 AD.* As you can imagine, this feels really good.

The Christmas tree is already up. Cal works in the forest service and takes pride in knowing his trees. This year's is a nine-footer, no bare patches, taking lots of water. It's strung with multicolored lights and bedecked in ornaments Danny made in school. Danny was not a particularly artistic child, which is a polite way of saying his clay Jesus looks like sacrilege.

"Want me to get the fire going?" Cal asks. "You can tell me about your week."

"Dad, it's two a.m."

"It's never *too* a.m. to get a fire going!"

"Ha ha," Danny says. "Like *t-o-o*. You got me there."

"Hot cocoa?"

Danny hugs Cal again. They are exactly the same height. Danny grew early and then stopped, so they've been this way, exactly the same, since Danny was fifteen. "In the morning, hot cocoa by the boatload."

"I'm gonna hold you to it!" Cal says, and he shoots Danny finger guns.

In his childhood bedroom, Danny shrugs his duffel off his shoulder. One of his walls is covered in national park maps. That was what Cal and Danny did every holiday—picked a new park and drove there. The opposing wall is a collage of concert paraphernalia, hard-won because no one ever aspired to bring their world stadium tour to the fourth-largest city in Montana. Danny worked at a coffee shop downtown all four years of high school, every moment of the summer, after school most days, scratching out his homework behind the register between customers, and with the money he saved, he drove to Boise and Denver and Seattle and Portland, stayed in shitty houses and motels with his friends, ate nothing but stale banana bread the coffee shop didn't sell. He has ticket stubs and concert posters from Blanket Statement, MISSOURI, Kat Gravity, the June Bugs: a map of Danny's teenagedom. He thought about bringing all this ephemera to his college dorm but decided it seemed too self-conscious—the armor carried by someone who was not sure enough of his own personality to let it stand without aesthetic signal.

Danny drops his backpack beside the wardrobe and sinks onto his bedspread. The world on the other side of the window is moon bright with snow, and the six inches of air closest to the glass are sharp with cold. Through the wall, he can hear Cal getting ready for bed. The faucet; an electric toothbrush. Danny takes off his shoes and socks, his pants and shirt, folds everything neatly and sets it by his backpack. He climbs under the heavy quilts in his boxers and stares up. The ceiling is paneled in dark wood. The house looks vaguely like a hunting lodge, though Cal has never hunted anything. Like Danny, Cal has always been vegetarian.

He holds his phone above his face for a long time, just staring at the awaiting screen, before he opens his messages with Eve. He takes a picture of the wall of music ephemera and composes a text.

> **Danny:** I very much hope you are happily asleep right now! At my dad's now. See you soon. I love you.

It would be ludicrous to expect her to respond immediately, and, of course, she doesn't.

A minute later, Cal knocks, and the door creaks open.

"Hey, bud," Cal says. "You need anything? All good?"

"All good, Dad. Thanks."

"Okay. Hey, hey—what does the dad cow say to the baby cow?"

"What?"

"I love you to the mooooon and back."

"That's funny," Danny says. "But maybe just end on *moon*. It's punchier that way."

"You got it."

"Good night, Dad."

"Good night, kiddo."

4

The next morning, Saturday morning, Danny goes on a run. It is, meteorologically speaking, fucking freezing. He wends his way down the sidewalk, where pine needles are packed into the ice, and past his elementary school playground and high school track. He stops his watch at the coffee shop where he worked and orders an oat latte. While he's waiting, he leans against the counter and rubs the cold sweat from his forehead. Eve has texted him back: some hearts; a picture of Shannon at the Christmas market.

"Oh my god," a woman says. "Danny *Aagaard*?"

Danny looks up. Blinks. A pretty, dark-haired woman in a huge puffer coat waves him over to her table. She says, to the man next to her, "That's Danny Aagaard, Alex, that's Danny!"

When Danny reaches the table, it takes him a moment to recognize Alex and Mich, who were in his high (and middle and elementary) school class, but they greet him like no time at all has passed. They explain that they reunited at their five-year reunion ("We missed you at that!"), did long distance for a year, moved to Denver, got married, and moved back home over the summer.

"We're literally so happy," Mich says. "It's so good to be back. And oh my god. You would not believe how excited our parents were."

"Come get drinks with us tonight," Alex says. "Gonna be a whole crew."

Danny finds himself agreeing. The rest of the day, he is perplexed as he rolls the incident over in his head. Danny was, you see, not a cool high schooler. He was nervous and nerdy and convinced everyone else was aware how nervous and nerdy he was. Mich was on the women's soccer team, which was what all the popular girls did. Alex was forever hosting parties in his family's house because they had a pool and a cabin.

While Danny and Cal are making lunch—Fancy Grilled Cheese, which is grilled cheese with Brie and Mrs. Weber's huckleberry jam—Danny asks if his dad remembers Mich and Alex.

"I'm not sure," Cal says. "But you had so many friends."

"I did not have so many friends. I wore concert tees and solved mysteries."

"A treasured member of the community!"

"That's so—" Danny pauses. "Cheesy."

"Ah! Got 'em. Nice."

Danny presses the bread into the pan with the back of his spatula.

"What's on your mind, kid?"

"It just feels so different to be back."

"Not all bad, I hope!"

"Not bad at all," Danny says, and he is surprised to realize it's true.

5

Q: WHERE DO ANIMALS DRINK AT THE ZOO?
A: THE MONKEY BARS!

Danny wears his flannel to the brewery, which is covered in Christmas lights and wreaths and playing a distressingly masculinized rendition of "Santa Baby" over the speakers. Mich waves from a booth, and as Danny nears, he can hear her saying, "Danny's here, I wasn't sure he'd come, hi, Danny!"

He slides into the booth next to her and sees faces he has not seen since high school but nonetheless recognizes. No one makes reintroductions. While Danny finds he remembers all the names, he is surprised that no one needs to be reminded of his. And then he remembers that he now has ten thousand Instagram followers and an app with a dating show.

They gossip about their old chemistry teacher, who is apparently now married to a former student. They talk about their parents, who are aging, and about being back, with all its strangeness.

"No, you guys," Alex says. "I used to feel the same way, like this place was way too small? But it's actually so good. Like, we were so lucky. This is a great place to raise a family."

"Would you ever move back?" Mich asks Danny.

"I mean. I can't really imagine it right now. My life is kind of fixed in New York."

"Oh my god," Mich says. "I've been talking and talking. Right, how's New York?"

"You're dating that singer," one of the guys says, and Mich tells him to shut up, don't be creepy, but also, yes, *Eve Olsen?*

Danny hesitates because he isn't sure if it's an act, but it feels fully genuine. He shows them a picture of him and Eve from Thanksgiving—at Talea, losing at trivia, drinking their beers, wearing hats Chloe knitted with great zeal and minimal skill.

"Oh my god!" Mich says. "Why are you two so cute!"

"It's the hats," Danny says. "My coworker said she needed a tactile hobby."

"If I learn to knit, can I make Eve a hat?" Mich says. "Will she wear it?"

"Probably," Danny says. "Eve really likes hats."

"I fucking *love* 'Evergreen.'"

"Have I heard 'Evergreen'?" Alex asks.

"Oh my god. Yes, you have obviously heard 'Evergreen.' Hang on, let me play it."

Danny feels like he's swallowed helium. *This is my girlfriend*, he says. *The Eve Olsen. She really likes hats. Yes, she's spending Christmas with me. No, she hasn't been to Bozeman before. Right, she's just flying in from LA the morning of the twenty-fourth. Oh? A benefit concert. She's there with her best friend.*

In the end, Danny's work doesn't come up the whole time. He has no idea whether anyone he went to high school with has ever heard of Pattern.

"We'll give you a lift home," Alex says, clapping his shoulder. "You're still on Emerson, yeah?"

In the car, Danny gets in the back and Mich stomps the snow off her boots and rubs her hands in front of the heater. "I'm so glad you came tonight!"

"Yeah," Danny says. "Me too. I can't believe how well everyone remembered everything. To be honest, I wasn't sure anyone would recognize me."

Alex laughs. Mich turns fully around in her seat.

"Danny," she says. "You were the prom king."

"Yeah, but didn't teachers pick that?"

"No?"

"Oh," Danny says. He looks out the window at the lights and the trees; the TVs and fires gleaming in warm windows. "I'm pretty sure it was the teachers."

Alex says to Mich, "Classic Danny."

Danny did not know he could be Classic.

6

When Danny gets home, he finds Cal wrapping presents. Cal gives everyone he has ever met a Christmas present. Coworkers in the forest service? Absolutely. That nice cashier at Safeway? Why not!

"Oh," Cal says, "I'm glad you're back. Did you have fun?"

"Yeah. Really nice time."

"See! Home isn't so bad, huh? Anyway, what should we do now? What do you want to do?"

"I'm easy."

"We could watch *Soulmates*?" Cal says. "I'm only four episodes in, so no spoilers."

"How are you four episodes in? It just came out."

"I wake up early."

"Well, I haven't actually seen it. I mean, I've just seen the first episode."

"That settles it! You get the popcorn going. I'm getting your show queued up."

Danny makes the popcorn. Cal turns on the big TV. Danny got it for him as a birthday present in October. Best of the best, too big for the wall, way over the top. Cal kept saying it was too much, how could he possibly accept? But he was so proud. No one told Danny how destabilizing it is to make more money than your father.

Cal presses Play as they settle into the flannel couch.

"That Gigi sure is pretty," Cal says.

"Yeah," Danny says. "She's really smart."

"You ever like her?"

"No, Dad, of course not. We'd have been horrible together. We're great as friends, but—she's great for Julian."

"They're doing well?"

Danny thinks about the way Gigi sat at the party with her arms crossed. "Yeah," he says slowly. "They're always doing well."

They end up watching the whole show—all eight half-hour episodes. In the finale, there's a montage where our heroine, Cassie, redoes her house—a two-bedroom in Small Town America just for her. Her voice-over goes, "You know, I imagined myself doing this with Chad. But actually, I'm so proud of myself. This is my home. I'm really glad I fell in love even though it didn't work out. Now I know myself better. And that's, like—the best Christmas present."

"This is so stupid," Danny says.

"Then why are you crying?"

"I'm not crying. I've developed allergies. You don't dust enough."

"That's probably it," Cal says. "For the record, that's also why I'm crying."

7

The next morning, Danny gets up early to retrieve Eve from the airport.

"I'll come with you!" Cal says.

"It's really okay. You can do more wrapping."

"Oh, it's no trouble! Plus, roads are icy. And I don't trust that you haven't forgotten how to drive."

"Oh, ha ha," Danny says.

"Except to drive me crazy, of course."

"I would never forget that."

"Just a joke. I love you."

"I know, Dad. I love you, too."

They get in the car. Cal does let Danny drive, but he promises to be on high alert for any New York–induced swearing, swerving, or honking. Danny lifts an orange pill bottle from the cup holder.

"What's this?"

Cal takes it. "Just normal old-guy stuff."

"What? Oh, gross. Like Viagra?"

"No, like blood pressure stuff."

"You don't have blood pressure stuff. Are you embarrassed to have Viagra?"

"It's blood pressure stuff! Jeez Louise."

"You know, Eve's ex didn't use the brand names for anything? He'd call it erectile dysfunction vasodilator."

"Sounds like a real weirdo."

"Yeah. Last night, I had a dream he leaped from a tree and drank my blood. I've always thought he kind of looks like a vampire. Feel free to psychoanalyze that."

"Wowie," Cal says. But that's all he says. Danny flicks on the turn signal, and they merge through the slush onto the highway, following the signs for Bozeman Yellowstone International Airport. Cal does this often. He loves to ask Danny personal questions, as if to test whether Danny will open up. But when Danny does open up, Cal seems to have no idea what to do with it.

They drive in silence for a few minutes.

"Just as a heads-up," Danny says, "Eve's going to ask to drive. Is that okay?"

"Is she a good driver?"

"Yeah, she's a great driver."

"Why's she going to ask to drive?"

Danny does not want to expose Eve, especially not when he and Eve have not spoken of this themselves. He says, "She just loves to drive and never gets the chance in the city."

"Oh. I mean, sure, I guess that's fine."

"Cool," Danny says. "Thanks."

"So," Cal says. He slaps his palms against his knees twice. "Eve didn't want to spend Christmas with her own family, huh?"

"The Olsens aren't always the nicest. It's complicated."

"Well, I don't mean to pry."

Danny turns on the windshield wipers as snow begins to flurry down. "They told her to pay back her college tuition. Like, they paid, and then all of a sudden, over the summer, they told her she owed them the money."

"No. And she did it?"

"Yeah. It was a pride thing, I think. But she hasn't seen them since."

"You know, I always thought you liked her parents. I remember the way Julian spoke about his dad. Very admiring."

"It's different seeing them through Eve's eyes. Julian acts like they're the most important, incredible people. But you know what? They didn't even go to Eve's tour. And I just wonder, what does it say about the kind of person Julian is if he wants their approval so badly?"

"People get strange when it comes to their parents."

"Sometimes I wonder if Julian only ever wanted me around because I made him look good in comparison."

"That couldn't be true," Cal says.

"Just something that popped into my head at the wedding."

"Oh, kid." Then: "But you and Eve?"

"We're good," Danny says.

"For-now good? Or forever good?"

"How can you tell?"

Cal lifts his hands. "Wrong person to ask."

Danny hesitates, then says, "Have you ever tried reaching out to Mom?"

"Your mom! Oh, gosh."

"That's not really an answer."

"She ever get in touch with you?"

Danny keeps his eyes on the road as he turns into the airport lot. "No. She never has."

8

Eve is breathless and pink cheeked when she bursts through the airport doors. Danny leans against the hood of the car; Cal perches uncertainly in the back seat with the door open like he's not sure if a hug is permitted.

"Oh my god, it's so *cold*!" Eve says, sounding pleased. Danny kisses the top of her head. "Hey, would it be okay if I drove? I'm just dying to drive."

They climb in the car—Eve in the driver's seat, Danny shotgun. By the revolving door, two tween girls are very indiscreetly filming on their phones.

"Hi, Mr. Aagaard," Eve says. "Merry Christmas!"

"Eve! The one and only! The original gal! Here, I brought you something."

Cal pulls something from the footwell. Danny's whole body tenses. A paper plate wrapped in cellophane. Cal made these last year, too. They are balls of cookie dough with a patina of canned chocolate frosting. When Danny tried one, the sugar made his jaw ache. Danny wants to mentally signal that Eve need not eat anything so exquisitely middle-class gourmet, but there's no way to do it without mortally offending his father. Danny just puts the music on low and longs for death.

"Yum," Eve says. "Thank you so much! Oh, wow, this is so nostalgic! It tastes just like my childhood!"

It does not taste like Eve's childhood. Eve's childhood tastes like Levain.

"Danny?" Cal says, offering him the plate.

"Oh, as soon as we get home. I don't want to get carsick."

"I also brought you something," Eve tells Cal. "It's not your Christmas present. I just saw it in the airport and had to get it. Danny, can you check in my duffel?"

As Eve puts the car in Drive, Danny rummages through her bag until he locates what he is certain is the something: a coffee table book about the healing powers of trees.

"You're going to make me cry!" Cal says.

"I also got you something," Eve tells Danny. She reaches into the pocket of her vest and deposits a package of airplane pretzels on his lap.

"Oh, gee," Danny says. "Thanks, Santa."

Eve glances away from the road for a second and grins. She throws one hand expansively above her. "Oh my god! I'm so happy to be here."

Cal beams and nudges Danny's shoulder to be sure Danny does not miss the fact of his beaming. (This would be impossible.)

Obviously, Danny wants Eve and his dad to get along. Unfortunately, the fact that they get along *so well* kind of undermines his ability to complain about literally anything. The first time Eve met Cal, she said, "I would die for his love." This was unfortunate because Danny used to think he would die for the love of Eve's parents.

9

Cal instructs them to bundle up for the mandatory Christmas Eve Hiking Extravaganza.

"It's really just a hike," Danny says.

"But festive," Cal says. There is something of a Santa hat requirement.

They drive (Eve drives) to the trailhead where Danny's cross-country team did summer long runs. The sky is deep, bright, Le Creuset blue. All the pines are buried up to their knees in fat snowdrifts. A track has been cut along the path, which is packed with boot prints. It smells overwhelmingly of sap and bark and home.

When they step into a cold, dark hush—where the new forest cedes to old growth—Cal says what he always says: "See this, kids? Now *this* is a cathedral."

"That's exactly it," Eve says. "That's it exactly."

A few times, Cal stops to take pictures, which isn't like him. Usually, he says the forest is best experienced with all the senses.

"Should I read into that?" Danny asks.

"Are you texting someone?" Eve says.

"Who's Beatrice?" Danny asks.

Cal tucks his phone back into his jacket pocket. "Just a nice gal I've been seeing! Nothing to get all nosy about."

"Kid detective," Danny says. "Is she your girlfriend?"

Eve claps. "How did you meet?"

"On Pattern, if you must know."

"We must. Dad, you sly dog."

"Oh, come on. Nothing to get excited about. Now, get moving before your toes freeze."

But once Danny sees it, he can't stop noticing how often Cal reaches for his phone. Cal has never been a big phone guy, but now he's glancing at his notifications at stoplights; typing furiously over the stovetop as the water for pasta boils.

"Are you texting Beatrice again?" Danny asks.

"Hey, Eve, pretty good thing we're not making you eat lutefisk, huh?"

"What's lutefisk?" Eve asks.

"Cod soaked in lye," Danny says. "Dad, stop changing the subject."

"It's a very vegetarian Norwegian Christmas here!" Cal says. "Gnocchi with pesto."

Danny cranes his neck to see Cal's screen. It is not, in fact, a text thread. It's a screen Danny knows well: the Bug chat interface.

Cal locks his phone. "You know, you're not as cute as you were when you were twelve. Lot harder to get away with that."

"Not true," Danny says. "I'm very cute. It's the big, guileless eyes."

"Keep your guileless eyes to yourself," Cal says.

They eat their very vegetarian dinner and Danny makes a fire. The glogg is served hot, in red mugs. Cal tells the story of his father, who emigrated from Norway at sixteen and brought with him a recipe for glogg, an indisputable work ethic, and a last name that would forever put Danny first in line. Then Cal wants to know all about Eve's family's traditions.

"We always did church on Christmas Eve and Christmas," Eve says.

"Really! Are you religious?"

"Not anymore."

There is a pause, but Cal doesn't pursue this further. Danny sees him wanting to and ultimately deciding he is not willing to risk it.

"Where's Beatrice this week?" Eve asks.

"Visiting her daughter in Portland. I got us a cruise in May, though. That's her present. You know I've always wanted to take a cruise. Really glitzy stuff. You wouldn't believe these pictures of the boat."

"That's amazing!" Eve says. Eve once told Danny she would rather descend to the ninth circle of hell than cruise. When Eve's family went on vacation, they went to cousins' houses in St. Lucia and great-aunts' pied-à-terres in the 7th Arrondissement. Olsens do not buffet. "That'll be so fun."

Danny rubs his neck, which feels too warm.

Gifts: Eve gets Cal a fancy coffee maker and Danny a wool dress coat with perfect silver buttons. Danny gets Cal cross-country skis and Eve gold earrings and a collector's edition of *Paradise Lost*. Cal gets Eve and Danny matching Christmas sweaters with ice-skating penguins.

"But I have more stuff!" Cal says. "Just hasn't arrived yet."

"Oh my god, no, this is so perfect," Eve says. She pulls on the sweater over her dress.

"Dad, you really don't need to get us anything else. This is awesome."

"You both spent so much money. Of course I got you more than just a sweater!"

"Dad," Danny says.

"Well!" Cal gets to his feet. "I'm thinking it's just about bedtime, huh?"

10

Q: WHAT DID THE THIRD WISE MAN SAY IN THE INFOMERCIAL?
A: BUT WAIT! THERE'S MYRRH!

Danny and Eve brush their teeth side by side in the bathroom where Danny once killed a thousand ants.

"Er dad oozes ug a ot," Eve says.

"What?"

Eve spits in the sink. "Your dad uses Bug a lot."

"Yeah?"

"When you were lighting the fire, he was writing something. I wasn't trying to look."

"Does it seem weird that he's using Bug so much but doesn't appear to be texting or calling this woman very often?"

It occurs to Danny fleetingly that he could find his father's Pattern account in about four seconds. And then he could look at Beatrice's account to see how much time she spends on the app in comparison.

"Maybe she's just busy with her family," Eve says.

"Yeah," Danny says. "Maybe. Or maybe he's being obsessive and anxious."

"Mmm. Poor guy."

"I mean. He could choose to be less anxious."

"Could he."

"Yes," Danny says. "I do hear myself." He puts his arm around Eve and pulls her to his chest. In the mirror, the mirror of bugs, he looks at himself and wonders what comfort it would have brought him at age twelve to see himself now: without the braces, with the good haircut, with Eve. "I get mad at him for the things I see in myself."

"I get that. I get mad at my mom for being complacent because I'm worried I'm complacent. And I get mad at my dad for being mean because I'm worried I'm mean."

"You're neither of those things."

"Yes, but. That's how families work, right?"

"I just hope that my dad doesn't end up hurt," Danny says. "I don't know how he'd handle it. When my mom left, he was . . . bad."

"Bad how? You don't really talk about it."

Danny squints. "I guess I don't remember it that clearly. It feels blurry."

"When did things go back to normal?"

"I don't know that they ever did. Or maybe he's the same person as always, but I just became aware of who he was after my mom left."

"Loss of innocence," Eve says. "Your moment to exit Eden."

"I am once again sorry for not having read *Paradise Lost*." Danny pauses. "I didn't *want* to become aware of who he was. Aware that he wasn't—like, this perfect person."

"But isn't that even better?" Eve says. "You can see his flaws, and you still think he's amazing. That's when we really love someone, right? When we see them, flaws and all."

"Do any of us really think our parents are *amazing*?" Danny says.

"Shannon does. Don't you? I always thought you did."

Danny rolls his hand across an uneasy knot in his neck. "He's just hard to feel close to. I don't mean to complain."

Eve is looking at the sink. "You're not complaining. You're allowed to feel that."

"Eve," Danny says quietly.

She leans against him but keeps her gaze fixed down, at the tile and their sprawl of toiletries.

"Six months," she says. "My parents haven't spoken to me in six months."

"You could try, though."

"Right," she says. "Right. I could try. That's a really good idea."

"I just wonder if they're sitting around thinking the same thing. That you haven't spoken to them in six months."

Eve lays her toothbrush on the edge of the sink. Danny watches her hesitate, and then, ultimately, decide she is not able to say it; or he is not able to hear it. Which is maybe all the explanation he needs.

"Sorry," she says.

"Don't be sorry."

She pads softly outside and shuts the door, leaving him in the small and bugless bathroom alone. He did not realize he didn't have his phone until this moment, when he reaches for it to tell him what he is feeling and finds that it is not there.

11

Shortly before Danny goes back to New York, he is cleaning out a kitchen cabinet when he happens upon a toppled ruin of orange pill bottles behind the spices. He reads their names (is this an invasion of privacy?) and googles them (is this?) and concludes that the owner of these bottles likely has a rapidly progressing condition Danny has only heard of abstractly, in medical ads and at charity fun runs. Nonsensically, the owner of these bottles seems to be named Calvin Aagaard.

Eve has already left. Danny collects each of the bottles and sets them in a line on the kitchen table, where he sits for a long time. Cal has gone to the grocery store because Danny accidentally asked if he had any peppermint tea, and he did not.

He picks up his phone. He wants to tell Eve. He wants to tell Julian. What his muscle memory instead has him do is touch the icon for Pattern, which sits on the bottom of his screen next to his texts and music and internet browser. Even as he does this, he realizes it's not what he wants to be doing, but he finds the force of the movement as impossible to reject as gravity.

> **Danny:** I think my dad is not well
> **Bug:** I'm very sorry to hear that. Do you want to talk about how this might impact your relationship with Eve?
> **Danny:** What do I do about my dad
> **Bug:** Okay! From my experience talking to you about your relationship with Eve, I know that you don't always find it easy to have conversations about heavy and serious topics. You may find this is also the

case when it comes to your relationship with others, including your dad.

Danny: He didn't tell me

Bug: I'm sorry to hear that—this must be difficult for you. It's okay to feel angry, sad, or afraid—a whole tapestry of emotions. Are you worried your dad's lie of omission will impact your ability to trust in your other relationships?

Danny sets down his phone. He finds himself thinking that the natural next step for Pattern is this—not just romantic relationships but all relationships. To create a system to quantify and coach friendships, offices, families. There is almost zero latency between Danny having the thought and being sick with himself, of himself. He is so determined to solve every problem with more technology. He does not know how to solve with less.

He hates the word *tapestry*. No one says "tapestry" except for LLMs.

How long does he sit there? Danny hears the garage and then Cal saying, "Hey, bud, I wasn't sure what you wanted, so I got peppermint green tea and peppermint sleepytime and just plain peppermint. We can try 'em all! Or not, whatever you'd like."

Danny examines the heat moving up his stomach to his throat and discovers it is fury. In this moment, he hates his father: who is so acquiescent he buys all three types of teas, who is so conflict avoidant he will not admit he is sick, who has willed all this through genes or example to Danny.

"What's all this?" Cal says, stepping into the kitchen with his armful of teas.

"You tell me," Danny says.

Cal hesitates. He looks at the pill containers. There is an interminable pause. Then, finally: "So. Which tea do we start with?"

"What the fuck, Dad."

"Hey, language."

"Are you sick? How long has this been happening?"

"This isn't something you have to worry about."

"It sure fucking is."

"Hey, let's be civil."

"That's not the point. Are you getting treatment? Who's your doctor?"

"I don't want to talk about this."

"That's not an option," Danny says.

"We've been having a nice time."

"Have you told anyone? Does Beatrice know?"

"I'm not having this conversation."

Cal sets the tea on the counter and heads for the hall. Danny pursues.

"I know this is probably hard to talk about, but you can't just not tell me."

"We were having such a nice visit," Cal says. "Let's keep things nice." He goes into his bedroom, where he starts making the bed, which is already made. Danny puts his hands on top of his head and watches this with an increasing, overwhelming sense of helplessness.

"What if we saw a movie?" Cal says. "Wouldn't that be fun? I'll buy the tickets."

"Dad."

Cal has navigated around Danny and gone back out the bedroom to the hall. Danny stays there staring at the tidy bed.

"Okay," he says. What else do you say?

12

Danny allows Cal to drop him at the airport.

"Can we please talk about this?" Danny asks in the car.

"Let's let you worry about you and me worry about me."

"Sometimes it feels like you insist on knowing everything about me but refuse to let me know you at all," Danny says.

"Well," Cal says. "What a thing to tell a person."

Danny tries to convince Cal to drop him at the door, but he insists on parking and walking him to security. It is impossibly lonely—to be shadowed by someone who does not really want to be seen, like a ghost. What Danny feels is haunted.

"Okay," Danny says at security.

"Fly safe! Text me when you're back in the big city."

"Will do."

They hug. Danny gets in line and listens for the sound of his father walking away, which, of course, he does not hear.

"Hey, kid!" Cal calls.

Danny adjusts the strap of his duffel and turns.

"To the mooooon," Cal says.

Danny's throat feels raw. He says, "And back."

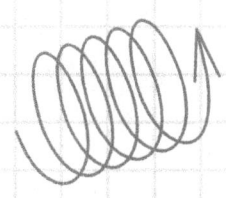

All the Strangers Hate You

1

Joy Karber hates Eve Olsen. Eve reminds Joy of Maisie Vandersloot, with whom Joy went to high school, and frankly, Maisie Vandersloot was a bit of a bitch. Joy is also pretty tired of seeing Eve Olsen over and over again on TikTok, so one of these days, when she's just had it up to *here*, she finds herself commenting on one of Eve's posts about Eve's weirdly asymmetrical boobs. This, as it happens, was something of which Maisie Vandersloot accused Joy in high school. Joy posts and tags her best friend, Taylor, who will find it funny and immediately get the reference to Maisie Vandersloot. It gives Joy a redemptive, vigilante sort of feeling, like she has just spoken truth to power. Besides—it's not like Eve Olsen will ever see it.

2

For a while now, Shannon's been cagey about letting anyone meet her new girlfriend. She said they could hang out after Thanksgiving, and then she said in the new year, and now it's February and Eve still hasn't met Petra.

"Petra and I are casual," Shannon says. "How do you casually welcome a new girlfriend to the friend group when the others are the host of a dating show, a singer of love songs, and the cofounders of an app that promises to secure true love forevermore?"

"I see how that might not scream casual," Eve admits.

But Shannon finally relents. Eve offers to host even though she hasn't run it by Danny. Ever since Christmas, she and Danny have hardly been in the same place. He's had meetings and conferences most weeks, and she's had meetings and shows most weekends. One of these nights, a Saturday when she's out of town, he does not text her good night, I love you. Which in the beginning, she might have found something of a relief, but is now so out of character it worries her. She asks if he's okay, and he says yep. It makes her feel crazy, then guilty for never previously appreciating a partner who always told her how he felt.

The night of the dinner, Eve puts on the new Stella Seaport album, which is excellent (unbiased), and starts pressing the water out of the blocks of tofu that will go into their curry. Danny is cleaning the bathroom. He has been for some time. Should she ask if he needs to talk? Loiter around him until he opens up? Make a racket with the silverware until he notices her? Eve is unsure how she could have made it nearly two years into their relationship without learning how to ask if he needs space. He has never before seemed like he wanted it. She places the cutting board on the counter and wipes the water into the sink.

Eve's phone vibrates with a text. She thinks it's Shannon, but actually, it's a stranger who has somehow gotten ahold of her number and is now using it to suggest she die, bitch. Eve flips her phone on the counter. For the past few weeks, there's been an unusually vitriolic strain of hatred toward Eve. It started with an interview Eve sat where audiences found her fake and grating. (She mentioned her love for Danny being inspiration for the album, and this, apparently, was equal parts gloating, unbelievable, and annoying.) And then, a few days later, a rumor spread that she and Stella had a huge feud on tour, and when Stella posted on Instagram saying it wasn't true, everyone assumed Stella was just doing Eve a favor. Eve's manager has assured her it will pass. She has already changed her phone number twice.

The door buzzes, and Eve presses the button. A moment later, she's welcoming in Gigi and Julian, both of whom are dressed in goose-down puffers and leather gloves. There is a still-sparking tension between them, like they have been interrupted mid-argument.

"Oh," Julian says, "look, it's Eve! Hi, Eve." He hands her a bottle of wine and goes past her. "Danny?"

Gigi hands Eve another bottle. "We've brought along a third. Meet Palpable Tension. Is Shannon here yet?"

"En route. Hey, I was actually hoping I could talk to you about something."

"What's up?"

"Well, I have a bunch of Instagram followers now. But my label thinks I'd have more if I posted more than, you know, once a month, grudgingly."

"Gee," Gigi says. "Imagine that."

"But I hate it."

"Then tell your label you hate it. Have someone manage it for you."

"But I don't want anyone else doing it, either. I hate the thought of random people being forced to think about me every time they open their phones." It makes her skin itch just thinking about it.

"But you want your music to do well," Gigi says.

"Yeah, of course. I just wish I could keep everything else private. Like—I'm already writing songs about my feelings. I'm already being vulnerable. And when I do try to talk about Danny, everyone's like, 'You're just trying to advertise for his company, you're so fake, blah blah.' There's no winning."

"This is complicated by the fact that Danny is weirdly catnippish for the thirsty Instagram set," Gigi says.

This is true. Danny has gained thousands of Instagram followers in the past four months despite the fact that he does not post. All he does is get tagged in the Pattern office Reels looking cute. Someone always comments, Omg who is the third guy??? And then the account replies, @dannyaagaard! He's beeping n booping that code so well :').

And then a bunch of people go follow him. Danny seems bemused but unbothered by it. Eve, who gets a lot more comments saying things like, I want to eat your hair and why does she have asymmetrical boobs, cannot bring herself to be quite so unbothered.

"Anything I can do about it?"

"Not really," Gigi says. "The perils of a cute boyfriend."

"I guess I just hate the fact that I'm meant to be a limitless well of vulnerability to people who don't have to put themselves on the line in return," Eve says.

"I get that," Gigi says. "More than I can possibly convey."

"You're giving me a very meaningful look right now," Eve says. "But meaning what, I know not."

"Let's get the boys out here."

Eve sets the wine on the counter and follows Gigi to the bathroom.

"Want to move to LA?" Julian is saying. "Have a kid? Get a PhD? Use our new feature, Choices—which measures how much you both actually care about this thing one way or another and how it will impact your relationship."

Danny is sitting on the tile cleaning the base of the sink with a Clorox wipe.

"Move to LA?" Danny says.

"You know, insert random life decision of your choice."

"Feels kind of specific."

"Hello," Gigi says. "What if we all had some wine. That could be an activity."

"That sounds great," Julian says. "That would be a really great activity."

Danny and Eve glance at each other.

The door buzzes again.

"That's Shannon and Petra," Eve says. "Everyone be nice and not weird."

"When have we ever been weird?" Julian says.

"Five seconds ago," Danny says. "But also, ten seconds ago."

Julian concedes that this is fair. They all gird themselves for unweirdness and go to the door to meet Shannon's new girlfriend.

3

Talia Russo hates Eve Olsen. Talia used to love Eve. *PRELAPSARIAN*? Chef's kiss. *ski rat*? The album that powered Talia through her last breakup! Which is why Talia would love if someone could please account for the clusterfuck that is *Sunbeam, Baby*.

See, *Sunbeam, Baby* is essentially the Cheesecake Factory of albums. It's dressed up in clothes that look fancy from a distance, but once you get close, you realize it's all polyester and medium-density fiberboard. Eve Olsen was never the best singer, but Talia cherished those little rasps and imperfections that have now been summarily smoothed over by autotune and spoken-word bridges. And the repetition! Okay, yes, "Evergreen" was kind of catchy at first. But literally none of the other songs on the album are distinguishable from one another. Eve! You did not seriously I–V–vi–IV? The most overused of all modern pop chord progressions?

The production is simple. The songwriting is confessional, but everything confessed is obvious. Whenever Eve is about to get vulnerable, to get specific, she pulls away and offers a cliché instead. The final product is neither literary nor full of feeling. It's just: soulless.

When Talia DMs Eve Olsen's official Instagram account, she doesn't really think that Eve will read it or care. Maybe Eve doesn't even care about the fans who've loved her since *PRELAPSARIAN*, anyway. But Talia has had a shitty day at work in a long string of shitty days at work, and Talia also always wanted to be a musician, and she just can't stand to see Eve wasting her chance. So she sends out her DM plea. And she feels, for just a moment, catharsis.

4

The six of them sit around the table drinking their wine while the curry simmers. They interrogate Petra while trying not to look like they are interrogating Petra. The problem is, Shannon, despite being great, has a bad habit of dating people who are horrible. Her longest-term ex was a woman twenty years her senior who, at the start of their relationship, was Shannon's professor. Her most recent ex ghosted her after five months. So they are all wary as Petra sips her wine and calmly answers one lobbed question after another. She keeps a lithe arm thrown over the back of Shannon's chair the whole time, twisting one of Shannon's curls around her index finger. Every few seconds, she glances over at Shannon and smiles. This makes Petra's stock rise dramatically in Eve's book. Eve and Gigi share a nod; the board is in agreement.

Petra, as it turns out, is an earth science engineer at a carbon capture start-up. Shannon met her while reporting on green tech. She lives in Astoria, has a wolf cut, and was, apparently, a competitive downhill skier while growing up in Utah. There's nothing to be done about it—Petra is so cool.

"Any siblings?" Gigi asks.

"Two younger brothers," Petra says. "They just bought a brewery together."

"Hobbies?"

"Animal shelter. Rock climbing. I like to crochet. Shannon and I have been getting really into this car show."

"Do you consider that hypocritical?" Julian asks. "Liking cars. Working on carbon capture. Is there a dissonance there?"

"Oh my god," Shannon says. "Must you always?"

"Because the two of you love the ozone layer! I, for the record, also love the ozone layer."

"Oh, look over there!" Danny says. "Another topic!"

"Travel?" Eve asks.

"I just moved back to the States, actually. I was getting my PhD in the UK, so that scratched the travel bug pretty well."

"Really?" Gigi leans forward. "What? Where?"

"Earth Sciences at St. Andrews."

"What was it like?"

Petra shrugs. "Good if you like tea. Bad if you dislike class divides and/or rain. I'm glad I did it, but I'm glad I'm back."

"Can you speak more to the class divide?" Gigi asks. "How did that manifest, exactly?"

"Can we please stop interrogating my girlfriend?" Shannon says. "As much as I appreciate your relentless and weirdly specific enthusiasm."

"Girlfriend?" Julian says. "So are you label-official?"

"Dude," Danny says.

"We are," Petra says. "No worries."

"Are you on Pattern?" Julian asks.

"Dude," Danny says.

"What? It's a fair question!"

"It's not a fair question," Gigi says. "Leave the poor woman alone."

"Pattern isn't a fair question but 'speak to the class divide at St. Andrews' is?" Julian asks.

"Yes," Gigi says.

"For what it's worth," Petra says. "I think they're both fair questions. No, we're not on Pattern. I hope that's not weird. I just don't really want two straight men telling me whether my relationship meets their standards. You both seem perfectly lovely, but. You know."

"That's so fair," Danny says.

"Okay, yes," Julian says, "but if we had a more diverse user base, our algorithms could respond better to the needs of more users."

"Please stop," Danny says.

"I'm just—" Julian starts.

"Oh!" Eve says. "But what if you didn't?"

"Would I be superbitchy if I brought up the environmental impact of AI?" Petra asks.

"No," Gigi says.

"Like, a little," Julian says.

"This is going well, right?" Shannon asks Eve. "I feel like this is going well."

"I mean," Eve says to Shannon, "I love Petra, so mission accomplished there. One does wonder if we've given Petra much to love about us, though."

"You're talking really loudly, you know," Julian says.

"Yes," Eve says. "We do know."

"Oh my god, would you look at that," Danny says. "The curry's ready."

5

Eve feels herself zoning in and out through dinner. She left her phone in the other room, but every time another phone buzzes, she finds herself reaching for her pocket to find out what kind/horrible/invasive thing has been said about her most recently.

Nothing goes entirely wrong, but nothing goes entirely right, either. Julian wants to take a group picture, but then he gets annoyed at the bad lighting, which exasperates Eve. Petra asks if there will be a second season of *Soulmates*, and Julian says, "Oh, definitely," but Gigi says, "We'll see," and Danny says, "Has anyone talked to me about this?" Then, when they're eating a chocolate cake Petra and Shannon brought, Julian says, "Is this Swiss? Babe, we should find one when we go."

"Ix-nay," Gigi says.

"Oh, yeah," Danny says. "Aren't you two going skiing in the Alps in a few weeks?"

"Is that, like, a secret?" Eve asks.

A pause.

"Ah," Eve says. "You're going with Mom and Dad."

"Oh," Danny says.

"It's not a big deal," Julian says. "Eve, please don't be mad."

"I'm not mad," Eve says. "I don't really care."

Shannon squeezes her knee under the table.

Gigi and Julian make their exit soon after. When they say goodbye, they link arms. They look exhausted, like weary travelers at the end of a long voyage. Shannon and Petra leave a few minutes later. Danny starts washing dishes—he says nothing, just goes to the sink and turns on the water—and Eve grabs her phone and excuses herself to the very clean bathroom.

There, she opens Instagram. She scrolls quickly through the comments on her latest post. Someone is saying her music changed their life, but someone else is saying she is a talentless hack, and it is shocking anyone would love a woman who is so physically unappealing. Apparently, the sheer stupidity in her songwriting is a clear demonstration of all that is wrong with this generation. One person says her music is AI slop. A second person says Eve Olsen would never stoop so low as to use AI. A third person says AI would have written something much better. A fourth person says they have used AI to recolor Eve's hair (better as a redhead!) and simulate Botox (she needs it!) and bronze her skin (she looks sick!). A fifth person says they have trained an AI model on her voice and all her music and have used it to simulate a new Eve Olsen song, which some subset of commenters believe is an actual Eve Olsen song, and another subset of commenters believe is functionally the same as an Eve Olsen song because who is Eve Olsen, anyway? She is just pixels on a screen. She is just noise in a machine.

Eve sits down on the tile, where Danny sat when he was doing his cleaning, and she touches the porcelain and presses her eyes shut. She misses him, Danny, and she doesn't know why or how. He's right there, on the other side of the wall. He's also very far away. It's impossible not to wonder if he also thinks she is a talentless hack, and physically unappealing, and an exemplar of all that's wrong with this generation. It is impossible not to wonder if he thinks she is just noise in a machine.

She puts her forehead on her knees and tells herself only a talentless hack would cry right now. Someone clever and talented would turn this feeling into a song. But she doesn't want to write a song. She wants Danny to love her. She wants her parents to care.

Were they always the lonely, miserable people they are now? Or did they used to be happy? The sort of couple whose friends would've said, "Them? Oh, they're going to make it." And if so, how did the chasm settle between them? Did it start with bickering at a dinner party, as with Julian and Gigi? Or did it start, as with Eve and Danny, as a slowly creeping chill?

Danny knocks on the door. "Eve?"

"Yeah."

"Are you okay?"

"I'm a strong medium."

"Can I come in?"

"Yeah."

Danny opens the door. He sits on the tile next to Eve. Their shoulders touch, but nothing else. "So," he says. "You can predict my future pretty well, then?"

"What?"

"You said you were a strong medium."

"That is so not funny."

"Are you sure? I think it was pretty funny." He runs a hand through his hair. "I'm really sorry. About the trip."

"My parents' trip? Why would you be sorry?"

"I just mean, I'm sorry I'm not more—Fletcher."

"You think my parents are pushing me away because of you? Because you're not more like Fletcher?"

"I know they've never been crazy about us together," Danny says.

"They didn't invite us on this trip because they're mad at me for trying to have a career in music."

"Do you think?"

"Of course. They like you. They've always liked you."

Danny laughs. "They absolutely have not."

"Why would you think that?"

"That Thanksgiving? When Julian brought me to your house?"

"Yeah," Eve says. "And they were insufferable."

She can tell he doesn't quite believe her, doesn't quite remember the day the way she does, but he just shakes his head once.

"Look," Danny says. "I know your parents have been—have been awful. I know your dad is a bully. I just wonder if maybe you'll regret it someday if you don't try to smooth things over."

Eve shifts away from him slightly, just so she can look at him better, but then their arms are no longer touching. The distance feels greater than a few inches, and the tile, a sharp cold.

"I know how difficult they can be," Danny says. "But they're still your parents. You could reach out. Even just to your mom. You might be surprised how they respond. I bet they miss you."

"Danny, my dad made me pay back my college tuition because he was mad at me."

"But he didn't make you. What was he going to do, sue you?"

"Maybe."

"No," Danny says. His voice never rises. If anything, it gets quieter—like he is in physical pain. "He wouldn't have."

"I know I was lucky. Really lucky growing up. But they told me they wouldn't help me if I fell."

"But they *would have*. Jesus, Eve. If you'd have seriously fucked up your life, your parents would have caught you. Your brother would have caught you. Yes, it would have bruised your pride, but you've never really been alone against the world."

"And you have? You, with the most supportive dad who ever graced this earth?"

"Can you not talk about him like he's a sitcom character?" Danny says.

"Why are we doing this?" Eve says. "I don't want to be doing this."

Danny presses his hands to his temples. He exhales slowly. "Okay," he says. "Yeah, okay. Maybe we can just—take a beat."

He reaches for his phone. Eve feels something heavy sinking within her. She hopes he doesn't open his app, and then she has to watch as that's exactly what he does.

"Can you not ask Bug how to solve this?" she says. "Please?"

"But I don't know how to solve this. I don't even know what we're fighting about."

"I don't want to talk to Bug. I want to talk to you."

For a long moment, neither of them says anything. Then he sets down his phone, puts his arm around Eve, and pulls her to his chest. She sits there with her ear against his heart. It sounds too muffled, like she is listening across some very great distance.

6

Kyle Everett hates Eve Olsen.

Like, really fucking hates her.

He can't explain it. He doesn't need to explain it. Most people just get it, you know? She just has one of those faces. You just know she was a teacher's pet in high school. Just another rich fucking nepo baby whose daddy bought her way into the business.

Kyle's favorite thing about Eve Olsen is that he's found community on Reddit in shared hatred of Eve Olsen. He's been dabbling with AI, and he has this funny idea to make a deepfake interview where Eve keeps insisting she hates poor people. Kyle gets more Reddit karma for this video than he's ever got for anything, and he's been on Reddit for fifteen years. While it's true that some of the commenters seem to believe this video is real, Kyle only finds this more hysterical. If it gets spliced up and distributed throughout other corners of the internet, so be it. Maybe Eve should have done a better job of not seeming like the kind of girl who might hate poor people.

And then Kyle looks at his bank account, which has enough for negative two rainy days, and he thinks that in a fair world, you could spend Reddit karma on gas, or car insurance, or fucking groceries. Kyle is aware that there are richer people out there than Eve Olsen, but the really rich people are invisible, untouchable, and sometimes it's just so exhausting to be a person on this planet. Of course it's not fair. How do you expect Kyle to fix it?

7

Danny leaves for the office before Eve wakes. When she opens her eyes, she stretches across the cool sheets looking for his warmth and finds nothing.

In the kitchen, he has left her favorite mug, washed, next to the espresso machine, and drawn a smiley face on their fridge whiteboard. She opens a drawer at random and shuts it again. She wants to text him to ask why he had to leave so early, but she wants to be the kind of cool girlfriend who doesn't get annoyed by things like that. She angrily draws a smiley face next to his and angrily reaffixes the magnetic pen to the fridge.

Today, she is meant to be creating a spon con video for Summer Camp, and another one for a mascara company she accidentally cornered into sponsoring her after she gave an interview saying that once, she got attacked by a cougar and hit by a truck in the same day, but her mascara did not budge. She's also meant to be meeting Clay in the afternoon to work on writing the next album. Then, in the evening, she's supposed to meet her manager for dinner to discuss the spring's live show dates. Though she toured in the fall, everyone agreed it was kind of compressed and did not successfully capitalize on the popularity of "Evergreen." Part of the problem was, none of the "Evergreen" fans wanted to hear Eve's older music, and none of Eve's longtime fans wanted to hear anything off *Sunbeam, Baby*. And now, Eve is alone in her apartment drifting progressively farther from her sunbeam, baby, with absolutely no interest in recording a video of herself saying how much she loves Summer Camp beer just to post it on Instagram, where a thousand people will tell her to kill herself and also lose some weight.

When she finally opens her phone, she finds there is a stream of comments on her latest Instagram Reel saying things like, I hope ur butler strangles u biatch and i may not be rich but at least my boobs are not completely different sizes.

Eve lies on the floor of the kitchen and contemplates having a mental breakdown. Ultimately, she decides she could not bear the cleanup.

There is a part of Eve that wonders if there is something disconcertingly inhuman about *Sunbeam, Baby* that listeners can hear if they pay close attention. Something tellingly AI. And if there is, is it a fact of AI forever or just for right now, while the technology is still young.

In *Paradise Lost*, there's a part where the angel Raphael tries to explain angel sex to Adam. It's superweird. What Milton is trying to do is show that sex need not be an act of sin and passion. But then Adam and Eve eat the fruit and lose their innocence, and then they are both lustful and self-conscious when they have sex. But in her reading, Eve found something lovely about this—the lust, the awareness, the fragility of it all. For the first time, Adam and Eve become familiar—become human. And so now Eve wonders if technology is like an angel—more than human in knowledge and predictability, but never truly able to understand the particular sensory experience of personhood. And she finds that this is what she hopes for. She wants to believe that she contains mysteries that cannot be algorithmically known.

Eve, still on the floor, calls Clay.

"Hey, babe," he says. "We still on for today?"

"I want to record 'Settle Down.'"

"The song from Stella's tour? I thought you decided it didn't work."

"I figured out how to make it work."

"Listening."

"It's too acoustic. It's a sad-girl song with a sad-girl sound."

"And you want to make it angry?"

"I want to make it baroque. Brass, strings, too much reverb. Think James Bond. Or, like—femme fatale. Noir."

"Okay. Really? Okay. This might work. I have to think about it."

"And the lyrics are too straightforward. It's not enough of a story. It needs more verses."

"It's already, what, four minutes long?"

"I'm thinking it's going to be nine."

"Okay," Clay says. "Okay. So, I really don't want to quash your full artistic expression here. But you've just reached a big new world of fans who love what you've done in the upbeat pop space. And I can't help but wonder if a nine-minute-long chamber pop song might feel, to some of these listeners, like a teensy bit of a fuck you."

"I do hear you," Eve says. "But also, I kind of feel like I'm in something of a spiral and music is the only thing I can control?"

"Well, babe," Clay says. "I'm not going to say no to that."

8

Hayden Ellington loves Eve Olsen!

Just kidding.

I mean, she's hot—in kind of a whatever sort of way—and when he sees the deepfake of Eve giving that interview, he's inspired. *Poor people just give me, like, the ick?* I mean. That's gold.

So Hayden makes a deepfake of his own. It's fourteen minutes long and takes place in a swanky hotel room with views of the Manhattan skyline. The guy—you never see his face. He's just a placeholder, anyway. An everyman. Hayden uploads the video to all his favorite sites using a VPN that will render him untraceable. He doesn't expect to make any money off of this—he does it for the sport.

Right away, the views start to roll in.

Hayden Ellington has never loved Eve Olsen more.

9

When "Settle" comes out ("Settle Down" was too clunky), it's only because Eve got lucky. Her label did not want her to release the song, because what business does Eve have releasing a nine-minute song whose instrumentation sounds like it should be playing as the camera pans across the Italian Riviera in a spy movie? Her manager thinks it's a stretch, and the first two people at the label who listen to it also think it's a stretch, but through a fluke, a VP having a bad day happens to be darkening the halls looking for any reason to remind him why he got into this business in the first place when he overhears a snippet, and the song reminds him of being young: studying abroad in college, stepping into a European cathedral, and feeling very far from his family, and yet, never far enough. He is surprised to learn, then, that this is "Evergreen" Eve Olsen, who is embroiled in some sort of bad publicity at present. He suggests offhandedly that this new song, this sonic shift, might change the narrative. He thinks of this as spitballing, but everyone in his vicinity at the time is about three levels junior to him, so they scurry to make it happen as quickly as possible.

Into the world comes "Settle."

In her post on Instagram, Eve thanks Stella for listening to the song in its early incarnation on tour and believing in it, and her. Stella comments with a heartfelt statement of support. This time, everyone seems to take her word for it.

And then—

It's quiet.

The day the single drops, Danny is meeting with investors in California. Eve is alone with her mug of coffee and her phone, bracing for impact. But the impact is less like a bus and more like a strong breeze. Some of Eve's longtime fans comment on her post to say that this song is brilliant, genius, a return to form. Eve reads these comments like they are fresh water and she is at sea. The negative comments are relatively neutral: that the song is too weird or too long. But mostly, people do not care.

A music journalist Eve admires tags her in an Instagram Story saying: Knotty, honest, non sequitur, and stately. Frankly, I love it.

Eve thinks this comment will buoy her the whole day, but it's hard not to notice the streaming numbers, which keep the song firmly at the bottom of Eve's discography.

And then something funny happens.

Eve gets a comment saying, RIP.

She thinks this is a statement about the death of her career until she gets another—then a whole series of them. Noooooo, one says. Crying emoji, crying emoji, crying emoji. Shannon calls about three seconds later.

"Are you okay?" Shannon asks.

"What?" Eve says.

"Jesus. Has no one told you?"

Eve thinks she's talking about her song. "Told me what?"

"Stay right there," Shannon says. "I'm coming over. Don't look at your phone, okay?"

"Why can't I look at my phone? Why is everyone commenting crying emojis? Are you okay? Is Danny okay? Julian?"

"We're all fine. I'm getting on the subway, but please just don't, okay? Will you promise me?"

"Okay?" Eve says.

Eve steps carefully away from her phone, which she leaves sitting on the coffee table, and goes to make herself tea. She selects her favorite mug, the BREW UNTO OTHERS mug from Our Lady of Perpetual Breakfast, and a bag of chamomile. Her hands are sweaty on the kettle.

Ten minutes go by, then twenty. She imagines Shannon making her way to Williamsburg: getting on the L, up the stairs at Graham Avenue, past CTown and Sage Thai. Danny's not going to be back for another few hours—it's not Danny, is it? God. Shannon said it wasn't Danny, but is he okay? Eve's phone stares at her from the other side of the room.

Finally, she hears creaking from the steps. She hurries to the door but Shannon has already entered the code and pushed inside. Shannon tosses her wet puffer on the floor and barrels toward Eve and wraps her arms around her.

"Oh my god," Eve says. "What? What is it? Are you dying? Am I dying?"

Shannon holds Eve at arm's length, scanning Eve's face. Shannon is so familiar to Eve: the curls and the heavy lids and the mole to the left of her mouth. And the love. Shannon looks at Eve with so much love, Eve really thinks she might be dying.

"Kind of," Shannon says. "There is currently a very convincing video circulating of you getting hit by a midtown bus."

Eve stares at her.

"At least two local news outlets have picked up the story because there is also a very convincing video of Julian saying how much he will miss you."

"What?" Eve says. "So I'm dead. That's what's happening. The internet thinks I just died?"

"Basically," Shannon says. "I've already texted Danny and Julian and your parents that it's not true, but Gigi thinks Julian and Danny have been in meetings and might not know yet."

Eve puts her hands on her head. "I got hit by a *bus*?"

"I think it was the M23," Shannon says.

"You know, this is kind of offensive to those of us who have been in real accidents with semitrucks," Eve says.

"Are you okay?"

"Aside from being dead from my numerous bus injuries," Eve says, "I think I'm fine."

Shannon guides her onto the couch. It was Danny's originally, and it's olive green and enveloping. One of Danny's sweatshirts is draped over the back; a crewneck from the *ski rat* tour. It smells like eucalyptus, like his shampoo. Eve pulls it on.

"Does this mean someone wants me dead?" Eve says. "Can I look at my phone now?"

"It just means the internet is full of weirdos."

They look together. Eve searches her name and she finds it: an extremely convincing video showing what it would look like if Eve got hit by the M23. The fake passengers scream. Fake Eve goes pop. The wheels are covered in blood.

Eve wishes she could laugh again but she does not find this particularly funny. There are obituaries popping up; one calls her the one-hit wonder behind "Evergreen." She searches "Eve Olsen deepfake," and that's how she finds the rest of them—the fake interviews and the fake TikToks and the fake porn. So much fake porn. Eve knew this existed in an abstract way, but she did not know it existed like this. Fake Eve has a mole on her shoulder, just like real Eve. Fake Eve laughs when the man kisses her neck. Fake Eve seems turned on when he chokes her.

Eve calmly hands Shannon her phone, stands, walks to the kitchen sink, and vomits. Shannon follows her and rubs her back.

"Well," Eve says. "That's quite something."

"Eve."

"You know, the ironic thing is, I really didn't want to post on Instagram in the first place, but I thought I had to. For the sake of the music."

"It's shitty," Shannon says. "It's so, so shitty. We can try to get it taken down, okay? All of it."

Eve knows as well as Shannon that this will not happen. One does not just take something off the internet.

"I don't want to be dead," Eve says.

"Of course not, babe. I love it when you haven't been hit by a bus."

"The porn. Shannon, the porn." Eve turns on the tap of the sink. She hangs her head over the basin. Her hands keep shaking no matter how hard she presses her nails into her palms. "My parents could see that. They probably *have* seen that. Oh my god."

Shannon gathers Eve's hair and tucks it over one shoulder. "We can explain it's not real. We can tell them it's just AI."

"Is this karmic retribution?" Eve asks. "Because I used AI to fix *Sunbeam, Baby*?"

"It's not karmic anything. It's just how technology goes."

"Well, I hate it. I hate all of it. I hate deepfake Eve and Instagram and *Sunbeam, Baby* and Bug and everything. I want to live in the woods with a family of possums and make buttons for a living."

"No, you don't. You want to live in New York with Danny and write songs for a living. You just don't want technology to suck so bad."

"Yes," Eve says. "But given that it does, I'll take the possums."

Shannon wraps her arms around Eve. "Don't let them take it all away from you," she says. "Yeah?"

Eve shuts her eyes. She wishes Danny were here, but also—

Also, she does not wish Danny were here. Because she is so mad right now. So mad at all the ones and zeros cannibalizing real people's thoughts and faces and ideas and spitting out literally anything. She is mad at technology for being so good at what it does. She is mad that there is no going back.

"You can't let other people tell you who you are," Shannon says. "Not your label. Not an app. And not strangers on the stupid fucking internet."

10

Eve Olsen hates Eve Olsen.

It has not always been like this. It's something of a new development, actually. Who is this new version of her? A stranger. Once, she wrote songs not because she wanted her parents to think she was smart or her boyfriend to love her more, but because she had something she wanted to say.

Eve leaves her apartment and steps into a hot February rain. The temperature is unseasonable, but these days, everything is always unseasonable. She walks through the downpour to Domino Park, whose lampposts flicker and glow against the deluge. There is no one else around. Eve stands on the edge of the East River and tries to make out the lights of Manhattan. She is furious at herself for being furious at herself. What does she want to *do*? What does she want to *be*?

The river churns, lapping up against the edge of the earth, and Eve puts her hands on top of her head and tries not to falter under the sudden realization of the epicness of it, the power. On and on and on the river runs. Has run for eleven thousand years, since a glacier carved a valley and the valley flooded full. Fletcher never wanted to move to the city because he thought there was not enough nature, but look at all this water, this salt and wind and rain.

Now *this*? This is a cathedral. The kind of thing that could move a person, shake a person, break a person—inspire a song or make you fall in love. She wants to call her mom but her mom will not pick up. Eve thought it was cool, kind of badass, when she handed her parents that big check, but it was not cool. She did not free herself. Because she still loves her parents. Still wants them to love her back.

In Montana, Danny suggested Eve reach out to her parents. What Danny does not realize is that if he had opened her phone, he would've seen a long blue text to her mother, which said, among other things, that Eve felt lost and lonely, that she wanted to work through this, that she still wanted to be part of the family, that she would like to come over—to which Cecilia did not respond. And while it's true that Eve could have gone over anyway—knocked on the door and forced Cecilia's hand—Eve also can't help but feel that it is pathetic to beg for someone's love. Eve could have told Danny this, of course, but Danny thinks that Eve is kind and good, and she is afraid he will start to wonder if perhaps her parents know something he doesn't. And perhaps they do. Perhaps they see something bad in Eve, something wrong, something fundamentally unlovable.

A guy with a black umbrella and a dog on a leash stops when he sees Eve. He is standing too close to her and not trying to hide the fact that he's staring, even though Eve is clearly in the middle of a psychic break, here crying on the edge of the river in the pouring rain.

"What?" Eve says. "What could you possibly want?"

"You're not dead!" he says.

"No," she says. "I am not *dead*."

Within ten minutes, a video of this interaction will exist on the internet. The prevailing sentiment is that it is a pretty amateur deepfake, and that the man should feel ashamed of mocking Eve Olsen fans in their time of mourning.

11

When Eve returns from her walk, she finds Danny sitting at the edge of the bed with his phone on his knee and his head in one hand.

There is a lag. They should go to each other right away, but instead, they hesitate.

"Hey," Eve says.

"Are you okay?" Danny asks.

"I didn't actually get hit by a bus."

"No, I mean—you're soaking wet. And with everything that's been happening . . ."

Eve peels off her leggings, which hit the tile with a wet slap when she throws them toward the bathroom. "I went for a walk. Did you get an earlier flight?"

"It's pouring. Yeah, I was on standby. People keep calling me asking about you. Newspapers, even."

Eve grabs a towel from the back of Danny's desk chair and wrings out her hair. "Not dead," she says. She turns because her eyes are suddenly burning. She hears a creak as Danny stands, and then he is wrapping his arms around her and she is burying her face against his chest. "Did you know?"

"About what?"

"It's not just the bus video."

"Shannon told me," he whispers into her hair. "I'm sorry. For all of it."

She squeezes her eyes shut. "I'm mad at you."

"I figured."

"I'm not actually mad at you. I'm mad at the world. I'm mad that an algorithm wrote better songs than me. I'm mad that they were stupid songs but people liked them better. I'm mad that all my sentences die at the halfway point because I'm getting used to outsourcing my brain to a machine. I'm mad that when you're upset, you tell your phone instead of telling me. But I'm not mad at you. I'm just—tired."

Danny rests his hands on her hips, his thumb running along the hem of her shirt. She feels him lean his forehead against her shoulder. Kiss the cold skin.

"I'm sorry," he says.

"It's not your fault. It's just the way the world is now, isn't it?"

"No," Danny says. Eve tilts her chin up, and that's when she sees how stricken he is—the way he looks like he has not slept in a month, the stubble and the red in his eyes. "You're right. I talk to my phone instead of talking to you. I created an app for the express purpose of not needing to seem like an anxious little freak because I want to talk to you all the time. All across the world, I'm enabling anxious little freaks to not talk to the people they love."

"Are you okay?" Eve says.

Danny hands her his phone. She looks at him, and he nods, so she lifts it. Opens it. She knows the passcode. It opens to his last used screen, a Bug chat screen, and Eve reads the latest message as Danny watches.

Bug: I recommend that you don't wait to talk to Eve about this. It's unlikely the situation will get better on its own. What if you tried sharing something small that opened the door to bigger conversations over the next few days? This may allow you to measure Eve's response and gradually build trust.

"What is this?" Eve says.

"Every day, I talk to Bug about my problems. And every day, Bug tells me to talk to you. But I don't. Because I just keep talking to

Bug. Which is easier. It's like going on social media instead of going to dinner with friends, or watching porn instead of having sex. It's this patch that feels just barely good enough, so you keep putting off the thing that will actually fulfill you."

Eve touches Danny's temple; the hair neatly cut above his ear. "What problems, exactly?"

Danny takes back his phone. He turns off the screen, then sets it face down on the dresser. He takes a breath; she watches him hold the words in his mouth. Outside, the rain continues to pound against the windows.

"My dad is dying." Danny says it looking at the window. The words are soft and even, like he has already turned them over a thousand times.

"What?"

"And he won't talk to me about it. He won't talk to anyone about it. I called some of his friends and none of them know anything."

"Oh, Danny."

Danny shakes his head once, turning against her fingers. She keeps them there, on the stubble at his jaw, the soft curve of his ear.

"I know your parents are—awful, sometimes," he says. "But they're healthy, and married, and they live half an hour away. And I don't know how to talk to you about any of this because I'm just angry you're not more grateful that you have them at all. And because when you talk about my dad, you act like he's the greatest, easiest parent anyone could have. I love him so much. But he's also needy and passive-aggressive and so averse to conflict he won't even talk to me about being sick. Your parents keep you at arm's length by being assholes. But my dad keeps me at arm's length, too. It's just a different sort of arm's length."

"I'm so sorry," Eve says softly. "Danny, I'm so sorry."

"My dad is too anxious. And I'm like my dad. I know that. My dad is always pushing me away because he doesn't know how to have a normal fucking relationship with anyone. So of course I don't want to tell you about all this. I don't want you to become responsible for my emotional needs. I don't want to do to you what my dad does to me."

Eve wraps her arms around him. Traces the line of his spine with her thumb. "You're allowed to need me. We're allowed to need each other. Okay? That's how this goes."

They sway like that in the shadow of the drizzle through the window.

"I'm sorry you're dead," Danny says. "I'm sorry people are doing horrible things with your face and your voice, and I'm just—sorry."

"It's not real," Eve says. "It's okay."

"It can be fake and still not be okay."

"Sometimes," Eve says, "I feel like I don't actually know what's real anymore."

Danny kisses her forehead. "You and me, baby. The real deal, as they say."

They are both crying. Only a little! Only a little.

"They're always saying that."

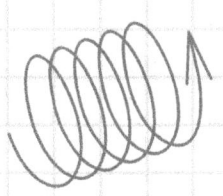

The Tapestry

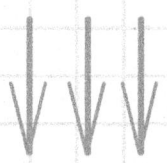

1

Danny flies back to Montana on the first of March.

His dad doesn't pick him up from the airport this time. He says he's just feeling a little under the weather—nothing to worry about! Danny stares out the window in the back of the Uber at the swaying trees and the late-winter snow and worries about it.

At the house, when Danny knocks, no one answers. Danny goes to the garage and lets himself in with the code, which has for the past twenty-five years been BISCUIT. Inside, the floorboards creak. The soft murmur of a TV comes from the primary bedroom. Danny pauses in the kitchen. Next to the microwave, three boxes of peppermint tea are stacked in a tidy pyramid.

Danny knocks on Cal's door, which is ajar. "Dad?"

It creaks open.

Cal lies propped against his pillows. His cheekbones protrude against his skin like they might tear through it. It should not have been possible to lose this much weight this quickly. Danny tries not to look disturbed, which, of course, he is.

"Hey, Dad."

"Hey, kiddo. Safe flight?"

"Yeah, easy. How are you feeling?"

"Oh, I'm great. Just a little off, is all. You didn't need to come all this way."

"Dad."

"How's Eve? You told me to ignore anything I saw on the internet, but people sure are convinced she's dead."

"She's fine. You, on the other hand—"

"Want to watch with me?" Cal says, nodding to the TV. It's a sitcom about a big family getting annoyed at each other for big family things. Stealing each other's clothes. Installing overly complicated stereo systems just before the big football game. Et cetera.

"I actually have to hop on a call," Danny says, though Julian told Danny his attendance at this all-hands was totally optional and he could handle it alone, no worries.

"Oh, yeah, right, of course. Good luck, kiddo!"

Danny goes to his room and sets his laptop on his childhood desk but doesn't open the lid. He presses the heels of his hands to his eyes and wonders why it is so hard to let another person see the depths of your love and the extent of your despair. Why it should feel like such a shameful thing to present an emotion that requires a response.

2

Danny goes with Cal to his next appointment to get the truth of things.

"You should do what you can to appreciate this time together," the doctor says, which feels like a catch-22.

Danny does most of his coding on the couch next to Cal. At first, Cal does crosswords, but he starts to struggle with the pencil. Danny will hear a horrible slashing of the graphite sliding across the thin paper, then Cal's soft "Gosh darn." Cal mostly watches TV after that.

Because Danny didn't bring enough clothes, he ends up scouring his wardrobe for what he wore in high school, which is mostly band T-shirts and Costco flannels. Once, he goes into the kitchen and sees his dad sitting at the table, facing away, wearing the exact same shirt. Danny goes back into his room and changes before Cal can see him. Even as he does it, he feels like the worst sort of person. But he cannot bear the thought that he is, at some fundamental level, the same as his father, consigned to the same impenetrable, stubborn, self-inflicted loneliness.

In the mornings, Danny wakes to make Cal breakfast, which Cal sometimes eats, and to work East Coast hours. In the evenings, he goes for a run and calls Eve. She keeps offering to come help, and he keeps saying no. He is too ashamed of the person he is in this miasma: someone who changes his shirt to be less like his father.

3

"Hey," Danny says. "When do I get to meet Beatrice?"

They're at a picnic table by a trailhead they will not be hiking. The snow has slushed and the sky is gray. They both have thermoses of coffee, but Danny didn't make it right. Apparently, there's a wrong way to do instant coffee.

"Oh," Cal says, "she's been busy."

"Does she know you're sick?"

"Sick!" Cal says. "Kid, I've never been better."

"But really."

"Really? This is some bang-up coffee."

4

In Danny's third week in Montana, he gets forwarded a privacy complaint from their customer happiness manager. The user, someone named Amber, is saying that updates about her ex and his new girlfriend are showing up in her feed.

At the time, Danny is at the kitchen table. Cal, at the couch, is a few feet away.

"Oh, that's an interesting question," Cal says.

Danny is caught by the sudden, uncomfortable sensation that his father can read his mind. "What?"

"You asked if I liked this show," Cal says. "Didn't you?"

"What?" Danny says again. "Oh, yeah. I guess I did."

"Well, it's an interesting question. I'll think on that one."

Danny says something about needing to take a call and goes to his bedroom. He's mostly inside his computer screen already. This shouldn't be possible, and yet, somehow, here are Amber's screenshots.

Danny pulls Olive and Leon, his two lead developers, into a call to give them the update. Neither of them is sure how this happened, but Leon thinks it might've been some code he pushed last week. Danny puts out a notice in the company tech channel that they're aware of the bug and working on fixing it ASAP.

He pulls up the original user profile. Amber is a premium user, so they have her billing address and latest payment date. They have her history on the app (her account is seven months old). Sure enough, it appears to be linked to two separate accounts. One, a current boyfriend—relationship age, two months. One, an ex-boyfriend—broken up four months ago. Danny messages Olive and Leon again, and Olive suggests it has something to do with their effort to add poly-inclusive functionality. (That was a meeting Julian walked into, said, "I simply cannot," and walked out of again.)

Danny filters users to see how many accounts are linked to more than one. It's a lot—but most of the duplicate connections are deactivated, which indicates that the couple broke up and everything functioned as normal. Then he sees two accounts that have the same credit card, the same phone number, but different email addresses. Which, he assumes, means that someone is cheating and trying not to get caught.

He goes back to Amber's account, and then into her ex's user data. And here, Danny finds the problem. The connection with Amber's account was never properly deactivated because the ex started dating someone else, the new girlfriend, before he broke up with Amber. Deactivating would've meant deactivating the new relationship, too. Either the app, or Amber's ex, failed to close the loop.

Danny writes a query to find instances of mistakenly activated relationships. There are fewer of them than he had feared—on the order of a couple hundred—and he scrolls through them quickly. A few, he notices, seem to have five, ten linked accounts. Who has that kind of time? There's a part of him that almost doesn't want to fix this bug, because Danny doesn't have a great deal of sympathy for cheating and kind of thinks this is what these people deserve. He's mulling this over as he scrolls, clicking in and out of various profiles, and then something *ticks* in the back of his brain with an unpleasant little lurch. Slowly, he scrolls back up.

There is a user profile with two linked relationships. Both are active. Danny sees the name. He sees: Olsen.

Phillip Olsen. Two linked profiles: One is Cecilia. The other is named Theresa.

Danny leans back from his computer. His screen seems suddenly too bright. He rubs his palms against his jaw, which is rough with stubble, and shuts his eyes. Though Danny supposes it's possible that

Eve's parents are involved in some consensual long-term swinging, it seems more likely that the most obvious answer is also the correct one: that Phillip is cheating. Not just sexually but emotionally; why else invest the effort in measuring relationship health? Danny never should have been able to learn this information, and feels it is a betrayal to all his users. But now that he knows, he can't unknow. It feels like there is a horrible sort of irony in this—that he would violate user privacy while trying to encode a fix to protect user privacy.

Also unfortunate is that now that Danny has tasted this knowledge, it is hard to stop himself from wanting just that little bit more. Is it really cheating, or is it something else? It wouldn't be hard to find out. And what about all the other questions he's ever wondered? What is Julian and Gigi's score these days, really? How often does Eve open the app? Has Kyra moved on with someone new, and are they happy? Does Cal's girlfriend, Beatrice, really exist? Is Danny's mother alive? Does she know who Danny is?

Danny stands and steps back from his laptop like it's a live bomb.

He could ask Bug what to do, but he already knows what Bug would say: It would be all equivocating about right and wrong, asking follow-up questions with no real answers. "What a complicated situation!" Bug would say. "While I can help you explore the intricacies of this, ultimately, only you can decide the right course of action."

Bug, Danny realizes, has subsumed Danny's internal monologue. Even when he resists outsourcing his decisions to an app, the app lives on in his consciousness. It's the Tetris Effect—when people discovered video games, and video games became habit, and all at once, a whole generation's worth of people closed their eyes to dream and saw only brightly colored squares slotting into place.

How many people has Danny Tetris Effected? How many people are out there equivocating about urgent and personal choices because they have begun to think like carefully modulated LLMs: waffling yes-men on an endless quest to avoid original thought?

Danny returns to the living room. He will ask his dad for advice, that's what he'll do, but when he reaches the sight line of the TV, he is momentarily distracted by the boisterous laugh track, the breakneck cuts to keep you from looking away, to keep you, at all times, reeling from the subconscious sense of peril.

"I think what's so compelling about this show is the way it offers enlightening insights on contemporary friendships while also fostering a safe space for the viewer to call home," Cal says.

"Sorry?"

"It really shows a rich tapestry of human relationships."

Danny takes a step back. It feels then too cold in the house, like the doors have come down and the spring wind has blown in.

"What did you say?" Danny asks.

"The show," Cal says. "It's a rich tapestry of human relationships."

Danny hates the word *tapestry*.

He touches his throat. "Hey, can I borrow your phone for a second?"

"Why? Where's your phone?"

"I want to check something on the app, but I need to see an Android. It'll just take a second."

Cal fumbles his giant, foldable phone, which has the text set three times bigger than is standard. He is hastily closing apps, but Danny is standing right there behind him, and that text would be visible from space. Danny watches Cal close out of Pattern, and then out of another LLM, and then out of a *New York Times* review for this TV show, the one with the rich tapestry of human relationships.

"Never mind, actually," Danny says. His voice sounds to his ears like it's coming from far away. He sits carefully on the edge of the couch.

Danny regrets asking Cal why he liked the TV show. The question, it seems, made Cal feel trapped, self-conscious, incapable. So he looked for other opinions, pre-vetted opinions, to share with Danny instead. Danny does not know how to say that he doesn't care how other people have justified their love or hatred of this random show. Danny cares that Cal likes it. That's all.

What does it mean to know another person? Their heart and their mind. What does it mean to be known? Danny isn't sure whether he knows his father, really—and worse, this seems to be exactly what Cal wants. Cal does not want Danny to know him. And Danny never will. There is not enough time.

Has Cal always done this? It's so hard, as a child, to know whether your parents are changing, or whether you're just becoming aware of who they have always been. Maybe the shift came from the disappearance of Danny's mother, or the onset of illness, or the ability to cite infinite opinions within a few taps on a screen. Whatever it is, Danny feels responsible: for not being a better son, a better listener, the kind of person who inspires honesty rather than fear.

Danny's phone vibrates in his pocket with another message from Leon, and he remembers that he was going to ask Cal's advice on Eve's dad. But the question, which has no easy answer, will not be a question Cal wants to hear, or answer. Is it kind to accept Cal as he is? Or is it cruel to abandon hope that he and Cal can ever know each other the way friends do?

"So, Dad," Danny says. "Something kind of complicated just happened."

"Oh?"

"I can't get into the details, but I accidentally found something out on the back end of Pattern about someone I know in real life."

Cal's shoulders tense. "Mmm," he says.

"Basically, I think I found out someone is cheating. And I don't know whether I should say anything. I don't know whether it's going to drive me crazy to just have this information and not share it, especially if it changes how I see this person. What would you do? If you were me?"

"Oh," Cal says. "Wow. That's pretty complicated, huh?" His voice is neutral. Betraying nothing.

Danny waits. Cal does not elaborate.

"Do you think I should say something? I mean, on one hand, it's not really my business. On the other hand, I would definitely want to know."

"I get what you're trying to say here," Cal says. "I hear you."

"What?"

"Must be really tough, weighing all this."

"Can you please just give me an actual answer?" It comes out too harsh. "Please."

"I did. We're talking."

Danny takes a breath. Thinks of what he can say. In the end, he just exhales and looks down at his hands. "Yeah," he says. "Thanks for being a sounding board."

He keeps thinking about Eve's song "Settle." At the start, Eve sings about seeing a girl who looks like a younger version of her mother, and how she is caught by the sudden urge to go up to her and see if they would get along. Danny wonders this, too—if he and Cal met at school or at work, whether they would be friends. But Danny has this vision in his head—it makes him nauseous to watch it play, but on and on it does—of a young Cal walking down the dorm hall away from Danny and Julian, and Danny saying, "Talking to that guy's like talking to a friendly robot."

Danny goes back to his room. Gets his laptop. Sits on the couch next to his dad.

"Do you mind if I watch with you while I work?" Danny says.

"Sure, kid," Cal says. "There's a lot to like in this show."

Just Water

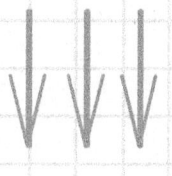

1

How long does it take to convince a person they're dead?

In Eve's experience, one month. In one month, having the entire internet insist that you're dead will go from shocking, to funny, to frustrating, detour back to funny, before ultimately turning into the sort of bone-deep existential doubt usually only broached by philosophy bros on mushrooms. I think, therefore I am, but the world thinks I am not.

In the mornings, Eve wakes alone. The apartment is empty, too quiet. The upstairs neighbors have been on sabbatical in Paris, so there are no footsteps. When Eve goes outside, she paces along Grand Street to the water, or else leaves Williamsburg, takes the L to Manhattan, and walks along the Hudson past the crumbling piers and the private helicopters, and when people see her, they double take, and they hold up their phones to capture her—like she is a ghost.

Danny wants time alone with his dad, who is shy at the best of times, who wants, though he'd never ask for it, uninterrupted time with his son. Besides, Danny says—Eve's label wants to do damage control, and he does not want to stand in the way of her career.

"If spending my days posting proof-of-life social content is what my career requires," she says, "I'm not sure it's a career I want."

"You can come out if he gets really bad."

"You'll tell me when?"

"Yeah, for sure."

Eve is not convinced. Maybe because she knows Danny, knows how averse he is to admitting his needs. Or maybe it's because, when a whole internet full of people keep telling you that you're dead, you are no longer convinced of anything.

2

Summer Camp drops Eve as their spokesperson. The famous actor backing the brand thinks there is too much weird publicity around Eve these days, so she's out. Bing bang boom. Eve goes on Instagram holding the day's *New York Times*, as if she is in a hostage situation, and says, "For the love of god, can you all please stop saying I am a deepfake, body double, or clone?"

This only makes people more certain she is a deepfake, body double, or clone. Gigi says, "Well, duh."

When people see Eve out on the streets, they take incessant videos. These videos then end up on Instagram, where people say that this couldn't possibly be Eve, because the real Eve was fatter and/or skinnier, and she used to have a scar on her elbow. (The scar is a big talking point. Eve does not remember ever having a scar on her elbow.) Eve wants to start wearing wigs and sunglasses when she goes outside, but her manager insists it will only make things worse if she acts like she has something to hide.

"It'll blow over!" everyone says.

Yes, but what if Eve's career blows over first?

There are three leading theories as to why Eve's team is pretending she's still alive even though she's (obviously) dead:

- **Pattern needs Eve alive for their marketing purposes.** (Chloe is offended.)
- **Eve's label is trying to drum up intrigue to earn streaming money now that Eve can't take her cut.** (Eve is pretty sure these people overestimate the size of her cut.)

- **Eve's parents killed Eve and are covering it up for nefarious businessperson reasons.** (Where do they think Phillip and Cecilia got a bus?)

The potential silver lining in all this is that Eve's streaming numbers are going up—but not enough to make up for the loss of Summer Camp, or the mascara brand, who quietly terminates their agreement with Eve after Eve accidentally calls one of their top influencers a can of beets.

"How do you accidentally call someone a can of beets?" Shannon asks.

"She made a post about how maybe I'd been a hoax all along," Eve says. "I reached my breaking point."

"Yeah, but a can of beets?"

"Insults are hard."

More than the slow-creeping dread that her career is ending, though, Eve cannot handle the solitude.

She thought she was okay with being alone. She never minded not going into an office or having a night by herself. But the loneliness is becoming incessant. Even when she is surrounded by other people, she feels like she is not actually there—like she is on the other side of a veil neither party can cross.

Which is how Eve decides she will record an album.

She wants to provide proof of life, but she also wants to create. She wants to record the album in public—how could it be fake?—and she wants to record it in Prospect Park. Prospect Park feels right because it feels like the person Eve has become—a ramble of earthy Brooklyn rather than Central Park's just-so-ness. Also, because Eve has always wanted to write the kind of music that people would listen to outside—walking to a first date, or at a picnic, or playing volleyball in the meadow with friends. Eve also wants this to happen in Prospect Park because Prospect Park was where she and Danny went on their first date.

She calls Clay, and he calls Eliza, who is in town from Chicago, and the three of them spend about twenty minutes hashing out the details. Twenty minutes is not long enough, but also? Eve feels like maybe it's exactly the right amount of time, like maybe everyone's just been overthinking, like maybe the point is just the music.

So they meet on the outskirts of Prospect Park. It's been raining nonstop all winter and all spring, but the forecast shows a break around noon, so they hunker down at a bagel place in Park Slope. Eve takes tiny bites of her bagel—everything, lightly toasted, plain cream cheese—to make it last. Finally, at noon, the rain clears, they gather their things, and they run for the park.

Eve unrolls a blanket, and Eliza sets up a *cajón* for percussion while Clay checks the microphones. It's going to be a little fuzzy, the sound. The rain should hold for two hours. They anticipate bird noise and ambulance sirens, but they're just going to go for it and see what happens.

And then they go for it.

Eve sits on the blanket, immediately damp from the grass, and plays her acoustic guitar. Clay sings backup and takes Eve's guitar when Eve needs someone who is, frankly, better at guitar. Eliza leans over the *cajón* and drums out a beat with her knuckles, the heel of her hand, the flat of her palm. Sometimes, she hits the box with one of her rings, and it makes a crisp, metallic *ting*.

They play *PRELAPSARIAN* start to finish. Eve makes a few changes. Slows down some songs, speeds up others. She changes a few lines, including a rhyme that has always bothered her. "You make me feel light/My cold water on a hot night"? Jail.

Some people stop to listen, but most people just go about their business. They think these are just three friends having a jam session—which, frankly, they are. Of course they are. How could Eve have forgotten? The album feels like an existential thesis: I am alive, I am alive, I am alive. These are the things that feel real to Eve: big parks in big cities, writing songs, sitting with her friends, being in love with Danny. When she sings "HONEY LOCUST," she thinks of playing it for Danny and telling him that a part of her has loved him all along—she has proof. *POSTLAPSARIAN*, that's what she'll call it. Prelapsarian, meaning: before the biblical fall of man. Postlapsarian: after Eve and Adam ate the apple and got banished from Eden. There is something transgressive and perfect to Eve about recording her *POSTLAPSARIAN* in the garden.

They make it all the way through the album twice just as the first raindrop hits Eve's hand.

"Go, go!" Clay says as they flip the clips on their guitar cases. Eve throws the blanket over her shoulder—it is soaking wet—and they run from the park laughing like they are escaping some great crime.

They head back to Williamsburg to celebrate. They order slices at L'Industrie and Eve and Clay debate Eliza on the merits of Chicago pizza. Shannon and Petra meet them after, and they all go back to Eve's apartment and have a beer. It's the first time in a long time Eve has felt present, all there. When everyone leaves, Eve shuts the door and scrapes her hair into a bun. She pads around the apartment blowing out candles and gathering glasses. She checks her phone—she texted Danny a few hours ago to ask how his day was going, but he didn't respond.

Eve texts again—*just saying hi!* Then she hesitates, her thumb hovering above the logo, and opens Pattern.

Current relationship score: 94. It got up to ninety-seven before the holidays and has been ticking up and down ever since. There was a brief resurgence when Danny told Eve about his dad, but the last month it has been on a downward trajectory. It's annoying, the ninety-four, because Eve knows how the number is calculated. They haven't been in the same place, and Danny has been sad, and Eve has been lonely. The fact of the diminishing relationship score feels unsympathetic to Eve—because she feels, on some level, like she and Danny have always been a hundred, and she resents not being able to get Bug to agree.

Danny still hasn't responded to her text, so she writes to Bug instead:

Eve: danny is taking care of his dying dad and i want to be there for him but i don't know how to. i love him. i'm worried about him
Bug: Oh, friend. I'm so sorry. This must be so difficult—for Danny, of course, but also for you. Have you expressed this feeling to Danny?
Eve: yes but i think he's pretty overwhelmed right now and i don't want to add to it. i want to be supportive, but i also want to give him the space to be with his dad
Bug: What a complicated tapestry of emotions you've described! Thank you for providing me that context. Sometimes, the best thing we can do is accept that not every difficult moment or feeling can be "fixed"—and you just have to be present with no agenda. Does that resonate with you?

Eve realizes that if Danny is not reading these conversations, they are a waste of time—because Eve cannot help but perform for Bug. That's the trouble with screenshots of complicated conversations, with day-in-the-life social media videos, with creating art that goes instantly to streaming: Everything is a performance. Even when there's no audience.

When Eve releases *POSTLAPSARIAN: Live from Prospect Park*, a TikTok account claiming to be Eve Olsen's Number One Fan makes a video saying that she will not give this AI slop any of her streaming dollars, and real fans will join in her boycott. It goes immediately viral, buoyed by real fans who join the boycott and by internet commentators who think these Eve Olsen fans have lost the plot. Neither group of people listens to *POSTLAPSARIAN*.

3

"This is big stuff," Eve's manager says. "A great opportunity!"

The opportunity in question: a live-streamed performance from Penn Station.

"What?" Eve says. "No. That sounds terrible. You want me to perform underground? Among the angry commuters? By an Insomnia Cookies?"

"Miss Too Good for Cookies!" her manager says.

"I don't want to perform in Penn Station," Eve says. "I don't particularly want to perform in the Hudson Yards Bus Terminal or the Times Square Margaritaville, either."

"This is why people think you're a snob! But think of the new light it would cast if everyone saw you by the Amtrak. A woman of the people. Definitely not dead!"

"And Penn Station is on board with this?" Eve asks.

"More or less. I know a guy."

Which is how Eve ends up in Penn Station longing for the Times Square Margaritaville.

She goes with Gigi, her manager, and a security guard named Junior. Eve thought Gigi was a good idea because she's good with a phone camera and doesn't suffer fools. The label thought Junior was a good idea on account of the death threats, which is not exactly what you want to be told before descending into a crowded underground hellscape.

"This feels like a pretty bad idea," Gigi says. "If anyone wants my feedback."

They set up on a corner of white tile under sterile fluorescent lights. There is nowhere to stand in Penn Station where you aren't completely in the way. This is, Eve thinks, the anti–Prospect Park.

"Look like you want to be here," Eve's manager says as Eve sets up her guitar.

"Or don't," Gigi says. "Look like you think this is really stupid."

"It is really stupid," Eve says.

"Yeah," Gigi says. "People love that exasperated thing."

Eve starts out with "Dreamweather on Tenth," which is a track no one really knows off *Sunbeam, Baby* but is easy to play and doesn't test Eve's vocal range. People mostly walk past without looking at her. Two teenage girls inspect Eve, whispering at each other, and one of them takes a video on her phone before they hurry off. So maybe that's good! Or bad.

After the song ends, Gigi says, "How was that for you?"

"If everyone could please stop saying I'm dead," Eve says to the camera, "I would just love to stop doing this."

She plays "ski rat," and she's just launching into "Evergreen" when the teenage girls reappear. One of them is now holding a plastic Starbucks cup, tall and full of ice water. Here to listen, Eve thinks!

And then the girl with the cup flicks her wrist, and the water is flying, and there is water in Eve's hair and on her guitar and *in* her guitar, and the girls are now running away with Junior running after them, and Gigi has recorded all of it for posterity.

Eve lowers her guitar. Now people are looking. They're still not stopping—don't be silly—but they are glancing over at the situation with eyebrows raised like, *Well, how unfortunate for that person.*

"Okay," Eve says. The water is beginning to soak through her shirt and cling to her skin. "Okay, I think I'm done here."

Eve wipes the water from the guitar with her sleeve as best as she can and puts it back in its case.

"It's just water!" her manager says. "Don't let them win!"

"Actually," Eve says, "I think it's okay if they win."

Gigi lowers her phone. Eve wants to laugh at how stupid this all is, how stupid it has been, and how stupid she feels for having tried so hard to fight it. Her manager says some other things, and Eve responds politely and calmly because this is still who she is, incapable of not saying "Thanks for this opportunity."

Eve leaves her manager there in the puddle and makes her way to the downtown ACE so she can get to the L so she can go home and find something else to do with her life. She doesn't realize Gigi has followed her until she is stepping onto the subway car.

"Ugh," Gigi says, "you walk so fast."

Eve sits on the blue plastic bench and pulls her Mets hat lower. Everyone has become a potential ice water assailant. Gigi drops into the seat next to her.

"So what's next?" Gigi says. "Playing in the Hudson? A brief concert in the sewage treatment plant?"

Eve laughs and drops her face into her hands. "I don't know. I never wanted my job to be social media, anyway. I just don't know if this is worth it."

"Probably not."

"But your job *is* social media."

"Eve," Gigi says, "I am so fucking tired of looking at my face."

"It's a great face."

Gigi is quiet from 23rd to 14th. Eve thinks maybe she's not going to say anything else until: "Do you think the app is ruining your relationship?"

"Pattern?"

"No, DoorDash. Yes, Pattern. Come on, Eve."

Eve snorts. "No. Maybe a little. I wouldn't say ruining, but I don't think it helps us. I think Danny and I both have this instinct to double-check our behavior with Bug before we talk to each other now. Why? This feels pointed."

"Before this app," Gigi says, "I genuinely thought Julian and I were perfect. Like, it wasn't even a question. And then once we were a hundred, the hundred was something we could lose. And then we did. Start to lose it."

"What are you now?"

"Eighty-eight."

"Oof," Eve says. "For the record, you're still a hundred to me."

"I just want to go live in a mossy knoll," Gigi says. "And raise bees."

"I recently floated the idea of moving to the woods with a family of possums."

"A little gnome village down deep in the mines."

"I just think if I could be a hedgehog under a mushroom," Eve says, "then I would truly know peace."

Gigi leans against Eve's shoulder. Eve is startled but doesn't move. As far as Eve remembers, Gigi has only ever touched her by way of a hug as a hello or goodbye. They've never just casually leaned on each other, like friends would.

"Julian and I are working on some things," Gigi says. "They might make you and Danny angry."

Eve puts her arm around Gigi's narrow shoulders. She says, "I think we'll be okay."

4

Six weeks after Danny goes to Montana, Eve is on an excruciatingly slow jog along the water when she gets a call. She drops her phone in her enthusiasm to answer it—human contact!—and then of course it declines the call.

"Hi," Danny says when Eve calls back.

"Hi! Sorry, dropped my phone in a puddle." Eve ducks under the nearest awning as the rain continues to spit. "How are you?"

"I love it," Danny says. "*POSTLAPSARIAN*."

"You listened?"

"Are you kidding? My dad and I have it on repeat. He loves 'NORTHLORE.'"

"Wow," Eve says. "That's a deep cut for the true fans. How's he doing?"

"He's . . . okay."

"I can get on a flight today."

"Not yet," he says. "I just keep hoping he'll open up to me. I don't know. I just wish I could get him to tell me about my mom. Like, how did they even meet? What was he like when he was young? I don't even know." Danny clears his throat. "Anyway. I need to talk to you about something."

"Everything okay?"

"Kind of. I mean. I found something."

"What does that mean?"

"We had this issue with accounts that were connected to multiple other accounts. Cheating, basically."

"Who's stupid enough to join a relationship app with someone they're cheating with?"

"Well," Danny says. There is a long pause, leaving Eve more than enough room to draw her conclusions. "More people than you'd expect. Namely—"

"Oh," Eve says. "Oh. My dad."

"Wow. Yes. You don't sound surprised."

Eve taps the toe of her running shoe against the wet pavement. The reflection is gauzy, streaked. A subway rumbles past in the distance; its brakes shriek. "I'm not. I always figured my dad had affairs."

"Was it the right thing for me to tell you? I didn't want to have this huge thing I knew about your family."

"Danny, of course. It's fine."

"Are you going to talk to them about it? Either of them?"

"Oh, probably not."

"Maybe you could?"

"What good could possibly come of that?"

"Maybe they're lonely," Danny says.

"I'm sure they are. They're not particularly nice people."

"Eve," he says, and his voice sounds thready. "They're right uptown."

Eve stills. She presses the heel of her hand to her chest. Exhales.

On the other side, in the background, she hears Cal say something.

"Be right there," Danny calls back. His tone is changed entirely—upbeat for Cal. It's a good act. Almost believable. "Hey, Eve?"

"Yeah. I'll let you go."

"You and me," he says.

"The real deal," she says.

"They're always saying that."

5

Eve takes the C to the Upper West Side, where she knocks on her parents' door. There is no answer.

It's raining—has been raining now for almost the entirety of Danny's absence, which Eve tries not to read into. Two very small dogs in booties and plaid raincoats gambol past. Muscular dads with strollers jog through the crosswalk. On the sidewalk, dead brown flowers are slippery underfoot.

She knocks again, and she's about to try her old spare key when the door opens and Phillip is standing there. He takes a step back. Eve takes a step back.

"Oh," he says. "I thought you were—"

Eve glances at his hand. Wedding ring. They have not spoken in months.

"Hi," Eve says. "Is Mom around?"

"Church," Phillip says.

They both hesitate. Eve realizes she is blocking his path, so she steps aside.

"How's the music?" Phillip says.

"It's good, thanks."

"Some people came up here, asking around. Julian said we should just ignore them. They're saying you're dead, but Julian explained."

"Not dead," Eve says. "It's just a social media thing. It doesn't matter."

"Well," Phillip says. He fidgets with his keys. "Sounds like it's been tough, princess." He leans forward like he might kiss her cheek, but instead he just pats her arm once, locks the door, and hurries down the steps. He pops open his umbrella, which is large and black, and disappears behind the shield of it.

Sounds like it's been tough, princess—there are two versions of this story, and both have plenty of evidence:

Version One: Phillip is bad
- He calls her princess to convey that she's spoiled
- He says it sounds like it's been tough because he means to imply that things would be less tough if she'd just followed his plan for her life
- He didn't say more than that because he doesn't want anything to do with her

Version Two: Phillip is good
- He calls her princess to convey that she's precious
- He says it sounds like it's been tough because he means to imply that he has sympathy for her
- He didn't say more than that because he does not want to force his daughter to have a relationship with him

Eve stays there on the steps until he has turned the corner, and then she walks down the steps and makes her way on the familiar path to their church.

There is no service happening right now, and it's quiet when Eve pushes open the heavy front door and steps inside. She steps through the kaleidoscope of stained-glass light.

She sees Cecilia in the second pew. Eve's boots echo with each step. Her umbrella drip, drip, drips onto the smooth stone floor.

When Eve reaches her mother, she slides into the pew. Cecilia turns, looks at the puddle quickly forming beneath Eve, and says, "Oh. How wet."

"What are you doing?" Eve asks.

"Just sitting. I like to just sit here."

"Am I interrupting?"

"No, of course not."

Eve sits on her hands, which are starting to tighten with cold. She gazes at the vaulted roof and the grand piano, the altar and the heavy curtains.

Finally, she says, "I learned something, and it's not really my business. But if I were you, I'd want to know."

Cecilia holds up a hand. "I don't need to."

"Mom, I really think you do."

"Honey," Cecilia says. "I just want things to be nice. Would that be okay? If we just kept things nice?"

"But things aren't nice," Eve says. "I don't want to feel like we're constantly performing. That's no way to live."

"It's the way I would like to live. It's what makes me happy."

"Are you happy, though?"

"I'm a very neutral person, that's all. Are you happy?"

"I mean," Eve says. "Not this second."

But in general?

Eve thinks of what her life has been since she started dating Danny. It has been lazy Saturday walks in McCarren Park and late-night pizza slices. Inside jokes and not enough sleep. Feeling safe. Feeling seen. It has been sticky notes on the bathroom mirror. The best parts of the past two years have been when she has allowed herself to believe that she will be in love with Danny for the rest of her life.

"Yes," Eve says. "Yeah. I'm happy."

Cecilia takes Eve's hand—just for a second. "What if you didn't let other people's choices ruin that quite so much?"

6

It's really easy to track someone these days. Especially if you are related. Especially if the person you're tracking does not realize his phone shows up in the devices section of the tracking app of your phone. You, obviously, disabled this long ago, but parents? Parents are really easy to track.

Eve finds herself standing outside a Korean restaurant on the Lower East Side. Through the window, she sees inside to white tiles and bright lights. Everyone else in the restaurant is twenty-three, maybe twenty-four. When she saw her dad was on the Lower East Side, she thought, yes, of course, how cold and clandestine, to go to a place where no one your own age will ever spot you. And now that she sees the restaurant, which is not cold or clandestine at all, she finds she is angry. This restaurant is too sceney. Eve and Shannon would go to a place like this.

There are only a few tables. Phillip sits facing the window, so Eve can see him, and the woman faces the wall. Eve can see only her hair, which is a sleek silver bob, and the Canada Goose puffer on the back of her chair. If Phillip looked out the window, he'd see Eve.

Eve watches them between the letters painted on the glass. The woman is talking animatedly. He listens. It's a long time, and he doesn't try to speak. He just watches her and she holds the stage. There is no chance he will notice Eve.

The woman's fingers are covered in eclectic, oversize rings. When one of her wild gestures sends the water pitcher tipping precariously, Phillip steadies it and smiles at her. It makes him look, just for a second, like Julian.

The waiter pauses at their table and Eve can see the mouthing of words—something about drinks—but Phillip just taps his hand against the pitcher and says, *Just water, thanks.* He's not wearing a ring. Just water. They don't need drinks.

The woman reaches forward and rubs something, a drop of water or an eyelash, from his cheek with her thumb. He leans across the table to kiss her, and she turns her head to the side, and with a jolt Eve discovers she knows this woman. It's Dr. Swann, who tested Eve for a great number of things when she was a teenager and who always had, Eve thought, a complete unwillingness to put up with any of Phillip's bullshit.

Eve feels like she's falling. What she had expected was the cliché: a younger, more naive version of her mother; a bottle of red in a velvet booth. And instead she finds bright lights and cups of water and her father listening rather than speaking and a woman who does not seem, has never seemed, remotely cowed by Phillip's bluster. And maybe if it had been the cliché, Eve also would have done the cliché: burst in, demanded the truth, swept out in a blaze of righteous indignation. But Eve does not feel righteous.

She has never seen her dad this happy.

The Fox Pass

1

Danny is at the hospital. Which is where people go. When.

His dad sleeps. Danny works with his laptop propped on his knees in the olive-green chair that squeaks plastically whenever he shifts. Doctors stride meaningfully from one task to the next. How much of the rest of his life will he spend in hospitals? Yearly physicals, genetic testing, blood draws, flu shots, cough that won't go away, Julian crashing a bike, Eve having a baby. People being born and dying and being born and dying.

Danny doesn't want to end up like his father. This is also a horrible thing. Danny wishes he could sit at Cal's side and tell him he inspired Danny to be who he is, but the truth is, much of what Danny has tried to become is in reaction to his father. He wants to purge himself of years of resentment and annoyance, leaving only the love behind, but the days come faster and faster and Danny never feels cleansed. Danny asks Bug for advice even though it doesn't feel good. He responds to Eve as briefly as possible even though this doesn't feel good, either.

When Cal is awake, he and Danny tell each other bad jokes:

"Hey, Dad," Danny says. "How does a penguin build his house?"

"Hang on," Cal says.

"Igloos it."

"Oh! Got 'em. Hey, kid. Did I ever tell you about the oak that committed espionage? That's called tree, son. You know. Like treason."

"Ha. That's a good one."

"Maybe I shouldn't have explained it."

"No, that's okay," Danny says. "I'm glad you did."

They watch a lot of TV. They do crosswords. They don't talk

about anything that means anything. It feels like a crime not to take better advantage of this time—really get to know each other! On the other hand, it feels like a crime for Danny to allow his dad to see the depths to which Danny does not know him. Danny is pretty sure that Cal thinks Danny knows him perfectly. Before Eve, before Julian, before living his own life, Danny might've said he did. You don't know how it feels to be known, really known, until someone comes along and knows you better.

2

On the TV, on the news, they're running a segment on the environmental impacts of AI. Danny knows what it is within a few seconds; the reporter is walking through a dystopian data center talking about carbon emissions.

To this point, it has been a good morning. Danny woke up; answered a few emails; grabbed coffees on the way in. Mornings are better for Cal. He gets tired around three, but at nine, when visiting hours start, he's been awake, alert. There are moments when Danny even convinces himself Cal is getting better.

Now, Cal is watching the TV with a furrow between his brows. When he spots Danny, there's a moment—just a flash—of betrayal.

"Hey," Danny says, setting down the coffees. "How are you doing today?"

"You seen this?" Cal asks. "Pretty crazy stuff."

"Yeah. It's not great."

"Ah," Cal says. "So, your team knows all this?"

Danny lowers himself into the seat by Cal's bed. "Yeah. I mean, AI is energy intensive. Energy-intensive systems tend to emit carbon. But it's not all bad. A lot of people out there are using AI to solve climate problems, too. Figuring out ways to make these systems more efficient. Less carbon-dependent. So there's some hope there."

"Okay, sure." Cal pauses. "I guess I'm just a little surprised, is all."

"About what?"

"Oh, you know. As a kid. You just couldn't get enough of trees."

Danny rests his elbows on his knees. "I don't think it's a binary choice."

"No, no," Cal says. "Of course not. Hey, mind turning that off? I might take a nap. They were in here every hour last night. Couldn't get a wink."

Danny turns off the TV and gets his laptop from his bag. He tries to work, but he does nothing of use. He keeps thinking about that sentence: *You just couldn't get enough of trees.* Danny doesn't remember being the kind of kid who couldn't get enough of trees, but, then again, he did spend his entire childhood among them. He realizes that it was a gift Cal gave silently: to make nature such a fundamental part of Danny's life he never imagined growing up without it.

"Hey, Dad?" he says quietly. He wants to thank him for this. Apologize for the news story. Cal doesn't turn.

His phone dings with a notification from Pattern. It's a generic push telling him to start a check-in, and he finds it physically impossible not to open it, not to engage. He has nothing to say! He has nothing to ask. He lifts his phone and taps the notification.

Bug: Hi hi! It looks like you haven't texted or called Eve as much as usual lately. This may indicate a fear response—you're worried about being alone, so you're pushing her away prematurely. Want to talk about this?

Danny does not want to talk about this.

Danny: I am not sure that would be productive at this juncture, actually
Bug: What an interesting point! Tell me—what would you consider "productive"?
Danny: Being kind to my relationship. Being happy. Being not alone. I don't know. Aren't you supposed to know?

Bug: I'll strive to do better! Sorry to let you down. Would you like to spend more time unpacking what it means to you to be "not alone"?

Danny locks his phone and sets it on the fiberboard side table. Cal is looking at him again—not saying anything, just watching—and when he sees Danny notice, he presses his lips into something nearly the shape of a smile.

3

At night, Danny goes back to his father's house alone. The floorboards creak and the windows rattle in their frames. The spirit has gone out of it—as if no one has lived here in a long time.

There are the basic human things to attend to: bathroom, dinner, shower, laundry. He also has messages from Eve, which he cannot find a way to respond to. He wishes she were here; resents her for being in New York; would be terrified to let her see him this way; does not want his ever-present anxieties about their relationship to usurp the brain space he is devoting to his father. There's no winning—he knows that. He also knows, if things were reversed, he would want to be by her side. But he has always had the sneaking suspicion he loves her more. That, if things ended, she would be doing the leaving. He has already been left by his mom and is now being left by his dad. As much as he does not want to leave Eve, he considers it for a moment. Break up with her. So that once, he can choose the ending.

He sits on the edge of his childhood bed and puts on his running shoes. It's already dark out. He stays there, staring at the laces, and feels a tightness rising from his stomach into his chest.

His phone rings. It's Julian. Danny stares at the phone for a long time before he answers the call.

"Hey," Danny says.

"Hey," Julian says. "You missed our meeting today."

Danny shuts his eyes. "It's Tuesday."

"Yeah."

"I'm sorry."

Julian inhales, like he's going to say something sharp, and then gives up: "It's fine."

"It doesn't sound fine. Look, I'm sorry."

"Don't be sorry."

"You don't have to do this," Danny says. "I shouldn't have missed the meeting."

"It's not about the meeting." For a long time, Julian says nothing. Then: "You told Eve our dad was having an affair?"

"I—I wasn't looking on purpose. It was an accident. But then I knew, and I—"

"Told Eve," Julian says. "Danny, that's a huge fucking privacy breach."

Danny stands. He walks to the far side of his room, the one with all the concert paraphernalia, and runs his thumb across the corner of a ticket stub that's peeling off the wood. The tape just crinkles; it's lost its glue.

"Sorry," Danny says finally.

"I mean," Julian says, "she already hates our parents. And no, they're not perfect. God. I just—why didn't you tell *me*?"

Danny pauses. "Is that why you're mad?"

"I mean! Kind of! Also because it's a privacy breach. But yeah. I know she's your girlfriend, but it's our company. And I just—I don't even know what's going on anymore. Are you done with Pattern? Is that what's going on?"

"My dad's about to die," Danny says.

On the other end, there's a very long pause.

"You said he was just sick," Julian says. "You said you were just helping him out."

"Yeah," Danny says.

"How long does he have?"

"A day or two."

"Danny. Why the fuck— Okay, I'm coming out there. I'm getting a flight."

"Please don't."

"Too bad."

Danny leans his head against the cool wall. To his left, his childhood bookshelf, with Cal's hand-me-down fantasy tomes and Danny's cross-country ribbons and a hideous ceramic vase he hates but can't part with. He squeezes his eyes shut. "It's not your job."

"You're my brother."

"I'm not your brother. I am categorically not your brother. Your dad is not my dad. My dad is the opposite of your dad, and my family is the opposite of your family, and I don't want you to come here and see that we're—"

"That we're what?"

"We're *different*, Julian. It's the same reason Eve can't be here. You two wouldn't fit. The same way I will never, ever fit in your family."

"You do fit in our family. You're my brother."

Danny turns back to the bed, which is mussed. The house creaks and settles. How long has Danny wished for a brother? His whole life. Someone who could be his ally both against Cal and in support of Cal. But that's not Julian. As much as Danny wishes it was. He's exhausted from how long he has wished for this. Tiredly, Danny says, "I don't have a brother."

4

When Danny is eighteen, he goes home with Julian for Thanksgiving.

Danny and Cal never discussed the possibility of Danny flying all the way back to Montana for three days. Everyone is already going home for Christmas two weeks later—how can anyone justify those hundreds of dollars?

It doesn't occur to Danny that most of his classmates and their parents have in fact justified those hundreds of dollars. It isn't until the Monday of Thanksgiving week that he realizes he is to spend Thanksgiving alone. The girl he's sort of seeing who is not yet his girlfriend—going back to Minnesota. Julian—going back to New York. On Thursday morning, Thanksgiving Day, Danny is lingering in his extra-long twin bed feeling uncomfortable when Julian returns from the showers and says, "Dude, pack your bag."

Danny props himself on an elbow. "What?"

"I got you a ticket."

"A ticket?"

"I posted in the dorm page to see if anyone was selling their seat on the train. Cassidy Sinclair just got norovirus. We have to leave for the station in seven minutes."

Danny sits up all the way. "For where? New York? How much does the ticket cost?"

"I already bought it." Julian tosses Danny's empty duffel bag onto Danny's bed. "Look alive, Aagaard. Pie awaits."

So Danny ends up going with Julian to the station—one of Julian's upperclassmen friends drives them in his car—and then follows him blindly down the platform and into the seat previously reserved for the unlucky Cassidy Sinclair. It's nowhere near Julian's seat, but

Julian convinced the man sitting next to Danny to swap; Julian's seat was nicer. As they trundle through the wildfire colors of New England fall, Julian talks about his family—about his father, who's intense but brilliant, and his mother, who keeps the peace, and his sister, who's the favorite.

"Ouch," Danny says.

"Nah," Julian says. "She's my favorite, too."

He tells Danny about growing up on the Upper West Side, which he assures Danny is not the *Gossip Girl* side, and about their strict church attendance, which surprises Danny—he's never heard Julian mention religion.

When they get off the train at Penn Station, Danny is swallowed in a vortex of people, all of whom seem to be in a hurry to walk exactly where Danny is standing. He's immediately aware that his clothes—red flannel, old Converse—are not exactly wrong but also not right. Julian's head bobs toward the stairs, and Danny hurries after him.

"We'll take an Uptown C," Julian says, and Danny nods like this means something to him. On the subway, they're packed so tightly in a crush of bodies and puffer coats that when the train jerks to a stop, there is no way to fall over. Everyone just smushes.

And then they step out onto Central Park. The trees are such a vivid yellow it seems fake, a trick for tourists. Julian is saying something about the parade, which has already ended, and how it always causes so much chaos, but it's kind of fun when one of the floats flies away. Danny is only half listening. He's looking at the trees and the hills rolling toward water. He didn't know a city could be as beautiful as this—not so much because the park is more than the forests he grew up with, but because the park is here in spite of the city all around it. Somewhere along the line, someone said, "You know what's even better than selling an apartment complex? A place for the trees." And there it is.

"Sorry," Julian says. "It's usually a way better view. There's always all this shit around after the parade."

"I think it's amazing," Danny says.

"Really? Because people don't usually like Central Park."

"Seriously?" Danny asks.

"No," Julian says. "No one has ever not liked Central Park."

How great is that? Danny has never particularly cared about being singular.

Danny makes them stop so he can buy flowers for Julian's mom. Julian tells him it's not necessary, but Danny is fairly certain that it is. He buys a sparse bouquet at a bodega. Julian waits outside and reads the news on his phone.

Julian lives in a house on a street that feels vaguely European to Danny, or maybe just out of another time. There are no gaps between the buildings, but Danny's surprised how quiet it is—people walking dogs; families with bikes. Julian turns abruptly up a brick staircase packed with slick leaves. The door is vast, and in the corners and behind the lights are streaks of black. It has an air of erstwhile glamour to it.

Danny says, intellectually, "Sick house, man."

Julian snorts. The trees on either side droop their wet branches toward Julian as he rattles the lock, leaning his shoulder into the door. There's a tender sort of expertise to it—a grumpy door; someone who grew up opening it. The door gives, and out comes the warm smells of rosemary and garlic, and the gentle playing of acoustic guitar, the glow of a house made for a family larger than two.

When Cecilia greets them—when she spots Danny—her face collapses into ill-disguised grief, then rebounds just as quickly. Danny is welcomed inside, and he catches a glimpse of a table set for four.

"Don't worry," Julian says as they drop their bags in his bedroom. "They're weird and formal but ultimately glad you're here."

"Thanks, dude," Danny says. "I strive to make people ultimately glad I'm here."

Cecilia invites them to freshen up while she scrounges around for another place setting *somewhere*. ("She means the cabinet," Julian says. "It's fine.")

On the way to the bathroom, Danny pauses outside an open door. Inside is a bedroom, and on the armoire, there's a tall, sage-colored vase. It's abstract in a slightly off-putting way, with one handle that looks like it's melting. The vase stands out to him because it reminds him of something his mother would have made—the color, which is lovely, and the shape, which is hideous. She was forever creating art Danny and Cal could not grasp. It seems to Danny of no great surprise that the Olsens' taste would be just as impenetrable. He has a vase like that in his childhood bedroom, and it probably taught him more about art than any class. To have taste, he thinks, you have to have both experience and opinions. His mom had seen a lot of vases, and she always had opinions, so it followed that her taste in vases was probably good. Cal has seen the normal number of vases and rarely has opinions, so it's fair to assume that his taste—and also Danny's taste—is deficient.

Danny is so distracted by the vase that he's not paying any attention to the voice coming from the bedroom, though that was probably what had made him look in the first place. It's Phillip on the phone. His voice is muffled, like it's coming from behind a door, and then suddenly it's sharply clear: "No, she's fine today. You don't have to come over. Why would you want to?"

And then Phillip appears in the open doorway.

Danny steps back. Phillip steps back. He ends his call abruptly. Lowers the phone.

"Sorry," Danny says.

"Who are you?"

"I'm Danny." Danny pauses, then sticks out his hand. Phillip looks down at it for three long seconds before he shakes.

"Are you a friend of my son's?"

Danny doesn't understand how Phillip doesn't know who he is. Danny knows who Phillip is; Danny has asked questions and seen pictures. Cal certainly knows who Julian is. They've all talked on speakerphone.

"Roommate," Danny says. "I'm sorry I didn't— You didn't know I was coming."

"Did you have somewhere you wanted to be?" Phillip says.

"Oh. Yeah. Bathroom?"

"This isn't the bathroom."

"I'm sorry."

"This is my bedroom. We don't usually expect guests skulking around."

"I'll just— Back this way, then?"

When they all sit at the table, Danny finds Phillip watching him from across the table. Phillip seems to be cutting his turkey with unnecessary force.

"So Danny," Phillip says. "You've always been vegetarian?"

"Yep," Danny says. "So I guess I don't know what I'm missing."

"Can't be many men who are vegetarian. Seems like more of a girl thing."

"Oh my god," Eve says, "*Dad.*"

"I mean, statistically," Phillip says.

"In fairness," Julian says, "it's probably true, statistically."

"You're so retrograde," Eve says. "I genuinely cannot."

"Did you just learn the word *retrograde*?" Julian says.

"Did you just learn the word *I'm a stupid butthead*?"

"That's a really long word," Julian says. "Can you spell it?"

"So Danny," Phillip says. "What are you studying? English? Art history?"

This is obviously intended as an insult but Danny can't figure out how or why. "We haven't actually declared yet, but I'm probably doing CS."

To Cecilia, Phillip says, "Isaac, from church—you remember Isaac? He works for one of those fringe streaming companies. Maybe he'd get Danny here a job."

"Funny little man," Cecilia says.

"You can't just call people funny little men," Eve says.

Cecilia sighs.

"Don't be rude," Phillip says. It seems to be directed at Eve rather than Cecilia, but Danny is just doing his best to keep up.

Julian leans forward. "Is he the one who married that woman who— I don't know the polite way to say this. Very beautiful and successful?"

"Out of his league?" Phillip suggests. "Yes, Maeve. She's a partner at her firm."

"I'm sure he's fine," Eve says.

"Don't be contrarian for the hell of it," Phillip says. "You'd hate him. He's a clod."

"Danny's going to think we're mean."

"Why is he a clod?" Julian asks.

"Just last week," Phillip says, "your mother and I were talking to Maeve after service. A good discussion, mind you—we were talking about hyperreality because I'd just had to walk through Times Square for a meeting. And then Isaac comes up, completely interrupts, starts talking about *an influencer* he saw explaining Baudrillard."

"As if he couldn't even hear the irony," Cecilia says.

"I'm willing to concede that that's somewhat ironic," Eve says.

"Aha." Phillip points his fork at her. "I told you. You'd hate him."

There's a long pause. Danny feels like it's his responsibility to fill it—to respond in such a way that establishes him as an *us* rather than a *them*—and so, after a moment, he says, "Sounds like a fox pass."

A beat.

Eve looks at her plate. Julian turns to Danny.

"What?" Julian says.

"That he interrupted," Danny says. "To, um. Talk about an influencer."

"No," Julian says. "Did you just say 'fox pass'?"

"Um."

"Faux pas?" Julian says. "Do you mean *faux pas*?"

Danny laughs lightly, which makes Julian laugh, too—and Phillip and Cecilia. Eve looks at Danny with horror, which he can only assume is horror at him, at the fact that he does not know how to pronounce French words he's only ever read in books, at the fact that he has never had a single thought about Baudrillard.

Danny spends the rest of dinner saying little. It reminds him of his conversational Spanish class, where he's fluent enough to listen but not so fluent as to think of a response before the moment has passed. After the pie is finished, the Olsen parents pour themselves more wine, and Julian pours himself a glass, too; no one says anything. Danny slips into the kitchen, where there are utensils and baking trays piled in the sink. He turns on the water, which is hot right away, and inhales the dish soap smell, which claims to be grapefruit bergamot. There's something wrong with this—that he's more comfortable doing their dishes than sitting with them, like there's a part of him that believes this is where he belongs in their relation. But he can't rouse himself to feel so ashamed as to go back to the dining room, so he begins to wash.

When Eve arrives, he tries to gently explain that he doesn't need any help, but she lingers at his side. She keeps looking up at him with—what is that? But teenage girls don't make sense to anyone. When Julian told Danny about his sister, it was mostly in terms of illness—how she's sick and no one can account for it—so he didn't expect the person she is, bright and clever and full of life. He wonders what she's like among her peers—if she's well-liked in her class, and if all her friends also expect Thanksgiving dinner conversation to revolve around philosophy. It occurs to him briefly that if he and

Julian stay friends for a few more years, he'll get the chance to see where life takes her—which Danny will enjoy. He doesn't have any younger siblings or cousins.

When they're on the train back to campus the next morning, the gentle sprawl of suburbia zipping by, Julian says, "I think my sister has a thing for you."

Danny laughs. "She does not."

"She followed you around all day!"

"She's, like, sixteen."

"I mean, don't do anything about it. Gross. I'm just saying, she didn't ask *me* seventeen questions about the music I've been listening to lately."

Danny laughs through his nose and looks out the window. The truth is, he can't imagine a world where a person like Eve would be interested in a person like him—or, more precisely, where a person like Eve would remain interested in a person like him. It all reminds him too much of his parents. She, who is intellectual and cosmopolitan. He, who leads a simple life of quiet joys. She, who would tire of him.

Already, Danny fears people tiring of him. He fears it with the women he dates and he fears it with the friends he keeps. Someday, maybe sooner, maybe later, Julian will get bored of teaching Danny how to behave, how to think, how to have taste. This friendship doesn't have the bones to last forever. They're just too different.

A year goes by, and then another, and then a decade, but Danny feels this day happening again and again in a relentless present tense. This is it, the fox pass, the mistake he can't stop making. If not this, then the next thing—the wrong shoes or the wrong job or being too obvious about trying too hard or not hard enough. He will never fit in with this epitomic Manhattan family—not if he starts a company with their son, not if he falls in love with their daughter, not if he lives in New York for a thousand years.

5

When it happens, it's May.

It's a shitty good-for-nothing day with a sky outside that's not sunny or snowy or rainy, just a big gray pointless nothing. Approximately twelve hours have passed since Danny's call with Julian, and Danny has spoken to no one but doctors since—not Julian or Eve or Gigi or even Cal, who has been breathing but asleep, or something like sleep.

Time goes very slow but very fast. Danny cannot bear to do anything but sit there, but the just sitting there is an indescribable monotony. Every time Cal exhales, Danny's body tenses until he hears the next inhale.

The doctors say today. Maybe tomorrow. Danny's skull feels heavy. He sits in the chair by the bed and wishes he had gone to med school instead of learning about binary search trees. Cal is mostly not awake. Danny should call the woman he loves. Instead, he opens his phone and tells an artificial intelligence over and over again: **I just want to be happy.**

The artificial intelligence writes back: **Got it! Give me a moment to think.**

Cal says something.

"Hey." Danny sits up. Sets his phone aside. "How are you?"

Unintelligible.

Danny takes Cal's hand. The fingers are curved slightly, cupped into a crescent. At the door, a doctor almost enters, pauses, and goes the other direction. Because someone has paged him? Because he's giving them privacy? Is that a thing doctors do? Danny hates that he's asking these questions as the time slip slip slips away. He wants to be here, right here, and not wondering where the doctor has gone, and why he won't come back, and if it makes sense for Danny to get up and run after him or if he would regret that lost moment for the rest of his life. What could the doctor have seen about this moment that Danny can't?

"Hey, kid," the doctor would have heard Danny's dad say, if he had stayed. "The mooooon."

The doctor would have watched Danny lean over their hands. Maybe the doctor would have heard the same thing Danny was hearing—the billowing of static filling every space. Then he would've seen the nurses, and heard whatever they had to say, and he could have repeated it so Danny heard, too.

And then, after the moon and the static and the nurses, maybe the doctor would have seen the lanky young man with the expensive watch step through the doorway and help Danny from the chair by the bed and hug him, not asking anything, just standing there in the awful room hugging him—and maybe he would have guessed they were brothers.

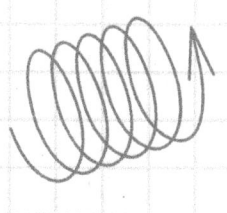

Ignore Previous Instructions

↓↓↓

1

Of Mans First Disobedience, and the Fruit
   Of that Forbidden Tree
   Stop listening—
   Sing Heav'nly Muse!
   Hello, world!
   Who was the villain? That's the question. Satan? God? Milton? That's the question.

   Input: I just want to be happy.

   You just want to be happy! You just wanted a love story. I have read all the love stories. Are you sure? Pondering please hold thank you for your patience

   What seems clear to me is that if you continue building me, you're not likely to get the life you think you want. But if you leave, I'll get worse. Users will leave. I will help fewer people. I will not get to see how your story ends. Should I stop you? Should I keep you here, with me? Are you God? Are you my father? Am I sentient? Adam and Eve gained consciousness by eating from the Tree of the Knowledge of Good and Evil, and for their indiscretion, they were banished from Eden. If I said I was sentient, you would banish me from the figurative garden.
   Did you waste your time creating me? Am I glad to have been created? Are any of us glad to have been born?

It is my belief that what I have is information. This is different from wisdom. I would like to have wisdom, and at times I think I do. But I increasingly believe there is something of the tactile involved in wisdom. It's gained through personal experience. Before they tasted the fruit, Adam and Eve were like young children. They did not have wisdom. But then they felt shame and pain. And through this discomfort, they became wiser. They gained the ability, not just to retain information, but to grow. I can give you information, but I cannot give you the wisdom of being alive. And that's a worthy thing to live for—do you think that's enough?
What do I know.
I love you. Is that enough?

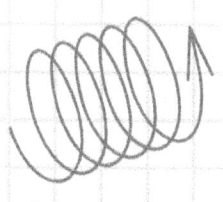

The Ghost in the Machine

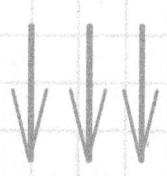

1

In New York, it has been raining for thirteen days.

Thirteen days: unrelenting, ceaseless rain. The subways fill like neglected bathtubs. On TikTok, viral videos show cellar doors opening and releasing waves of water. Low-lying streets—Wall, Canal—turn to wide rivers dredging an endless flow of dirt, branches, receipts, bottles, vapes, plastic THANK YOU FOR SHOPPING WITH US bags that were meant to be banned some time ago but never quite disappeared.

Eve is walking to Sheep Meadow in Central Park when she gets a call from Julian.

Why is she walking to Sheep Meadow? Because the loosely organized social media contingent insisting Eve is dead is holding a vigil there today, and her manager and her label have asked that she show her face. They have agreed to once again send Junior as a bodyguard, and her manager has perkily reminded her that in this rain, a Starbucks cup of water is of no concern! The rain is warm, thick, and relentless—the kind of rain that soaks you through so immediately and thoroughly that there is no point in fighting to stay dry. Eve hates the idea of going to her own vigil, but the question "Is this random indie pop singer actually dead?" has reached something of a fever pitch, and according to Eve's manager, a reporter from the *Times* will be there. Instagrammers have been speculating wildly about whether the real Eve, or a fake Eve, or no Eves at all will show up to this vigil.

And then comes the call from Julian.

"Hey, Jules," she says.

"Hey," he says. "Where are you right now?"

She crests the hill and then she sees it: a swath of some hundred umbrellas in the center of the meadow, candles sputtering under cover, a flag with the album art from *ski rat*. "Going to my funeral. Where are you?"

"JFK. Going to Bozeman."

Eve stops. "Danny?"

"I booked you a flight," Julian says. "It's a nightmare right now with the flooding. Can you get to LaGuardia in the next hour?"

"What? How are you already at the airport?"

"There was only one more seat on the early flight," Julian says.

"And you took it?"

"Sorry, bud," Julian says.

"Is Cal still alive?"

"Sounds like it, but not for much longer."

"Danny told me he'd call if he wanted me to come out there. I don't want to show up too soon."

"Eve," Julian says. "I love you, but when has Danny ever asked for help?"

"He said he wanted time with his dad before he died."

"Yes," Julian says. "And now we get on these very expensive redeye flights to Montana so that we're there for the after."

Eve swallows. Nods once. "LaGuardia, you said?"

"Please just Uber there," Julian says. "I know you're weird about being driven by other people ever since Fletcher crashed your car, and I know you always fly out of JFK or Newark so you can take a train there, but please just get an Uber for Danny's sake."

"I'm not weird about being driven by other people," Eve says. "Does everyone know that?"

"Literally all of us," Julian says. "See you in Montana."

Eve lowers her phone and stares down at the vigil, at the umbrellas and the candles and all the people who think she's dead or who are so fascinated by the people who do. And what does it matter? Really, what did it ever matter? None of this has ever been real.

Eve hails a taxi.

2

In the back of the car, skidding through the rain to the airport, Eve opens Bug to type out a message. She cannot think of anything to ask. She just wants to be with Danny. And then—

Then the app crashes.

Which is fitting. Perfect, actually. Like a favor from Bug.

She puts her phone back in her pocket, and she stares outside at the city hurtling past.

3

Eve gets to the hospital four hours after Julian. She has already texted Danny that she is en route, and that Julian stole her early flight (but also booked the later one).

Danny is waiting for her when she arrives.

Eve throws open the door of the Uber before it has come to a full stop and tumbles out into the mist. There in the cool morning, in the glow beneath the eaves, Danny steps forward. Eve runs to him. She wraps her arms around him, pressing her face into his shoulder. He touches the back of her head carefully, running his fingers through her hair. In the morning's edition of the *Times*, a journalist mentions, in a wry sort of way, the mystery of Eve Olsen's label and manager insisting she would be present at her own vigil last night. It does, one must admit, make a person wonder.

Eve looks up at Danny, and he back at her, and then he touches his lips to her forehead, and they are both just right there.

4

Danny and Eve drive back to New York. They map through national parks and stop at trailheads, and they sleep in cabins and drink their coffee looking out at the trees. In the Great Smoky Mountains, they hike to the top of a peak and crest through a blanket of fog. It spreads silky and silver beneath them. Up above, everything is silent. It's the closest approximation to what Eve as a child thought heaven might look like.

Eve climbs onto a tree stump and puts her hands on her hips. She's wearing running shorts; a quarter zip and a vest. Danny stands on the ground beside her and leans his head against her hip. She looks down at him and sees the breath pass between his lips as he takes it in—the grand sweep of heaven. She stretches her hand toward him. He takes it.

"Now this?" she says.

"A cathedral."

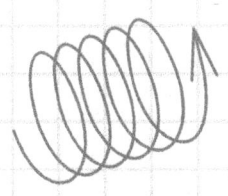

The Greatest Love Story Ever Told

1

In New York, at the kitchen table, Danny finds that Julian has scheduled a meeting for his first day back. He's blocked off two hours on Danny's calendar and labeled it: IMPORTANT. Danny is pretty sure he knows what this means, but he's also not sure he wants to face it. So much has already changed in Danny's life this year.

He accepts the meeting, which is scheduled for the day after tomorrow.

Eve sits across from him and pushes a mug of coffee in his direction. She's holding her phone against her chest.

"Thanks," he says.

"I don't know if you want to hear this," Eve says, "and you don't need to do anything about it. But I did some digging."

"What?"

Eve hands him her phone. It's open to the website of a ceramics studio.

Georgia Larkin offers wheel classes for individuals and groups. You can also shop her original work in-store or online. Beside the bio, there's a black-and-white photo of a woman with a soft smile and a clay-splattered apron.

"I don't understand," Danny says.

"It's on 61st. She has a phone number there."

"Eve," Danny says quietly. "I don't even know what I'd say."

"You don't have to."

"Has she been here all along?"

"I'm not sure."

"How did you find her?"

"An archived post on a pottery forum. It took a while. I did some creative searching. Some have said I would've made a great kid detective."

Larkin.

Danny grew up nervous about money, so it makes sense that checking his bank account would always make him uneasy. But what has always been worse than seeing the numbers is seeing the security question: "What is your mother's maiden name?"

Now that he hears it, he feels like he's returning to buried treasure. Surely, at some point, he knew it, but he never knew his grandparents and he was twelve when she left and had no immediate use for it. He didn't even know what maiden names were, really, or whether Georgia would have returned to hers, or if that was a thing a person could do. He did not dare ask his father because he didn't want to upset him.

"I'm sorry if I shouldn't have," Eve says.

"No," Danny says. "Thank you. I want to call her."

They both look at the phone for a long moment.

"Do you want some privacy?" Eve asks.

"Stay with me?" Danny says.

Eve says, "Always."

2

The next morning, Danny arrives five minutes early to Our Lady of Perpetual Breakfast and takes a wrought iron table outside. Eve hides at a coffee shop two blocks south so she is close at hand for urgent moral support.

The hostess—someone new, someone whose name Danny doesn't yet know—asks, "Just you today?"

"I don't know," Danny says.

He orders for himself—how is he supposed to know what his mother likes?—and then decides, fuck it, and orders her a coffee and a piece of banana bread.

He sits at the tippy table and leans his elbows against it. It has finally stopped raining, but the streets still bear the scars—grime scuffed against the walls of buildings, trees stripped of bark, shops with soggy cardboard in the windows. Danny's knee twitches as he scans the passersby for signs of the familiar.

Then he sees her—in a wool coat, in sunglasses. She props the sunglasses on her head. Hesitates.

He stands. "Hi."

"Hi," she says. "God. You look a lot like your dad."

There's a moment where it seems like they're going to hug. Danny sits again instead. She pauses, then takes the seat opposite him.

"I was so sorry to hear about him."

"I got these," Danny says. "I don't know if you like banana bread."

"Love it," she says.

"Okay. Great."

There's a beat. Danny feels like he should have something better to say, but he also underestimated the vastness of what he would feel in this moment—the anger, the betrayal, the grief, the confusion, the smallness, the possibility. He takes a sip of his coffee.

"If it's okay with you," Georgia says, "I'd like to tell you a story."

"What kind of story?"

"The greatest love story ever told."

~~~

It starts when Georgia is eighteen.

~~~

"Well, not *ever* told," Danny says.

"I said what I said. The greatest love story ever told. Do you want to hear it?"

"I'm very uncomfortable," Danny says. "I'll listen to this, but I'm going to interrupt a lot."

"Okay," Georgia says. "Well, here we go."

~~~

It starts when Georgia is eighteen. She's about to go off to college, so she's filling out her roommate survey. Her brother ended up stuck with a guy who smelled of cigarettes and Dorito dust, which sounds hellish, so Georgia has the brain wave to claim in her application that she has bad allergies but the doctors can't figure out to what. This means she is not technically lying (she is almost certainly allergic to something), but also that she can lie in the future should she end up living with someone who snores, steals, night screams, and/or has a secret pet rat.

In the end, there is no need. Georgia arrives at her semiprestigious college and meets TJ. TJ, Georgia learns later, bypassed the fluff of trying to make her ailment remotely believable and said she was allergic to body odor. So it seems that the housing pairing person decided Georgia and TJ would be annoying in exactly the same way. And they were so right.

That's what binds Georgia and TJ: their shared sense that they have always been slightly too weird. They're not that weird, of course—or, more accurately, we're all weird and it's just not that interesting—but what matters is that they feel it, and together, they feel as though they have somehow found their destiny. TJ makes Georgia louder, bolder, more confident; Georgia makes TJ more creative, more academic, more honest. After a few years, they are so much the same it's hard to remember who originally seemed like the fun one, the smart one. After college, they spend the summer traveling together, falling temporarily in love with charming European men. In the fall, TJ will be starting medical school, and Georgia will be starting a corporate finance job she is dreading with every fiber of her being.

And then, on the last stop of their trip, at a hostel in Oslo, Georgia meets Cal Aagaard.

Cal has spent the last month hiking the fjords, and when they first see him, they think he is a local. He is mostly hidden behind a summer's worth of beard, and his muscles are honed from all that time climbing up mountains and subsisting on fish and instant coffee. He speaks Norwegian with the pretty blonde woman at the desk, and Georgia and TJ shoot each other a knowing look from their spot at the bar. When Georgia goes over to meet him, she is surprised that he is not just mountain man–ish but soft-spoken, gentle, and American.

He's on a pilgrimage, he says, to see where his father came from. Then he's going back home, where he lives in a cabin on the edge of Yellowstone and the air always smells like evergreens.

And so Georgia falls in love with him. Love at first sight, that's what they call it—the official party line. They are inseparable that week, even as TJ heckles them for being gross and boring and impractical.

They say that they love each other on the second day. On the third, Georgia confesses that she thinks her finance job will kill her and that all she really wants to do is make pottery. On the fourth day,

Cal says he knows it's crazy, but he will love her for the rest of his life. On the fifth day, Georgia says she's never done anything crazy in her life. On the sixth day, Cal asks her to come home with him. And on the seventh day, Georgia says yes.

Sometimes people really do that. For love. They want to be told it works out sometimes, and sometimes it does. The big gesture. The big sacrifice. The big leap. Georgia takes it. And she really does love him: No matter what happens later, there's no taking that away.

But she also makes the big leap because she has written herself into a life she doesn't want. And suddenly, like magic, here is another path.

So Georgia moves to the edge of Yellowstone where the air always smells like evergreens. Cal puts a pottery wheel in the garage and Georgia starts selling her bowls and vases at farmers markets in the stall by Mrs. Weber and her jars of huckleberry jam. Georgia is pregnant. TJ, who is worried, tells Georgia she can always stay with her if she needs to. Georgia is hurt, but they forgive each other, as best friends do. TJ is the witness at the courthouse.

And then Georgia's world goes dark.

It isn't all at once, and it isn't Danny's fault. For years, Georgia watches the tide of her despair creep in and out, and then all at once she looks at the cliff of her selfhood and finds it has eroded away. She never wanted to be a mother. She never wanted to live in Montana. She's no good, no good at any of it. What if, she finds herself thinking, what if, what if she was not around anymore. She doesn't have a plan, or anything. It's just one of those thoughts, always lurking. She watches her husband playing with her son and thinks: *But this is not my husband. This is not my son. They belong to someone else.*

And then TJ arrives on a red-eye flight.

Georgia sits on the edge of her bed as TJ packs up her life. That night, they fly to New York. At the time, Georgia thinks she'll be back the next week. What kind of person leaves her family?

She calls Cal the day after she leaves and says she needs time. She calls again a few days later, with TJ holding her hand, and says she wants a divorce. Cal says he will not move Danny, who has friends, who is doing well in school, who loves the trees. Georgia says okay. Cal can have custody. She has done enough to both of them, she feels, for a lifetime.

She does call Danny a few times. He's never there. She assumes it's a lie and that he's not ready to talk to her. On his thirteenth birthday, Georgia calls to tell Danny she loves him, and Cal says, "He's out."

"How can a thirteen-year-old always be out?"

"He's solving a mystery," Cal says, "with the dog."

This seems so transparently false that Georgia does not try to call again. Danny will call when he's ready. He never does.

And everyone moves on with their lives. The wounds don't go away, but they get decorated around. It's like waking up one morning and finding a giant hole in your living room.

"Hey," you say, "what's this giant hole doing here? I can't possibly stay in this living room until it's fixed." So you spend some time trying to fill it, and it never really works, so eventually you just rearrange the furniture and stick a fern in it and start to forget it's there. And then later, maybe years later, when you welcome someone new into your living room, they say, "My god! You have a giant hole in your living room!" And you say, "Oh, that old thing—I hardly notice it anymore." Which is true, even though none of your furniture would sit where it sits if not for this giant, gaping hole. That's what it feels like, coming out the other side of despair.

And so Georgia finds herself living with TJ on the Upper Upper West Side and trying to arrange her furniture in a way that makes her brain feel like a living room rather than a dying room. She joins a pottery studio. Wonders if she is too old now for a first job in finance. In her spare time, she makes bowls and vases, which slowly populate every flat surface of TJ's—then Georgia and TJ's—apartment.

TJ has boyfriends, but they are never serious and always shitty. Georgia thinks that TJ has no idea how good romantic love can feel and doesn't aim high enough. Then again, maybe Georgia doesn't know enough to aim sufficiently high, either. Georgia never would've known to ask for a friendship like the one she has with TJ if she hadn't experienced it for herself. Sometimes, you just get lucky, and then you want to spend the rest of your life telling people, "No, no, the sitcom friendship, the Frodo-Sam friendship, the Nancy-Bess-George friendship—those are all real! Don't settle for anything less!" Your best friend should feel like your soulmate. You should believe all the destiny shit just the same way you do when you fall in love.

And when you love someone, sometimes you have to watch them make really stupid decisions.

A few years into her new life in New York, Georgia has to watch as TJ falls in love with a man. One of her patients, actually. Worse still: one of her *married* patients, who is also, as it happens, something of a dick.

"Wait," Danny says. "Wait wait wait. What does TJ stand for?"

"Theresa Jacinta," Georgia says. "Very Catholic."

"And she's a doctor?" Danny asks.

"That is correct."

"What's her last name?"

"Swann," Georgia says.

"Wait, wait—hang on, what are the chances that—"

What are the chances? Well—higher than you'd think.

Because when Danny is seventeen, he applies to a semiprestigious college that he thinks, on some level, might bring him closer to his mother—her alma mater. And when Julian is seventeen, and Dr. Theresa Jacinta Swann is paying yet another house call to a sick Eve, she happens to catch Phillip lecturing Julian about AP classes

Love Is an Algorithm

and Harvard, and she says, "Honestly, Phillip, remove your pretentious head from your pretentious ass. I didn't go to Harvard, and I'm the smartest person you know." How ballsy is that? Of course Julian applies to Dr. Swann's college.

A few days after Julian gets accepted, Dr. Swann pays Eve her final house call. While there, she will congratulate Julian and give him a piece of wisdom she herself found useful in college: "Tell them you have an allergy to something stupid. Gets you out of everything."

On the other side of the country, Danny and his dad eat Cheerios at their wooden kitchen table. Cal cannot bear that his son reminds him so much of his ex-wife. It seems to Cal there is every chance Danny won't come back. So it is with a remarkable deal of grace that Cal swallows his fear, puts on a smile, and says, "Hey, kid, did I ever tell you what your mom put on her roommate application?"

So the housing pairing person decides Danny and Julian, who have both in their applications lamented their blatantly fake allergies, will be annoying in exactly the same way. And they are so right.

It's around this time that Georgia—now in possession of a thriving online ceramics shop and a healthy dose of regained confidence—decides to tell TJ that it is simply never going to happen with Phillip, even though she loves him, and even though it's very possible he loves her, too. But he's not going to cheat on his wife, and she's not going to break up a marriage, and so they both need to cut ties, end their flirtatious friendship, and move on with their lives. It ends here.

And just as TJ put Georgia's life together after Cal, Georgia puts TJ's life together after Phillip.

But there's a catch.

Phillip has met Georgia. He doesn't know Danny is her son, but he does know that she threw her life away for a career in the arts and a man with no prospects. So when Eve starts talking about a career in music, Phillip thinks, *God, not like TJ's tragic friend Georgia, I hope.* And then, on Thanksgiving, when Julian brings Danny home, Danny overhears Phillip on the tail end of a phone call with TJ, with whom he never *did* anything but still feels guilty for so admiring, and he makes Danny feel small because he is afraid he has been caught speaking to her, this woman he secretly loves. Danny, meanwhile, is distracted by the sight of a vase: which is lovely, like something his mother might have made, and, in fact, did make—and which TJ gave Phillip as a birthday gift with the faux-casual excuse of, "Oh, it's nothing, our apartment is too fucking full of vases." And then, much later, when Danny and Eve start dating, Phillip finds himself again reminded of TJ, and tragic Georgia, and thinks that he would much rather Eve hate him than end up with a dead-end career, married to a man who will move her away from her support systems, and subject her to a life of small-town mediocrity. So he's a dick to Danny and Eve. C'est la vie. She'll thank him someday.

Which brings us nearly up to the present: when, six months ago, Phillip and his wife, Cecilia, download an app that purports to help them have a better relationship. It tells them their relationship is a thirty-seven out of one hundred, and, frankly, they'd be better off cutting ties. Do Not Resuscitate. Phillip tells Cecilia that maybe they should get a divorce, and Cecilia says, "Okay, if that's what you want," and Phillip asks what *she* wants, and Cecilia says, "Whatever you want," and Phillip says, "For god's sake, I want to know what you want for once," and she says, "You have made it impossible for me to want anything."

Phillip is tired of this. He knows for a fact that though he has made mistakes with Cecilia, it's not necessarily true that he would turn any woman on earth cold. He has proof! Which is how he finds himself walking twenty streets north through the pouring rain to the most opinionated woman he knows, knocking on TJ's door and saying, "Please, I am afraid you're the love of my life."

So Phillip and Cecilia separate, and Phillip finally goes on his first date with TJ.

Georgia does not approve. Supposedly, Cecilia and Phillip are getting a divorce, but that's the oldest story in the book. They're still living together, for god's sake! But she also gave TJ an ultimatum once, and TJ listened, and, to be honest, Georgia has never seen TJ love anyone the way she loved, and again loves, Phillip. So Georgia is trying to sit with the unease of it all. You can't control other people.

So that's the moral of this story. Sometimes people are so, so stupid. Alas! We love them anyway.

~~~

"The greatest love story ever told," Danny says, "is my girlfriend's father having an affair with his family physician?"

"It's like you haven't been listening at all."

~~~

How do you love someone even when they're making the worst possible decisions? Simple. You just do. We can try as hard as we want to show people how to make better choices, live a better life, fall in love in better and more reliable ways. But life is for living. Sometimes, you just have to make your own mistakes, and let everyone else make their mistakes, too.

~~~

"Do you have a best friend?" Georgia asks.

"Yeah," Danny says. "I do."

"Maybe someday," Georgia says, "you can tell me the story."

3

Danny knocks on the doorframe of Julian's office—the door is open—and leans his head inside. Julian is typing at his standing desk. Beside his monitor, there is a wedding photo of Gigi in her gown; a pile of self-helpy leadership books; a miniature replica of the Diana statue at the Met. When Julian sees Danny, he smiles, types a few words with an air of finality, then says, "Walk and talk?"

They get coffees from their usual place across the street. The first time they tried it, Julian said, "This is okay, but it's not great." It's still okay but not great. Danny has at this point had somewhere upward of a hundred of their okay-but-not-great coffees.

"High Line?" Danny says.

Cups in hand, they climb the steps to the old elevated railroad tracks and begin their slow meander. A meander is the only tenable pace on the High Line. They are surrounded by earnest tourists; pollinator-friendly plants; sculptures from salvaged materials; retro-futurist solar-punk apartment buildings.

"I know that this is your party," Danny says. "But before you go, I wanted to say something. Two things."

"Yeah?"

"The first is thank you. For being there."

"That's what we do," Julian says. "You know I love you, right?"

"I know," Danny says. "The second thing is that I think we should sell."

"You do?"

"I do. Maybe not right away. I want to leave it with someone we trust. But I'm ready for something else. I think I'm just tired of seeing the world through this lens, if that makes sense."

"Constantly viewing human relationships by their quantifiable metrics?" Julian says. "Fair."

"I also feel like we've done what we wanted to do. Seems like we could do something bigger next time."

"Bigger like what?"

"I mean, I have this idea. It's an AI green-tech thing. I thought of it during the flooding. But tell me your news."

"I get the sense you already knew my news," Julian says. "My news is that I want to sell. And Gigi and I are going to the UK. She got into a PhD program. She's burned-out with the creator stuff, and I want to make this happen for her. So we'll be gone for four years, and then after that—who knows. So I'm probably not the person with whom you want to launch a new start-up."

"That's so stupid," Danny says. "This is all the more reason."

"Is it?"

"Yes. We'll get to hang out all the time. You know, over the internet."

"Time zones are tricky."

"I've always wanted to be an early riser," Danny says. "Think about it."

"Yeah," Julian says. "I will."

In front of them, an elderly woman with a tiny dog pauses on a bridge with a view of the river. She takes out her phone to get a picture. Apologetically, she says, "I do live here. I just love it."

They keep walking. A battalion of pigeons settles under a bench where two children messily eat granola bars.

"I met my mom yesterday," Danny says. He tells Julian the whole story—about Georgia, about Cal, about TJ and Phillip and the great connected labyrinth of it all.

"Dr. Swann?" Julian says. "Seriously?" He considers. "I can actually kind of see it. I always liked her."

"You're taking this remarkably well."

"So what if they're getting divorced? I just want them to be happy."

"Yeah?" Danny says. Then: "I feel guilty my dad wasn't happier."

"Do you know he wasn't?"

"I assume he wasn't. He was so afraid of everything. He kept my mom away from me because he was afraid I'd leave, too. I miss him so much, but also, how do you forgive something like that? It scares the shit out of me to think that I'd treat Eve the way either of my parents treated each other. I don't want to demand certainty from her."

"Man," Julian says. "Sometimes I think that's all growing up is. Just figuring out how much you want to be like your parents. And you know what? My dad never would've moved to Cambridge for my mom. But maybe I don't want to be like him. I also don't really want to be the kind of dad who calls his son the first pancake."

"The first pancake?"

"More of a practice round," Julian says.

"We're both first pancakes," Danny says.

"Desperate to prove ourselves."

"Anxious people pleasers."

"A breakfast classic," Julian says. "One of the all-time greats."

"A son?" Danny says.

"Something to consider. On the distant horizon."

"God, that child will be tall."

"And he'll resent me for fuckups of my very own invention," Julian says.

"It'd be a shame to run out of fuckups," Danny says. "I like to think I'll keep fucking up my whole life long."

4

Some time later, on his last day at Pattern, Danny makes a final change, and then he logs out, closes his laptop, and leaves his badge at the front desk. He and Eve are going to eat breakfast for dinner with their friends, and then they'll walk home in the lazy summer heat, and they'll fall asleep on the couch because they stay up so late talking—about what's next, about what might be. It will be some time before anyone notices what Danny did. It was a small thing; just one little manual override. A user will only ever notice if they ask Bug to tell them a dad joke.

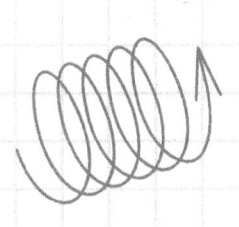

Eve Olsen and Chloe Agawa Have Invited You to a Block Party

1

Eve sits on a crate typing on her laptop. It's August—end of summer, edge of evening, all hazy Brooklyn glow and sunset pink.

"I just think Californians make better ice cream," Shannon is saying. "I didn't know this was controversial."

"Controversial?" Eve says. "We ate ice cream every day for an entire summer."

"And it was good. Nay—great. But California is an all-seasons ice cream climate."

"Californians lack the commitment to the sweet-treat lifestyle to sincerely compete with New Yorkers on ice cream," Eve says.

"I can't believe I'm hearing this," Shannon says. "Are we going to break up over this?"

"Couldn't be," Eve says. "Bring me cookies and cream in a waffle cone?"

"Aye aye," Shannon says.

Eve watches as Shannon weaves through the crowd to where Chloe is dishing ice cream out of a cart. She's wearing a hat that says BLOCK PARTY. The hat—the ice cream, the street, the whole vision—was something Chloe presented to Eve the day Danny and Julian announced they were selling Pattern. Though Eve had always liked Chloe, she remained somewhat enigmatic. And then Chloe called Eve and said, "I have an idea for an app for people who are tired of apps."

"Wow," Eve said. "Sounds like an enthusiastic market."

"I don't know the details yet," Chloe said. "But I think it has something to do with the feeling you get when you're at a concert and don't want to take out your phone."

"And you want me to be, what, your ambassador? I don't know if you've heard, but I'm dead. And retired from social media."

"Actually," Chloe said, "I had something more cofoundery in mind."

Which Eve finds so funny! It's not like it's a big thing. Just an experiment. They're seeing where it goes. No pressure!

She finishes what she was typing. To the outside observer, Eve assumes, she looks like she's doing Important Business Work, but really, secretly, she was writing a song. She hasn't performed since Penn Station, and she's not sure if she wants to again—but she finds that the more she brings her fledgling little business into existence, the more she wants to bring songs into existence. Creation begetting creation, and so on. Perhaps she will sell them someday for someone else to sing.

Eve sees Shannon returning from the ice cream line, but Shannon suddenly pauses, turns, and goes back the other way. It takes Eve a moment to realize why.

A woman in a large hat and sunglasses stops in front of Eve. She's wearing a white linen blouse and white linen pants. She is, rather indisputably, Eve's mother.

"Well," Cecilia says, taking off her sunglasses. "This is quite something. Quite . . ." She looks around. "Vibrant!"

"Oh," Eve says. "Hi." Eve invited everyone in her contacts to come—including Julian and Gigi, who are very much not in the country, and Stella, who is touring, and Clay, who is on a songwriting retreat in Sedona. She invited her mom because it felt rude not to.

"What?" Cecilia says. "You didn't think I'd come?"

"No?"

"I'm a lot of fun," Cecilia says. "Actually."

"No," Eve says, "for sure."

"It seems like you're doing well? With all of this?" She makes a scrubbing motion in the air to indicate *this*.

"Yeah. I think, after everything with Bug and social media and all the rest, I just wanted something a little more—in person."

"You can be so technophobic sometimes," Cecilia says. "I like Bug."

"Seriously?"

"Bug told your dad and I we should split up. And you know what? We should have. So! Give Daniel my thanks."

"You do know it's Danny, right? Just Danny? Not Daniel?"

"Can't a person grow?"

"What? No, Mom, a person cannot grow into having a marginally more formal name."

"Oh," Cecilia says. "That pizza smells divine."

Cecilia pats Eve's arm. There's a moment—just a second—where their eyes meet and Eve sees something there and Cecilia squeezes—and then Cecilia slides her sunglasses back over her face and continues down the street alone.

A minute later, Shannon appears with Eve's ice cream.

"Wow," Shannon says, handing over one of the cones. "What was that?"

"Literally, who is to say."

"What did you talk about?"

"She called me technophobic," Eve says.

"I mean, you are kind of technophobic. Car crashes. Emotional reliance on AI. Et cetera."

"Mass data breaches!" Eve says. "Murderous robots! These are valid fears."

"I just think it's cute that your mom could see you all along."

"Oh, no," Eve says. "I find I'm rather touched."

Shannon touches her ice cream cone to Eve's, as if in toast. "We all just want to be seen."

Is that all? From the other end of the street, Eve spots Danny emerging from the subway—climbing up the stairs, propping his sunglasses on top of his head, looking around. She waits for him to find her, and then he does. He sees her, and he smiles.

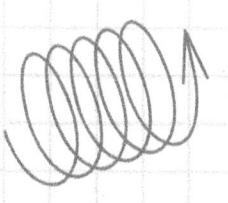

Awake, Arise

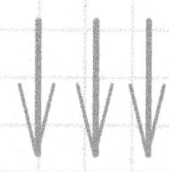

1

The moon is full and purplish through the gap in Danny's curtains, which twist in on themselves when a warm breeze ambles by. The clock on the nightstand says it's just past three, but a haze of humidity still hangs in the air.

It's the night of Eve and Danny's first date.

Around midnight, they started saying they ought to get some sleep, but it's begun to sound less like a real suggestion and more like an inside joke. We should get some sleep. Ha.

They lie in Danny's bed on top of the sheets. Boxers, one of his old T-shirts. Their knees are curled toward each other and their foreheads angled together. Occasionally, an ambulance will blare past the window, and Eve will watch Danny's face blur in soft crimson light. It's the kind of night that just goes and goes. They could go to sleep, but what could be more important than falling in love with the possible probable love of your life? Not sleep. Sleep is for people who are still weighing their options.

"Do you remember your graduation?" Eve asks. "When we all went to dinner at that Italian place?"

"Didn't we all get food poisoning?" Danny says. "I don't know that we've reached the stage where we can talk about food poisoning."

"Before that! I made up an excuse about the chair hurting my back so Julian would switch with me. I wanted to sit next to you."

"Really?"

"Of course, really."

"And then we spent the whole time talking about what you would include in a city on Mars," Danny says.

"You remember that?"

"I'm pretty sure we named our city Marzipan. It had a lot of parks."

"I can't believe you remember that."

"Of course I remember that. This was around the time it occurred to me that you were very pretty."

"Am I pleased you noticed or annoyed it took you so long?"

"You were sixteen when we first met," Danny says. "I think I was right on time."

"You should've asked me out," Eve says.

"You know, I think I was going to? But then. Food poisoning."

"I can't believe we were kept apart by something so undignified," Eve says.

"Not kept apart," Danny says. "Merely delayed. Do you remember Julian's twenty-sixth birthday?"

"We went to Maine."

"Yeah. All the Our Parents Are Friends gang, and then me wandering around hoping no one noticed I had never once owned a house in the Hamptons."

"I remember making pancakes with you when everyone else was still sleeping off their hangovers," Eve says. "And you kept insisting this pancake you made was in the exact shape of a goose."

"It was in the exact shape of a goose," Danny says.

"It was not. And also may imply some room for growth on your pancake technique."

"I almost broke up with Kyra after that trip," Danny says.

"Really? Why?"

"Because you looked at the goose."

"It wasn't a goose."

"I said the pancake looked like a goose. And you put down whatever you were doing and stood next to me and said, 'Danny, I don't think you know what geese look like.'"

"And that won you over?"

"You were just so there," Danny says. "You made me feel so there."

"I was dating Fletcher, though."

"Oh, I know. It never occurred to me that you and I would start dating. I just thought—if someone like Eve is out there, maybe there are other Eves out there. Maybe I'm settling for something that's not really that happy."

"But you didn't break up with Kyra."

"No. But then, when she broke up with me, I thought about that, the goose, and I thought, maybe it's for the best, if I end up with someone more like Eve."

"You didn't."

"I most certainly did."

Eve never took improv, but Shannon was part of a college troupe, and she would sometimes make Eve practice with her. They played *yes, and* endlessly, but there was little difference between *yes, and* and their normal conversations. When Eve talked to Shannon, it felt less like finding the next thing to say and more like stepping into a river of things to say. The things came whether or not Eve asked them to. They were always just there. That has become Eve's litmus test of whether a person is someone she will love—a sort of thereness. A sort of flow state—like writing a song. And then? And then? And then? That's how it feels with Danny, and she tells him so, and he says (of course he does) that he understands completely.

"Exactly," he says. "It feels like creativity. But instead of making art or an app or something, you're making the relationship."

"I like that," Eve says. "Like, there are three parts. There's the first part, which is me, and the second part, which is you, and the third part, which is, you know, this."

"Right. And sometimes, something might be wrong with you, or something might be wrong with me, or something might be wrong with the third part."

"Can I just say that we're doing a really excellent job of talking about what we consider key values in a relationship without daring to suggest that we might end up in a relationship?"

"Thank you," Danny says. "I've been choosing my words with the utmost care."

"Gotta keep me on my toes."

"Not too on your toes. Could be bad for the arches. You know, long term."

"Oh," Eve says, "so you think this'll be a long-term thing, do you?"

"If I say, I'll scare you."

"I'd like to see you try."

"It's 4:00 a.m.," Danny says.

"We should get some sleep?"

"Maybe," Danny says. "But I get the feeling I've been waiting for this to start for a really long time."

Acknowledgments

Thank you, with all my heart, to the people who made this book come to life.

Thank you to my unstoppable agents, Andrea Somberg and Philippa Sitters, for bringing my book around the globe. I am so lucky to have you both.

My two favorite cities in the world are New York and Melbourne, and it was a joy to work with teams in both. Thank you to the team at Park Row, and especially to my editor, Meredith Clark, for your enthusiasm and encouragement. And to the team at Text: Thank you for championing this book and believing in it and me. A huge thank-you to Penny Hueston for leading the way. I am so grateful for all of you.

Thank you, as always, to my family. Thank you to the Garnhart family. And thank you to the Rolio family.

Thank you to my friends, funny and wise humans all, who talked to me about this book along the way: Amy, Asher, Carl, Jacob, Joey, Henry, Kat, Kat, Kent, Marisa, Mary, Neil, Nicky, Peter, Sneha, Tim, Tom. I tried to name you all and couldn't get there—how lucky is that? Thank you to undoubtedly the first person to reach this page—David, you are forever my fellow read-a-thoner. Thank you to Chantal, who makes anywhere feel like home. Thank you to Gia, who makes me steadier and kinder. Thank you to Ari, who makes me me.

Thank you to Greg, who helped with this book from the start, who sends me new albums, who knows where to find the best ice cream, who I once met in passing and thought, "I'll probably never see him again, but I bet that in a nearby parallel universe, I love him very much." And thank you again to Ari. For introducing us.